Various Heroes

Various Heroes

Earl Brogan

NORTH STAR PRESS OF ST. CLOUD, INC.
St. Cloud, Minnesota

First Edition: June 2013

Printed in the United States of America.

Published by

North Star Press of St. Cloud, Inc.
P.O. Box 451
St. Cloud, MN 56302

www.northstarpress.com Facebook - North Star Press Twitter - North Star Press

To Jan and anyone else who believed I'd finish writing this. Thanks for your long-term confidence.

Various Heroes

One

ONCE IT WAS THE RANGE of the vast Killarney Mountains, the largest peaks North America has ever seen, putting to shame those young upstarts the Rockies. Over the centuries erosion, glaciers, and the effects of the vast inland sea wore down the rock until now just the weathered roots of those mountains still remain. The stone sleeps under the glacial till dreaming of the ice sheets and remembering their lullabies.

This is the Keweenaw Peninsula.

The land here is rugged, having been raised as a mountain range when it was king of a continent. Even though brought down in size and surrounded on most sides by Lake Superior, it still remembers the days before the glaciers. It remembers a time when no people walked the landscape, and it wouldn't much matter to it if that time came again.

Pines, poplars, maples, cedars and a variety of other trees, plants and wildlife share the peninsula with man. The mountains rather like them. The roots tickle beneath the surface and the animals keep their noses to the ground and know the land as no man can. The land remembers.

It can create an attitude, and sometimes it is unforgiving to the latecomers who have settled here on its surface.

The first men came following the game. The great herds drew them north as the glaciers receded and the land opened up. Once here they discovered and became some of the first to use the copper abundant in veins on the exposed cliff surface, and with fire and stone tools they brought it out and worked it into shapes both practical and fantastic.

They sensed the mood of the land, its ruggedness, long winters, and unconcern for humans as well. Winter starvation led to stories of the Windigo and Grey Walker, which they passed on to their descendents.

In time their presence gave way to a new influx of travelers. These newcomers, too, came for the copper, but they also came for lumber, the fish from the great lake and a homesick longing for farming in land that was just as bad as that of the Old Country they had left behind. The great-great-grandsons and granddaughters still live here although they, like the land itself, change but little.

Much further to the south and east, a group of men sat together at a long table in an antiseptic room. They were used to coming together to decide the questions of how this nation was to be run and exploited, and now their attention was turned to this once glacier-ridden land. The time, they felt, had come for decisions, and they, they felt, were the men to make them.

One stood before a long, large map of the Keweenaw and the surrounding Lake Superior. His laser pointer occasionally paused on features of the map as he addressed the others calmly and coolly with the sense of well-briefed authority.

"This place is made for our purpose. Granted, there were some questions about using land so close to the Great Lakes, but as you know, our subsequent plans have taken that into account. The mine shafts from the last round of copper mining are still there. The population is marginal at best and really presents no state-wide influence or voting bloc. Jobs are virtually non-existent and are becoming rarer with the ongoing downturn in the economy. Many of the people there are at what would be considered the poverty line anywhere else in the country and either stay from a lack of ambition or an overabundance of loyalty to their roots and the area. We can handle those. The movers and shakers, such as they are, move on to greener pastures and leave the rest behind.

"In recent years they have become used to government interference in their affairs," the man continued. "Yes, there is a sense of resentment, but that is nowhere near as strong as the sense of futility in fighting the system. Again and again when they have come up against the powers that be, it was the common folk who took the beating and the powers did just as they wanted. The people are used to it. I have no reason to believe they will be a problem."

"What about grassroots organizations or outside agigroups, sir? Is there a chance of anyone stepping in there to organize and pull these people together?" a man asked.

"I don't believe so, Jenkins," came the reply. "They've been pulling in seven different directions for so long rather than cooperating to take on much smaller players than us that I don't believe any 'movement,' per se, is possible.

"I also have the assurance and the green light from our Washington friends. They are sending two of their best field men into the area soon to get a feel for the whole atmosphere up there. We'll await their report, of course, before we move on, but obviously we've considered all the questions germane to us."

He paused and looked at Jenkins before continuing. "If we really thought there was a real potential for problems, we wouldn't be having this meeting now."

Jenkins, knowing he had been rebuked by his senior, nodded in agreement and sat back, making a mental note to never question prior planning or fieldwork again, at least not in open session.

The man before the map waited to see if other questions would arise. Of course there were none, and he went on.

"In addition, an 'accidental' infusion of chemical contaminants, PBB to be exact, was introduced into the state as a whole ten years ago. Additionally, heavy metals and tailings from the mining days, making the whole area a Superfund site, has helped to acclimate the people to forces beyond their control. This, along with the economic climate of the state as a whole, and the

Upper Peninsula in particular, has the population in a suitable mindset for our plans.

"Of course, there may be individual citizens who may sense the course their area is on and our plans for it, but, as stated, they are fragmented and the chances of their pulling together in any real, meaningful way are slim at best.

"As I said earlier, I have called you together basically to brief you on progress to date, and to assure you all we are moving forward. There is money to be made here, Gentlemen. Let us make it together. The operation at this stage will be called 'Overseer.' If there are no further questions, we'll adjourn."

Two

THE TOWN OF PHOENIX was not the garden spot of the Keweenaw Peninsula. In fact, in many ways the Keweenaw Peninsula was no garden spot itself. The usual wisdom had it that winter lasted nine months out of the year and the mosquitoes and black flies ruled for two of the three remaining months. That last month, though, actually split in half between spring and fall, made it all worthwhile.

The town itself was a lot like the people who lived in it, with an architectural mix as broad as that of the ethnic mix of groups that built it. The heart of town was roughly nine blocks long and four blocks wide with the odd bulging addition. The houses were mostly two-story wood or brick homes with the occasional mansion of sandstone or wood with cupolas and porches. Most of these hung together one block off the main street, creatively named "Main Street," and were clustered where the business owners and mining officials used to live. Where fire or the collapse of a building from snow load had created an opening, ranch-style homes or doublewides had sprung up like saplings in a fire-cleared forest, but for the most part, the homes had been built about a hundred and thirty years ago.

In the business district, all three blocks of it, the buildings were mostly brick or sandstone buildings two or three stories tall. The peaks of each were adorned with cornices, statuary, the name of the builder or owner, and the date of construction. The uniformity of brick or stone was not accidental, but rather the effect of a building code instituted after the wood buildings of the original downtown had gone up in smoke in 1887. The occasional wood exception often bore the false front façade of a wall squaring the front off in old west fashion. Most of these structures were or had been bars, and the bullet holes in the wall from a late nineteenth century gunfight still marked the interior walls of one.

The mixed drive for the need for a quick building boom and civic respectability had created a schizoid cross between Eastern, in particular Massachusetts, architectural fashion and Western frontier practicality. Rising above the rest of the town was the sandstone city hall with its three full floors and domed spire.

The largest of the three churches in town was Roman Catholic, built by "voluntary" donations made by prominent Catholic businessmen and successful farmers after a visit from a particularly effective parish priest who may or may not have discussed blessings and curses with the generous or recalcitrant. A sandstone structure like City Hall, its stained glass windows and twin spires lit the long winter nights and provided a landmark visible throughout the area. The other churches were more modest protestant structures, but each provided its own fine points and marked the seeming piety of the community. The proliferation of bars and taverns may have indicated otherwise, but let's assume the positive for piety was well founded.

Roy Shea walked down the streets of Phoenix on his way back home. He looked up automatically at the identification and year blocks of the buildings he passed out of habit. Given time and reason, he could probably tell when each had been built from memory, but a part of his walk to and from work each day included this touristy gawking, just as it included the automatic wave in response to a passing car honking hello as it drove by.

His interest in history and people made him wonder what the original builders of the city would think if they could see it now. There had been dreams built into this town just like any other. It had taken determination, money, hard work, and more than a little vision to lay a stake here and carve out a town in what in the nineteenth century, if not now, could logically be considered the end of the earth. What could have drawn people here?

Turning up the corner past the bank he walked up the blocks, entered "residential" Phoenix, and approached his own neighborhood. He passed the round tower of what had once been a brewery magnate's home, truly a mansion for the local area, and thought again of what it must have been like to stand in front of it when it was new in 1898.

Across the street was another of the town's most impressive structures. This had been the home of a mining company executive, and its set of carved sandstone lions had undoubtedly been brought in at great expense by water as the master stroke of completion for the robber baron who had made his fortune with the copper stripped out of the hills by mostly immigrant workers who risked life and limb at slave wages to make the owner's fortune.

This had been a moneyed neighborhood in the old days. Home to families of newfound wealth, position, and patronage who placed a part of the wealth the area had provided them on display here, but saved most for sending to banks back East in Boston or New York. The sons and daughters of Eastern society had fairly often come to this wilderness to make their marks before returning to their respective and far more civilized communities.

The rich were gone now and replaced by pale imitations, doctors, lawyers and college professors who made Phoenix their bedroom community and commuted to work in the larger nearby cities of Houghton or Calumet. They found these old homes irresistible, and although the prices were outside of the local citizens' reach, the new owners found the prices matching the proverbial song when compared to real estate values in the real world south of the Mackinac Straits.

Shea could remember having been in one or two of these stately homes as the guest of classmates who had been descendents of the original builders. Some of the old families had still lived here through his elementary and middle school years, only to up and move with the accumulated interest raised on the capital earned by earlier generations before the final closing of the mines took place in the 1970s.

He occasionally had wondered what had happened to some of them, but it was highly unlikely that any of them would return, let alone the wealth that had left.

A block up, Shea came to his own street of much more humble, but with just as many years' lineage, homes. These had been built to house the workers whose labor had made the executives' dreams come true. Most were built to the same basic plan, essentially two-story boxes. Today, these housed more descendents of the original owners than the homes of the barons.

Generations of the same families had been conceived, born, and raised in these houses. In time they were inherited from parents or grandparents, and were passed on to children or grandchildren. These were true family homes in neighborhoods where folks shared the same trials and hardships across backyard gardens and fences.

In recent years, when the old families packed out to look for work or died off, many had emptied and been purchased by newcomers, but an inordinate number were still in the hands of the descendents of the original owners. Others, like Shea's place itself, were no longer in the same family, but had been taken up by folks of the same local stock.

Some of the streets still retained that neighborhood feel despite the changes since the original owners found themselves unexpectedly holding the titles to their own homes in the trickle down wealth of the boom period for the Keweenaw mines.

Roy walked past the empty lot on the end of his own block. He was never really sure, but suspected that the lot had once held a house like his since lost to fire or relocation. Either that, or the plot had been left open as a buffer between the workers on his street and the boss's home on the next corner. Perhaps it was there to discourage the offspring of the Massachusetts-bred from running with a child whose parents still spoke Finnish or French at home.

He truly reached his own territory when the houses stopped having backyards and started having back hillsides. The foundations of his home and those on either side of him had been carved into the sides of a steep creek gully. Some of the original owners had terraced the back hillsides for gardens, gentile tea houses, or merely a place to take a level seat. Since these houses had been built before indoor plumbing, when outhouses were the rule, such concerns had been important.

At first sight of his own home he automatically thought, *I'll have to finish painting this place soon.* It had been a passing fancy for over seven years now. Someday it would get done — with the possible exception of the front peak, fully three stories above the blacktopped drive because of the ground floor basement. *It might get done this summer,* he thought.

As he walked up the steps he could hear his wife and daughter discussing what still needed to go into the baking. "More chocolate chips, Mommy," Erin pleaded. "We want 'em gooey."

"There's already a full bag of chips in there, Erin. We want you to keep your teeth," his wife replied.

Jeri worked mornings at the lab in the local clinic and spent the afternoons with their two children, Erin, aged seven, and Sean, aged five. Roy and Jeri both felt it gave her a chance to keep her hand in at work yet still be home for the kids during their formative years. Besides that, like anyone else up here, they couldn't make ends meet comfortably with just one salary.

"Hi, hon. How goes it? Looks like you're having fun," Roy greeted his wife as he walked in the kitchen.

"Not bad, Roy. Erin and I are getting some baking done. We'll get dinner going, too, but you'll have to start the charcoal—hint, hint." Jeri grinned. "Remember, I've got my Friday class tonight."

"Charcoal? I take it that means I'm cooking? That's fine," Roy said as he reached in the refrigerator, grabbed a Leinies long neck, and popped the top off.

""I remembered about your class, too. I'll probably take the kids down to the park or out to the boat while you're gone." Roy continued on into the living room and set down his pack.

"How'd it go at work today?" Jeri called from the kitchen. "Kids a little antsy in the nice weather?

"Not any worse than us. I swear I don't know who gets more sidetracked when these late fall days are as nice as they are today. Still think we shouldn't start school until October."

"Well, you'd be starting next week then anyway." Switching gears, she said, "Turn off the TV if you want. Erin and I weren't watching anyway, and Sean is out back playing on the hill."

"By himself?"

"I'm keeping an eye on him through the window, but feel free to go out and check."

Shea walked over to the back window and looked out at his son playing in one of the few level places in the back. "Looks like he's fine, Jeri. I'm going to put on some music, if you don't mind." Shea hit the PLAY button on the CD player and the first strains of Van Morrison's "I've Been Working" filled the room.

"Van might have been working," Jeri called through the doorway, "but I think the verdict is still out on you."

Shea walked back to the kitchen doorway with the beer in his hand. "What's a man got to do to get some respect in his own house?"

"Maybe get his wife one of those and start the charcoal?"

"Your wish, m'damn wife," he said, bending over to get the beer from the bottom shelf. It was one of his favorite times of day, getting back to his family after the daily session with other people's teenagers. "And the charcoal is coming up. I'll get Sean to help me."

He bent down to kiss Erin and headed outside, calling for Sean as he headed to the deck.

After supper and Jeri's departure for class, he sat down with the local newspaper —all twelve pages of it —while the kids played on the porch.

As usual, there wasn't a lot to read, just the headline articles, local news (mostly arrest reports and newsed-up gossip), the obituaries (on the second page, since the editor had the good sense to realize that was the most read section of the paper), and the comics on the last page. These he read to Erin while she curled up in his lap and Sean tried grabbing the paper from his hands.

One article on the front page dealing with the local scene did catch his interest. "EXPERTS SAY FISH STUDY EXTENDED" read the headline. This was the latest big thing in the area.

Recently the nearby Linden Lake, a backwater on the portage canal, had gained fame as having the highest concentration of fish with tumors in the entire U.S., if not the world. "Experts" from the local university and downstate Lansing with the DNR, neither usually filling the locals with confidence, were tripping all over each other trying to find the cause. Most really had no idea, but almost all the articles mentioned the fact that the lake had been the recipient of raw sewage from nearby communities and tailings from the local stamp mills for ages. A number of the older former employees of United Chemical, the mining company responsible for most of the digging and processing done in the last hundred years before they up and left for greener pastures, coincidently ocurring with an increase in environmental laws and violation fines, remembered shifts of men being ordered to take out barges filled with barrels that sank like stones when rolled into the lake. Some of them leaked and left a surface residue discoloring the water and stinking up the air. This had gone on for decades.

No one was going to put his neck out and actually place blame, but everyone seemed inclined to think all that surreptitious dumping had something to do with the condition of the lake and its fish. In the meantime, everyone was warned not to eat fish from the lake, and the more alarming reports questioned the sensibility of swimming in it. All the local medical people like Jeri had known for years that the incidence of cancer in the area was disproportionally high, and this was looking like a possible link. At any rate, everyone was following the reports, and a lot of people wanted to get into the act—and the newspaper— with their own theories.

Shea read to the end of the article, "Samples taken from the lake will be sent for testing to both the DNR central office as well as to the Center for Disease Control in Atlanta. The community is advised that an answer may be forthcoming."

What the hell, thought Shea. *Our tax dollars at work.*

Fish tumors were the last thing on his mind as he lay beside Jeri later that night with the quiet all around them. *Things have been going well,* he thought. *I wonder if there's a shoe about to drop.*

As he fell asleep, night settled over the Keweenaw. Except for the late night lake shore parties where high school students fought against sleep and sensibility, all was quiet.

Three

TWO WEEKS LATER and five hundred miles to the south, a federally owned unmarked Ford was being packed quietly and efficiently by two men. The IDs in their wallets said they were employees of an international chemical company. Paperwork in their briefcases said they were on their way to the U.P. to do a land use feasibility study on the holdings the company still owned in the Keweenaw. Two laptops on the back seat held, among other things, a number of files of people of interest in the Upper Peninsula.

The two men, one white and one black, worked well together. They both stood an average-looking height, were of moderate build, and neither had any outstanding physical features that would make a casual observer sit up and take notice. Neither gave the appearance of being spies or agents, but both had been, and still were, just that.

When the car was packed they turned out of the lot of the government office building and made their way east across the state to I-75, where they turned north. They would drive as far north as the Mackinac Bridge tonight and stay in one of the many modest motels in St. Ignace. Tomorrow they would continue north to the Keweenaw to begin the investigation for their report.

It would be interesting to see if foreknowledge would have changed their plans. Would it change anything if they already knew that the Company does make the occasional mistake and that all parts of the U.S. are not necessarily a part of the country? It probably wouldn't have made a difference, but it would have been interesting to see for sure.

Something else was still up and about, too. A chuckle ran through the area. Something, perhaps with a sense of humor, was waiting for things to start happening.

Four

THE UPPER PENINSULA, although east of the Mississippi River, was somewhat slow to be settled. Reports of copper had been made as early as 1765, but the area did not attract settlers like the Lower Peninsula, Ohio, or Indiana. It wasn't until the copper rush of the 1840s that any real influx of men trying to exploit the area's potential wealth took place.

Even the way the U.P. became part of Michigan was somewhat left-handed. When Michigan Territory was first formed, its settlers believed it extended further south than the present border and did not include the U.P., which was considered an empty, barren and frigid wasteland.

But Ohio, already a state, had other plans. In the infamous Ohio-Michigan War, itself more full of foofaraw than real action, Ohio won the claim to the southern 470 square mile border between Michigan and Ohio. Michigan received the U.P. as some sort of sop to the feelings of its future voters.

The first copper rush brought the first flood of would-be miners. Hundreds, if not thousands of otherwise probably sensible and practical men turned their noses north, booked passage to the Great Lakes and made their ways to the Keweenaw expecting to find masses of copper like the Ontonagon Boulder, displayed for twenty-five cents a peek in Detroit during October of 1843.

All of these men felt sure they would make their fortunes picking copper off the ground, not realizing that the rumors of winter and predatory bugs throughout the year were far more true than those of quick riches.

By 1845, most of these early amateur prospectors had discovered that it wasn't going to be that easy, but there was money to be made for the intrepid or lucky. True, most of it would go to the financial backers investing in what became the larger companies and not to the men digging the ore, but there was money to be made.

The first few tentative claims mostly failed, but as investment money began rolling in to the few successful digs, true mining companies began to develop. By the 1860s, there were over thirty different companies, mostly backed by Eastern money, throughout the Keweenaw. Over four million dollars in investments were poured into the wilderness, and a select few began drawing dividends.

The mining camps began to grow into towns and immigrants began to pour in from all over the world as the word spread.

The Cornish in particular felt the draw as the tin mines of Cornwall began to play out. The companies welcomed them with open arms. Here were the best miners in the world, accustomed to long hours and the dangers. Here a man who had been an ordinary shaft worker could become a mine captain on the basis of his experience. Here they could make from fifty to a hundred dollars a week doing what they did best. They came in droves.

They spoke English and fit in well. They didn't cause any untoward problems and listened to the company men who controlled their lives. They became part of the community and got ahead.

The Swedes, Germans, and Norwegians quickly and early became major parts of the ethnic mix. All three seemed to assimilate and settle right in. Educated and quick to take to the English language and the American way of doing business, they fit in as well as the English speakers and moved in basically without a ripple, but adding their own ingredients to the ethnic soup.

Of course, others came as well. The Irish who had arrived in their famished hordes during the Great Hunger made their way to the U.P. They were looking for whatever they could find, and a lack of mine experience was no real problem. Many of them ended up in the mines, and at a time when "No Irish Need Apply" was the rule throughout much of the country, their strong backs were welcome here.

They weren't the Cornish, and the mine owners kept a closer eye on them, but still their numbers grew. Irish societies grew overnight, and the taverns in many areas took on the character of pubs from the Old Sod.

The Italians found their way to the Keweenaw mines after the Irish, but they more than made their mark. They reluctantly signed on to the mines, squirreling away their wages until they could open their own businesses. Italian newspapers, clubs, and social groups sprang up throughout Calumet and the larger towns. These hotbeds of free speech pushed their own brand of socialism and lamented the failure of the revolution back home, but many members of this particular group were more than happy to try it here. Anti-Italian propaganda ranged from their politics to rumors of the consumption of songbirds by these Southern Europeans in the English language newspapers, but this group of new settlers dropped in for the long haul.

On the heels of the Eyeties arrived the Finns, in some ways the strangest group of all to the English-speaking inhabitants. They moved into logging, fishing, and, of course, the mines. The dream of the Finnish immigrant was his own farm, although choosing to try to farm in the U.P. showed a distinct lack of discernment on their part.

Split among themselves into two factions—those who dropped the old ways like used tissues and assimilated and those who wanted to hold on to their culture and language—Finnish farms and small communities rose throughout the area on the outskirts of the mining towns. The Finnish newspapers and magazines reported the respective successes and failures of the sons and daughters of both groups, but settle in they did. By 1896, they had established Suomi College in Hancock, on the edges of the Quincy mine operation, for their children. For the most part literate, Lutheran, and political, they immediately began riling the English-speaking community.

Although the Finns and Italians were divided in many ways by ancestral geography, religion, and temperament, they seemed to understand each other—which was more than any other group could do for either of them. They were able to work together.

The list goes on—the Poles, the Germans, the Russians, the Hungarians and Croats all arrived in turn and settled into their neighborhoods in Red Jacket and Laurium. Even the ubiquitous Chinese laundry was serving the needs of miners by 1890. The string of mining communities lining up on the ridge of the Keweenaw kept growing until ninety thousand were eking out a living north of the Houghton canal.

Union organization began, too. As with the nation, an undercurrent of socialism, brought over with immigrants but adjusting to its new home, was going through growing pains. This growth was to have an immediate and lasting effect on the Upper Peninsula.

Demands for better wages and conditions were followed by protests and strikes when denied by the companies.

Many of the main instigators came from the Italian and Finnish communities, while often the English-speaking and more authority-bound nationalities wondered what all the fuss was about.

After all, they reasoned, weren't conditions in the mines all right when compared to those elsewhere? The companies paid the men really no more or no less than others elsewhere. They supplied the homes of the mining families for only dollars a month. Workers with United Chemical received health service for themselves and their families for only a dollar a month. Water of good quality was supplied. In Phoenix, workers had the right to keep cattle on the common grounds the company kept, and in Calumet a company-owned library of thousands of books in dozens of different languages was available for workers and their families. Why, United Chemical had even started a broom factory hiring miners blinded in accidents. What was there to complain about?

True, the mines were cold at the top and hot down below. They were dark and vermin-infested, and it was true there was always danger—especially in the days of open flames and blasting powder. The possibility of a cave-in was constant, and the variety of ways to get injured in the above-ground operations was unlimited as well. This, however, was mining. Conditions were like this all over.

Besides, the things those Socialist Finns and Italians were calling for would cost money, and that would lower the dividends paid to stockholders who had put their money in good faith to finance the mines which provided these jobs. Why should they lose out to make the Copper Country a workers' paradise? It was just un-American.

So there were troubles.

Men went to work with guns in their lunch totes. The tools of the mining trade made especially nasty weapons. A blast might accidently go off early and perhaps catch someone who was not quite yet behind an embankment wall. An ore cart may get away from a trammer and crush a hand or foot, or even a head. A ceiling support might give way. A fire might even break out among the refuse gathering in the corners of the shaft. But these things were expected. It was simply the way things went below the ground.

In 1913, things came to a head. The workers, gathered from many of the companies, both large and small, that dotted the Keweenaw, voted for and demanded recognition of the Western Federation of Miners as their union and drew up a list of demands.

When the companies pulled together and refused across the board, they insisted conditions in the Keweenaw were good and would not warrant allowing such a "Godless and socialistic" movement to take root in U.P. soil.

In the last week of July, the miners called a strike. The companies presented a united front and held out. They realized full well there were more workers where these came from. Paid strikebreakers and replacement workers, many of the latter not knowing what they were walking into and how their newfound label of "scab" would affect their lives, were brought in by the trainload.

Violence flared up almost immediately. Credit in stores was cut off to men going on strike, and violent altercations between business owners and men trying to feed their families became routine. Men on both sides were intimidated, beaten, or shot. Arson took out company buildings, and workers were forcibly evicted from their homes. Dynamiting punctuated the air near unguarded railroad crossings and mine structures and shafts. The local authorities, clearly in the pay of the copper bosses, arrested and beat strikers at will. Assassinations—outright murder—were carried out by both strikers and the "Citizens' Alliance" vigilante groups.

At the urging of the bosses, Governor Ferris of Michigan sent in state militia to "restore order," and the strike district was put under martial law. When mounted troopers breaking up a pro-strike demonstration on Sixth Street in Calumet trampled a young girl to death, the message was clear to the workers: We are the government and we are not on your side.

By September, the area was attracting national attention as a battleground. Sporadic yet frequent outbreaks of violence grew more common despite the presence of troops and the arrival of Waddell men hired by the companies. "Deputies" and paid Ascher guards patrolled company interests and didn't much care what they had to do to keep their assigned areas pacified.

National figures began to take part. Mother Jones, the patron saintess of the workers and their families, arrived to speak out in favor of the union. Clarence Darrow conferred with Governor Ferris and traveled to the strike zone itself to speak to workers. Even President Wilson was approached, but failed to enter into the discussion.

All such involvement, of course, drew the ire of the mine owners who detested what they saw as outside agitation in their demesnes. Their unofficial organs, the English language newspapers, although claiming impartiality, began referring to the strikers in general, and the Finns and Italians in particular, as too socialistic for American life. "The Finns, due to their experience with the Repressive Tsarist state see violence as the only solution. They and their Socialist brethren, the Italians, wish to wrap themselves in the red flag they consider redemption despite what well meaning and patriotic citizens desire and work towards," announced *The Citizens Gazette.*

By August some of the strikers, mostly Cornish and English speakers, were ready to hang it up for various reasons. Sickened or cowed by the violence or tired of harassment from their neighbors, they voted to return to work if promised protection and arbitration by an unbiased committee, free of the taint of either the owners or the Western Federation of Miners.

They, however, were only one group out of many.

An "Italian mob" attacked the shaft house of the mine near Painesdale. Two deputies protecting the property were slightly injured while one striker was shot dead and two more seriously injured. The mob came nowhere near what was claimed to be their target.

Three nights later, shots were fired into a boarding house full of sleeping strikers. Four men were wounded while a fifth died immediately after being shot at point blank range through an open window he was sleeping near. Although six "deputies," all, incidentally, members of the Citizens' Alliance, were later arrested, none were found guilty of any wrongdoing in the speedy trial with its all-English-speaking jury.

A federal investigator on the scene reported that the violence simply was taking its toll on the good people of the community, and that many English-speaking workers and a smaller number of foreign-born admitted "to be confused of why the strike took place at all." "Why," one said, quoted in the report, "the conditions here are not that bad. In fact, they're better than any mine I ever worked."

Clarence Darrow suggested, "All gunmen of whatever stripe ought to be banned from the three counties. Yes, that includes the small minority among the union driven to violence, but they're not the worse and every right thinking citizen knows it. Those deputies are just hired thugs. They flat out can kill a man if they want, and too many of them want." A week later a group of demonstrators were fired at from the cover of a copse of trees on a hill overlooking their parade route. No one was seriously wounded, but the attempt still rattled them.

One man said, "I don't mind the shouting, but the shooting is what gets tired. Whoever those boys were, bad shots or good, they made me drop a bottle." This "translation" was widely repeated in the general English-speaking press, who added that, "Taverns are frequently the starting and ending points of these so called 'parades' so the inveterate drinker may have his drop of 'liquid courage' before feigning moral outrage at what they consider the recalcitrance of the owners."

The foreign language newspapers printed the names of those they suspected of being involved as shooters and suggested an appropriate response. For this, two newspaper offices found themselves ransacked by deputies, with the editors detained for inciting violence.

In the first week of October, an American flag was knocked to the ground from the hands of a striker at the head of yet another parade. In the near-riot that broke out following the incident, all sides soundly renounced the patriotism of the other while doctors treated the dozen or so with mostly minor injuries in the name of the general good.

Forty-nine strikers and "outside agitators" including Anne Lockwood, a Chicago socialist leader, were rounded up in response to "this most recent affront to common decency. The lack of character and morale fiber among those most recently incarcerated is a sure sign of the degeneracy bringing violence to our community," as the papers reported.

Despite this note of the moral high ground, soldiers by now had been barred from entering local taverns, and the children of strikers were being targeted at school and driven from the premises with the tacit approval of many of the teachers.

Still, there was more than enough ill will to make things even uglier.

Henry Engel, a well-known if not much loved local sheriff, was walking home after his nightly rounds. Over the course of the previous three weeks he had been in a number of altercations, arrests, and just plain attacks on strikers in the bars and on the streets of Allouez. He had earlier that evening personally beaten three men in a fight at the base outside of Gallagher's Saloon when he had informed them they weren't allowed on the premises. Usually this came from no decree but his own and was only a sign that he was looking for a fight. Two of the men had been knocked unconscious, and the third had lost teeth. All were beaten bloody. When two other deputies arrived he had the three hauled off for resisting arrest.

As he walked past a copse of trees, a voice thick with some eastern European accent whispered out, "Hey, you there, Engel. I hear you like to beat men. Come here and try me."

With a grin Engel stepped off the path looking for more fun.

Witnesses later said at least seven shots had been heard.

Engel was found shot dead. Neither side was too grief-stricken over the man, but the companies had lost a particularly vicious tool, and that called for some retribution.

Two strikers, both Finns, walking home from a union meeting were picked up by armed horsemen. Their bodies were found dumped down shaft number three the next morning. A printed notice informed the public that justice had been done and Sheriff Engel was avenged.

It was quickly discovered that both men had been in Hancock the night of Engel's shooting in Allouez.

Train lines in and out of the mining district were attacked and dynamited repeatedly in the first weeks of November. A house boarding Ascher men in Allouez burned under an early snow in the last week of November while crowds gathered to jeer at the company fire brigade, which could do little to stop the destruction. General Abbey received reinforcements and the area covered by martial law was expanded to include all of the three main counties of the mining district.

"We need the extra manpower if we are going to succeed up here on the range," Abbey was quoted as saying for the daily newspapers. "The problem here is the sheer number of these ne'er-do-wells who have their own military experience everywhere from South Africa to the Philippines. I must have the manpower to keep the peace."

None of the reporters present pointed out that there didn't seem to be any peace to keep—at least none said anything out loud—but the general consensus was that things were out of hand and public opinion might just be starting to stray toward the miners on strike. It was hard to ignore that most of the violence in the towns was brought on by hired guards and deputies. Troopers were banned for displays of public intoxication, but many of the fights had started on military sweeps of the streets to keep the peace, and many of the enlisted soldiers involved seemed to exhibit a snootfull often only overshadowed by that of the officers present.

A last call went out from the company to forget the union, return to work, or pay the price.

Most everybody agreed that times were tough, but more trouble was brewing.

Five

SIGNS BEGAN TO GO UP as the Copper Country entered November of 1913. "REMEMBER THE LITTLE ONES! A CHRISTMAS EXTRAVAGANZA FOR CHILDREN WILL BE HELD CHRISTMAS EVE AT THE ITALIAN HALL. FOOD AND A GIFT WILL BE MADE AVAILABLE TO ALL," they said. Even the English papers acknowledged that bringing a little joy into the lives of children who had little would be a Christian thing to do, although a couple suggested that allowing the snakelet to grow into the snake may not be the American thing to do.

Up the stairs to the second-floor ballroom of the Italian Hall climbed hundreds of children, their mothers, and the occasional father. Almost everyone there was an immigrant or the child of immigrants. These were people for whom English was at best a nodding acquaintance. Finns, Croatians, Italians, Poles, Russians, Swedes, Hungarians, and an odd sprinkling of Irish jostled in the food and gift lines. Songs of the season were sung out in many languages and keys. The piano played the melodies most thought of as familiar, but the cacophony of language would have made Babel blush.

As the night went along a little joy was spread. Children used to doing without were full and happy. Parents with too many worry lines on their faces were able to forget for a while what their lives were like and how precarious the futures of these cheerful children were. For a little while they were happy.

For some, it was the last happy memory of their lives. For some, it was their last conscious thoughts.

"Fire!" was the cry. Children, most of them Finnish, began to panic and ran for the stairs. Some mothers joined them. Older sisters took their siblings' hands and rushed to the staircase to escape from the second floor before flame and smoke overtook them.

But there was no flame, no smoke. There was only panic.

Children and steep stairs, high and narrow, were not a good combination. The first little girl fell towards the bottom. Soon others were tripping over her, and then more tripped over them. The screams began.

The screams toward the bottom of the stairs were soon choked out as the life was pressed out of the children beneath the crush. A father waded into the mob on the stairs, grabbed his daughter and tossed her back up to the top before he fell under the press of people. His daughter survived. He did not, nor did his wife or son ahead of him on the stairs in their attempted escape.

The last to enter the staircase couldn't proceed—the staircase was filled from risers to ceiling—and so they were saved. They stood there at the top and looked down into the carnage on the staircase. The moans of the dying competed with the silence of the dead. It was a sight the survivors would carry with them to the day they died.

The doors at the base of the stairs were opened, but it was impossible to extricate the bodies from the sheer weight of the compressed mass above. Ladders were brought and run to the second story windows, and men began to remove the injured and dead, bringing them back up to the ballroom and laying them in rows upon the stage.

The calls for missing children in a dozen languages were split by the wails of recognition as bodies large and small were brought up into the light. The Christmas tree, now completely incongruous to the scene it overlooked, still had lit candles—the only flames that had really burnt—on its branches.

Survivors were brought down the ladders as the clearing of the stairs continued. The vast majority of children and parents who had been in the room survived, but some families had lost all of their children. It was the immigrant community—Finns, Croatians, and Hungarians in particular—who had been the hardest hit. It was their children stacked upon the stage and their lives torn apart. The same people most intent in the strike had the hearts torn out of them in the minutes of the panic and the hours of the recovery of bodies.

The stories started immediately. The men who screamed "fire" had worn Citizens' Alliance buttons. The panic was intentional. The doors at the base of the stairs had been held by laughing strikebreakers to prevent escape as the press of bodies grew before them. The whole incident had been engineered by the copper bosses. The stories spread in ripples and waves, beginning that night and continuing on through the community, the world, and time.

No one could prove them, however. The people at the base of the stairs who might have testified to the intentional holding of the stairs were dead. No one outside of the building had seen or heard the start of the panic. No one had heard orders or laughter.

The witnesses who had survived above gave conflicting stories, too. Some claimed a tall man in a long black coat had shouted "fire" in the ballroom itself. Some kitchen workers said they had seen sparks outside the window as if from a chimney fire, but none of them said they had shouted. Some said they had heard nothing before the panic began. Others said they heard shouting, but the shouting was of the Christmas celebration among the children. Perhaps, they suggested, the Finnish and Hungarian children had misunderstood? Could a mistaken cry of joy in another language be taken as a warning of fire in their own?

Newspapers local, national, and foreign reported the story and the speculation. Pictures were reproduced of stacked bodies, the chaos left over in the hall, funeral corteges, open graves, graves being filled, and weeping survivors.

No one would know for sure what caused it, but the incident took the life out of over seventy party goers, the community, and the strike.

And if a full envelope and a train ticket were passed to a loyal worker by a company executive in the parlor of one of the big homes in Calumet that Christmas Eve night, there was no witness to the scene who ever spoke a word about it.

The union at first refused the offer of support from the mining company executives. "We'll bury our own rather than accept help from killers," said the union president, William Moyers, in an interview on Christmas day while a train full of coffins was awaited from further south.

The spirit of the movement was gone, though. Some men who had lost children or wives simply packed up and left following the burials. Families headed out West for a new start. A surprising number of single men with no direct connection to any of the bereft families simply faded away to parts unknown.

A group of armed vigilantes showed up at Moyers's hotel room on December thirtieth. He was taken from his room, roughed up, shot in the leg, and delivered to the train station, where he was summarily driven out of town. He would only see Copper Country one more time, when he returned under military protection for the inquest into the Italian Hall tragedy.

The inquest itself reached no real conclusions. The speculation over intentional cause, the various witnesses in and out of the building, the competing agendas of striker and mine owners, "Americans" and immigrants were all brought forward, but to no real purpose except to say an inquest had been done.

By February, the strike was over. Most men returned to work. The die-hards either voluntarily left the area or were refused work of any sort. Help from other unions and the Western Federation of Miners dried up as they realized just how much of a lost cause this particular campaign had become.

There was a certain degree of smug satisfaction and back slapping in mining company offices and at the Miscowaubik

Club, the private dining and watering hole of the local hoi polloi. Most wouldn't say all recent events had been good things, but they certainly had to admit that the outcome was agreeable, as well, of course, as inevitable. The English language newspapers reported a return to "law and order" and "the American Spirit of enterprise." The "deputies" left for greener conflicts while the Waddell and Ascher Companies cashed their checks and accepted congratulations.

The Finnish and Italian papers moved on to other topics dealing with problems in their respective homelands and the victories and defeats among their immigrant groups in other parts of the country. After a short time the Italian Hall itself returned to business as usual, and except for an odd echo or appearance on winter nights over the ensuing years, the ghosts of the children were for the most part seemed to be laid to rest in the trench graves that had been dug for them.

Occasionally someone came forward with a new "revelation" or even a confession—it was remarkable how often over the years the drunken confession to having been the one to call fire was made in bars and taverns, even when the confessor wasn't old enough to have been born in 1913—but the event itself grew fuzzy in local memory. Still, it had its effects. It would be another thirty years before the mines unionized and fifty-five years until another range-wide strike took place. Even Woody Guthrie's song "1913 Massacre" couldn't keep the event current in popular, national culture.

So quiet, of a sort, settled over the Keweenaw. An acceptance of one's lot became a part of the local make-up for the most. Workers had been put in their place and had learned their lesson, which was something business leaders, politicians, and others would make use of in the future.

Six

ROY AND PETE, stream fishing poles over their shoulders, walked along the Superior shoreline from the Tobacco River. Stamp sand beaches stretched out as far as the eye could see from here—which really wasn't that far given the fog coming off the lake. The skyline itself disappeared a few hundred feet off shore.

"What's wrong, Pete?" Shea asked, continuing the conversation that had started on the drive to the river. "I mean, what is it that's filtering out of our lives and where does it all go? I never dreamed I'd be asking these kinds of questions after high school, but I am. Where's everything that was promised?"

"I don't know, man. I mean, I know what you're asking, but I don't have any answers. Sure, I remember . . . we were all going to live on the same street someday. Each one of us was supposed to have made it somehow. I guess each of us figured we'd do a little bit better than everyone else," Pete said with a smile, "but we'd all have made it."

"That's pretty much the way I've got it down, too, except we never could quite agree where that street would be, right? Was it going to be New York, Galway, or somewhere in Australia? At any rate, I sure as hell never expected to still be here."

"Australia! That's right. I used to stay awake nights trying to decide how I was going to tell my folks I was moving to Australia. I knew leaving would hurt their feelings, but I figured being successful would make it up to them. I even figured I could write about the big leave-taking scene in the big book in the future."

"Didn't work out that way, did it? Here we are still twelve miles from where we started talking about it all those years ago. Over fifteen years and we're still waiting," Roy said. "I mean, being gainfully employed, married and having kids—all that stuff is fine. I even like my job, but it's not what was in the plans. It's not the same, is it?"

"Nope, it's not."

They walked on for a while without saying anything. The fog continued to swirl away from the shoreline. Occasionally either Pete or Roy would pick up a flat piece of sandstone and skip it off the swells half-heartedly making it to shore. Neither talked, but they were still sharing the same thoughts.

Roy was the first to break the silence again.

"I think we ought to start a new political party, Pete. A movement, maybe. I'd call it the 'Citizens in Exile Party,' and all of us who have that feeling that somehow we've been taken, that we're not living in the U.S. of A. we're supposed to be living in could join. You know, the one with the Pilgrims, not the Puritans. The one that had the cowboys and Indians, not Wounded Knee. The one that had the melting pot, not the wall keeping out the illegals in Texas. The one that gave everybody a fair shot and won all the wars."

Roy sighed before continuing. "Where'd that place fucking go? Is it still out there somewhere and we just haven't got the word? Was it a dream that came out of the Depression and our folks wanting more for us than they had? Was it a dream that faded when we woke up in bed with that asshole Reagan in the '80s?

"I just don't know, Pete, but if it was a dream, maybe it's time we all rolled over and went back to sleep. Maybe that's why we're all on a trip for downers and Darvon. Maybe we figure the dream's still there if we can just get to it again." He paused. "We're just sure of ourselves anymore."

"Hell, Roy, I'd be happy if we could just hold on to our own little corner. Look what we've got coming down on us again—getting used and abused by Lansing and the Lower Pee. We're used to it—being their playground, I mean. You know, kept for a recreational ghetto for the folks downstate. This time, though, it looks like Uncle Sam is getting in on it, too. First Seafarer and Elf, next a building boom of federal prisons. The Waterways control bill to take away any say we have in our own streams and lakes. All this talk about a 'protective containment area' for nuclear waste and relaxing the environmental protection so leach mining can be done for national security? Does it matter who is trying to shit us? It all means we get dumped on, right?"

"Yep," Roy answered. "But that's the way it's always been here. It's just new bosses rolling in behind the old bosses. First the mining companies screw us and rape the land over real good. When people started asking for a larger piece of the pie what did United Chemical do? Decide the natives were too restless and the profits too small, sold out to someone from overseas for a tax write-off, and left us here holding the bag. We're used to being taken for a ride, and as long as we expect it, someone's going to take advantage. I suppose the feds feel it's their turn now.

"Somehow it feels different this time, Pete. Sure, the mining companies screwed us, turned the lakes toxic, left everybody with mounds of poor rock, concrete, and rubble in their backyards, and outside companies still own most of the land, but they left us here where we could still use it, like this beach. But the federal government now—that's something else. These guys play for keeps. I swear they won't be satisfied until everybody here is filled with mercury, PBBs, and radiation and glows in the dark. They want us so bad—our land, that is—that they'll do anything to drive the last Yoopers out and turn the whole area into one 'Enter at Your Own Risk' park. Hell, this administration probably has a contingency plan to pave over everything to make it easier to truck in the waste."

"Paranoid a little, Roy? You've got it bad, boy."

"Remember the old adage, 'Just cause you're paranoid doesn't mean they're not out to get you.'"

"Yeah, I know."

Except for the breakers in the background, it was quiet again.

"But I remember another adage, too, Roy. What's Jefferson Airplane sing? 'Up against the wall.' Let's say, just for the sake of argument, that you're right. That they do want to send our water from Lake Superior to Las Vegas. That they are set on putting weapon systems that are never going to work or be needed in our backyard. That they do have plans to use the mines for radioactive and toxic storage, and they're not too concerned about what solution mines dump in the streams and us. Say you're right. What do you propose we do about it?"

"Got me scratching. I have no idea—not one single effing idea on what we do about it. That's what bugs me maybe more than the chance they do have a watertight, foolproof, no fail plan. I don't know what to do about it. Maybe there's nothing to do."

"Organize, Roy? Protest? The revolution that never came? You want to don a plaid beret and run through the underbrush burning government installations? A little Che Guevarra action, man? Want to send a letter to Castro and ask for foreign aid or a military alliance?" Pete was wearing his sarcastic face at this point.

Roy stopped walking and turned to him. "Don't laugh, man. I mean, yeah you're taking it too far, but maybe a little of this is just what we need. Treated like the third world, act like the third world."

Pete raised his right hand in a power salute over his head and stood at attention. "Long live the revolution!" he called. "Power to the people! Let the former miners, loggers, and farmers unite! Time to get off our collective asses and join the collective! Long live our friend, the machine gun!"

Roy punched the edge of his hand into his friend's sucked-in stomach, doubled him over, and ran like hell back to the car, dodging the sticks, stones, and epithets from the quickly recovered behemoth behind him.

Seven

WELL, GENTLEMEN, I assume everyone has gone over the details of the prospectus of Project Overseer. Are there questions or suggestions?"

"I assume, sir," said Newsome, "you're asking us if we see any loopholes left open that they may find? I think I speak for all of us when I say, if we reach the implementation stage, there's nothing they can do even if they want to."

There was a general nodding of heads in agreement from the men sitting around the table.

"Then I can count on support from you and your departments when I bring this matter up before the boss?"

Newsome realized it was a rhetorical question. Again, he was met with general agreement.

"Then we proceed. As soon as the report comes in from the two field agents, we will go on to step two. To put it in the vernacular, I believe we have them by the short hairs, and I, for one, have no attention of letting go."

Eight

ON A BEAUTIFUL LATE FALL DAY at the lake, with the kids both napping in the screen tent, Jeri and Roy had a little time to themselves. Hand in hand, they walked the short distance down to the beach, until finally, still in sight of the screen tent where the kids played by the cabin, they sat on an old, beach-washed pine from one of the log rafts that broke up on Lake Superior nearly a century before. Logs such as these littered the beaches a few decades ago, but they were getting scarcer as eventually they were cut up for firewood or reclaimed by local entrepreneurs looking for the high grade, straight-grained lumber that could not be found anymore now that the old growth was long since logged.

The sight of the huge pine on the beach at their camp had always given Shea a touchline to the past. They made him think of what it must have been like in the old days when rafts of logs such as this were towed down to mills on Superior's shoreline. Occasional squalls, especially in the early spring when the loggers' winter harvest was on the move, tore loose logs like this. Some became waterlogged and sank to the bottom, long preserved by Lake Superior's cold water. Others, like this one with the iron tow hook still embedded, made it to shore and eventually met a different fate.

They were both quiet for a time as they sat and watched the waves.

Through Roy's mind ran pictures of other beaches where they had sat together, running back to Isle Royale, a forty-mile-long island in Lake Superior, where they had first met. Just two kids themselves then, gawky, uncertain, and just starting to learn about the possibilities in the world around them, they had a break from the teenage blues that seemed to follow their friends and them around on the mainland.

Through three months of work and play in the isolation of Isle Royale they came to grips with who they were and what they meant to each other. Over the summer they grew together, finding out that the adult games could be more than fumbling around the backseat of a car with an almost insane desire for relief.

The island, corny as it sounded, had been a magical time and place for them. True, the work was no great shakes, but that wasn't the point, From June to the end of August, they and their thirty-odd—and some of them were pretty odd—coworkers, all college age whether they were actually attending during the school year, had lived, worked, ate, played, fought, and often loved together. With no cars, televisions, siblings, parents, and very little real pressure, they had almost no distractions to keep them from paying attention to the minute, the now.

Despite spreading out all over the country at summer's end, a bond grew among the summer workers. A lot of long-term friendships and no small number of marriages had developed out there, and Roy and Jeri's was one of them.

Every so often they talked about how it had been and both occasionally had a bout of homesickness almost too strong to bear for those pine-covered, rocky shores, but they had developed something that survived the exile, and both would always be grateful for the summers there.

That was what Shea remembered, now sitting on another Superior shore with the woman who had grown from the girl he had met twenty years before. Everything they had been through, and just as with any couple there was a lot they had gone through, came back to him and he found himself realizing again that he'd go through it all once more to reach the now they were in today.

Jeri was smiling next to him, and he was about to ask her what she was thinking about when she turned to him and said, "We've been lucky, haven't we? We've managed to make it so far. First the college years when we just had each other and our friends, then we got the jobs and the house, now the kids . . ."

"Don't forget the dogs and the camp here, honey."

". . . and the dogs and the lot. We're some of the lucky ones, aren't we. A lot of our friends never made it this far."

"I'd sure say so, Jer. There's been the times I wasn't sure we would make it through, but somehow it's come together for us."

"Then why are you so worried, Roy? I know you've been brooding lately, and I know it took a lot for you to send that letter to the *Gazette* and that you thought it was necessary. You never take a public stand like that! What's got you thinking things are going to change for us?"

"It's not afraid just for us, Jeri. It's for everyone up here. We're just included in the general grouping. It's for all the screwballs we've got up here—all the small town people, the workers, the unemployed, our retirees. It's for Erin and Sean, you and me. It's for the guy around the block with the killer dog and the derelicts we see in the bars. It's for Pete, Jim and their wives and kids I'm worried. I don't want to be, but I think I have to.

"I just don't want to see things go to hell for any of us. I don't want to see it all go bad up here, and I'm beginning to think there's not any way it won't. Places and people like us, we've been screwed over so often we don't even ask for the Vaseline anymore. Just got sand in it anyways."

Jeri gave him the "you're getting carried away" grin—about fifty percent concerned and fifty percent lovingly mocking. "Do you realize what kind of crazy you're starting to sound like? Next you'll be walking around Calumet muttering about the plot to take the turnip out of pasties."

"Yeah, well, I can guess how it sounds, but I just don't want things to go bad."

She took his hand and leaned back against his shoulder. "All right, you go right on worrying if it makes you feel better. After all, it's not like it's the first time."

"What do you mean?"

"Remember when we first met? You told me that story about how your Lutheran minister scared you kids with stories about the second coming and the judgment, and how when he said no man would expect its coming, you made it your job to purposefully expect Armageddon so it couldn't come. You're doing the same thing now, aren't you?"

"Yeah, I remember. I also remember how terrified I was when I realized one day a whole week had gone by without my thinking about it—and the relief when I realized since we were still safe, someone else must have been expecting it. But it's not like this makes me feel better. It's . . . it's like something I've got no control over. You know, like an obsession, and I'm afraid the whole thing is just eating at me."

Somehow Roy felt drained. He just sat there, Jeri tucked in next to him. Finally he felt the warmth of his wife against him and calmed down. He allowed the flow from her to fill him, renewing his mood.

"There's one thing you're sure right on about," he said. "We have been lucky, and that's something I won't allow myself to forget." He took her in his arms and just held her like they had long ago on that other shore, like they had even since.

Later, they both walked back the forty feet or so to the screen tent, where the two kids had just started making waking noises. They had their picnic and played on the beach with the kids and dogs, and, for a while, everything was just fine.

Nine

FIVE HOURS FROM THE TIME they had left the straits, Newark and Paalo arrived in Phoenix. The two men had mostly been quiet during the long hours of driving. Both, as usual, had their own thoughts, and neither really had felt the need to talk for the sake of talking. They had been partners long enough to feel relaxed in the relationship.

What had been going through the mind of one was very different from that of the other, however. Paalo had been pleasantly surprised as they headed north. The shoreline and the trees, the occasional deer, and the openness of the land had brought back memories of the Pacific Northwest and vacations with his family when he was a kid. He saw himself in the backseat of his parents' station wagon again and felt the same childhood anticipation of "when do we get there?" growing. He seldom thought about any of the years before he had joined—actually been recruited for—the Shop. He found himself looking forward to this area for operations.

To Newark, however, it was starting to look more and more like a foreign land. Raised in big cities, his only real exposure to the "outdoors" had come in the military, and the lands he had served in looked nothing like this. It didn't look anything like that here, but it was starting to have the same feel. For the first time in a long while he had the sense that he was going "in country" again. He kept looking at the small towns they passed through for some familiar sight, some sense of identity, but it just wasn't happening.

When they arrived in Phoenix it was still early afternoon. They went straight to the small one-man realtor operation the Shop had connected with for lodging. The motels here were too open in the small towns, and rather than face the scrutiny of the locals they had decided to rent a house close to, but outside of town.

Ben Gibson, the realtor who handled the renting of a property owned by the local sheriff, Troy Pershing, was surprised when the two clients walked into his storefront. These were not, emphatically *not*, his usual customers. Not that it made any difference to him. He was able to disassociate himself from the people he worked with as long as they had money. He seldom asked questions or looked at customers' money too carefully, and he never talked about his renters or their ways.

He was a quiet man, and except for one lapse unfortunately discovered by the sheriff, he had had no problems staying that way. And he practiced what he preached. Hell, hadn't he been able to keep even a hint of gossip out of the air when he rented a house to Sven Perk's boy when he'd returned from college with three male friends? Being what it was, in this town it could have been a major scandal. The thought of spreading the word hadn't even occurred to him. Perk himself had thanked them three weeks later, after they left.

He didn't usually handle rentals owned by other people, but Pershing's property was the exception. The sheriff and he were *not* friends, but it was Pershing who had talked to one of the young girls who cleaned for Gibson and found out there were services rendered not on the usual job description. Pershing had actually pulled him over one night on a local back road and explained the situation and how he came to find out.

"Now I don't want to make trouble for you, Ben, but you know how this would look if the word got out. You're an upright member of the community," he had said in a tone that said he really thought Gibson was anything but upright, "but I also know you're a man of discretion. I can be, too.

"But understand: you owe me one. I know about you and that little Martin girl you have 'cleaning' the sale homes with you. Now don't try to deny it. I have an excellent source. She'd even give a description of your dick if I asked for it. Just rest assured that I know, but you might as well keep on screwing the little half-wit if you want. She looks like she might be fun, but when I pulled her and her boyfriend over and found the bottle they had, it didn't take too much persuading—I only had to tap the boy once—to get them to tell me about all kinds of things going on around here a good cop would like to know. Couldn't help but think the boyfriend was a little surprised to hear about her and you, though. At any rate, I'll be getting in touch one of these days for some kind of gentlemen's agreement."

So as part of his payback, Gibson handled the rental, without commission, of course, of a piece of property outside of town owned by Pershing. Gibson went ahead and made sure it was ready to go by the time the clients, Pershing said they were two professional friends of his, arrived in Phoenix. He always had his doubts about renting the place, however.

Few people had stayed in the place for very long since the last of the live-in owners had died. That had been Roy Shea's grandfather, if Gibson remembered correctly. It had a history of being bought and sold a number of times, but no one held on to it for very long, and eventually Pershing had added it to his holdings for back taxes.

Most of the sales had come as a loss to the owners, but they hadn't seemed to have minded as long as it was sold. The last owner before Pershing had simply walked away from the place. He couldn't get a local to touch it, and the locale wasn't attractive to out-of-towners who usually went for lakefront rather than hobby farm.

So, through the vagaries of real estate, Pershing had it, and through the vagaries of "law enforcement," Gibson managed the property. He had rented it out long-term a number of times, but the renters always ended up leaving—sometimes even losing deposits to get out of a lease—but despite managing a problem property, Gibson was a pragmatic man and had done the best with what he had. He had told Pershing when the sheriff complained about the place not making enough money that a depreciation loss sometimes came in handy at tax time.

Which is why, with some consideration, he was prepared to accept the security deposit and hand over the keys to these two who had just walked in his office.

He briefly wondered if it was a mistake.

"Mr. Gibson? I'm John Paalo, and this is my associate, Thomas Newark. I believe you're holding a rental property for us?" one of the men asked.

"Sure, gentlemen, but just call me Ben, okay?" he said as he shook their hands. "Sheriff Pershing was quite particular about my having it ready for you." Pershing, of course, was not the type to have any such concern. Gibson wondered briefly about what possible connection these two could have to the sheriff. They were certainly out of his league, as Gibson could immediately see.

"I was just out there two days ago to make sure the water and power were both on and that the place was aired out and ready for your arrival," he continued. He didn't want to mention he had gone himself since it was hard to get any of his usual workers to go out there. It wasn't a popular property.

"'Aired out'?" asked Newark. "I hope the place isn't a dump."

"No fears, Mr. Newark, it's just that it's been empty since the last long-term rental, and I wanted to make sure it smelled fresh. Long-term renting is the usual for this place. You gentlemen just happened to sneak in-between." A little white lie never hurt in business.

"Would you like to go across the street for a cup of coffee on me while I fill you in?" Gibson continued.

Newark continued to speak for both Paalo and himself. "No, thanks. If it's all the same, it's been a long drive and we both have a lot to do before tomorrow. We'd just as soon head straight out if you don't mind."

"Well, sure. No problem at all. I understand. That trip upstate is a killer.

"Why don't I just get my keys and you can follow my truck out there?"

"That'd be fine—Ben, you said it was?"

"That's right. If you stay with us awhile you'll find there's little use for a `mister' in conversation up here, Mr. Newark."

Gibson realized just how that had sounded as he led the two men from his office, locked the door, and headed over to his truck.

Ah, hell, he thought, *they probably take us all for backwoods hicks anyways.* He started his truck and pulled out onto the empty street. Newark and Paalo were right behind him.

The two vehicles moved down the short main street of town, turned the corner at McWatts, the local ma and pop grocery store, and headed towards the bridge across the Traprock River. From there it a short run to Millwash Road, where they turned again.

Newark, sitting in the passenger seat, asked Paalo, "You notice anything about the town so far?"

"I was wondering when you were going to say something. You do kind of stand out back there, don't you?" He gave one of his rare smiles and added, "Maybe we were just on the right side of the tracks."

"Right side? Damn, that town's not big enough for a right side or wrong side. This whole Phoenix berg looks like it's on the wrong side. I haven't seen another black since—what was that bog town—Marquette?"

"Something like that. Well, look at it this way. The Shop sent us as a team, and they know what they're doing. Besides that, maybe you can impress the locals with your suave, urbane manner."

"Screw you, man," chuckled Newark. "Look, he's turning up that hill. Maybe we're here."

They had been following Gibson up a gravel road and across a small crick, but now he had had turned up a steep, dirt drive. They pulled in behind him, went up the drive, and parked beside his truck. The two men got out of the car as Gibson climbed out of his truck.

Paalo immediately turned to look over the drive back the way they had come. The valley and lake stretched out below. About three miles across the lake sat Phoenix.

Hell, he thought. *Newark's right. It's not big enough for a right or wrong side. It's hardly big enough for a right or left.* He turned and walked to the porch where Gibson unlocked the door and held it open for his two clients.

"This is the place, gentlemen. I haven't had anyone in here real recently, but like I said, it's all ready to go. I think it'll meet your needs." He stood aside to let the two men enter.

Newark and Paalo walked across the enclosed porch and through the door to the kitchen. They looked over the stove, the pearloid Formica-topped table, and the pantry with the refrigerator. A breakfast nook was through a short archway at the end of the room, and along the long wall where the stove stood, twin archways led through to the living room.

On the side wall nearest the entry from the porch was another closed door. "What's this?" asked Paalo, opening the doorway to discover a set of steps heading down.

"That's the basement, Mr. Paalo. On this side the stairs head down and in the next room runs the staircase leading up to the bedrooms. Like I said, I think it'll meet your needs," said Gibson. He swept an arm before him. "The kitchen, pantry, and breakfast area, of course. Through here is the living room," he added, walking through the nearest archway. "Bathroom door's over there near the base of the stairs. Up them, of course, are the bedrooms and a little room which would work as an office, which I think you requested.

"There's a large wood room through the other door in the porch, and that's the basement door under the staircase there. Would you like me to show you any more?"

44

"No, I believe we can find everything all right, Ben," Paalo said. "The deposit check did accompany the inquiry letter, correct? I hope that covers everything for right now."

Gibson smiled, "To be honest, it more than covers everything for at least two months. I wrote back to your office explaining that when I received the check and letter, but they just said you'd take care of it at this end."

"Well, let's not worry about that for right now, Ben. Let's just let it ride. If Newark and I end up staying any longer to settle out our business here, we'll make sure we've got it all worked out before we leave. If we leave in less than two months, consider it a tip for services rendered. Now, as I said, there's a lot we have to accomplish, and so I believe we can take it from here?"

For a moment Gibson felt like he had just been dismissed without having to give a full tour. "There's lots of good fishing around here, fellows. A few tumors in the bass from Linden Lake, but the stream fish are good."

"That's fine, Ben," came the response.

Now he knew he was dismissed.

As he walked out and got into his truck again after a hurried and somewhat embarrassed goodbye, he wondered again about his two new renters. *Guess I'll just have to wait to see, but those two guys don't act like any United Chemical men I've ever met,* he thought.

Just as he was climbing into the cab of his pick-up, he looked back up at the farmhouse. For just a moment he thought he saw a hand in the upstairs window holding back the curtain. It didn't look like the hands of either of the men he had just met.

He climbed in, started the truck, and started to pull out, but then he hesitated. He sat there for a moment without moving, and then said out loud, as if reminding himself, "I do believe they said they could take it from here." He punched the gas, kicked up some dirt, and headed down the drive back to the real world.

Ten

NEWARK AND PAALO WALKED through the small home checking out the rooms and the view from the windows. They made a thorough inspection of the upstairs, discovering a long storage closet built into the eaves all along one of the long walls. They then made a run-through of the ground floor, including the bathroom—Paalo flushing the toilet experimentally—and the woodshed. Finally they made a tour of the basement. It was about as dark and damp down there as one might expect from a place over a hundred years old. All in all, though, Paalo and Newark were satisfied. The house was adequate, if unexciting.

Essentially, the building was a two-story square with a one-story addition including the bathroom—the house itself had been built long before indoor plumbing—and the extra woodshed room tacked onto the side by the drive. The windows were small and irregularly spaced from the outside view, but that was only because of the set-up of the rooms inside. Downstairs in the main section were three rooms. A living room took up half of the available space. A Heatrola with a mica screen was placed on the wall between the archways leading to the kitchen. An open set of stairs along one wall led to the upstairs rooms, with a doorway at the base of the stairs leading to the bathroom.

The rest of the downstairs held a kitchen that took up about two-thirds of the rest and contained the built-in pantry. The rest was taken up by the breakfast nook.

The upstairs was divided into three rooms, all very small, and a walk-in closet, actually a crawl-in storage area along the slant of one walls eaves. Of the three bedrooms, the one at the top of the stairs was the largest, but the least private. Others had to walk through it to get to either of the other rooms. The smallest room was the brightest, having a large window facing southeast out over the fields. There was a doorway that led into the crawl space in this room, too, and another doorway in this room led to the third bedroom. When the doors were open, it was possible to see into each of the other second floor rooms from this one, and anyone moving through the second floor would be visible.

The third bedroom was low ceilinged on the eave side and dark. Only one very small window looked out. All were papered with designs once bright to the point of garishness, but now faded and dull.

The furniture, such as it was, was functional and old. The beds were metal-framed with mattresses that had definitely seen better days. End tables dated to the twenties had little redeeming value except their ability to hold lamps and tissue boxes. Montgomery Ward's chest of drawers took up room, lazing against the walls in each bedroom. Two of the rooms had straight-backed wooden chairs that looked uncomfortable from a distance and proved this characteristic with closer inspection. The only things that stood out were a military footlocker and a framed collection of medals, ribbons, and newspaper clippings hanging on the wall in the third bedroom.

These were actually from Roy's Uncle Karl, who had died a hero in World War II. When Roy's parents and aunts had emptied out the farmhouse after the death of his grandfather, the mementos had been inexplicably left behind, although Roy's mother had recovered and hung onto her brother's letters. Roy had tried to get the collection of medals and clippings back from one of the later owners, but when he refused out of simple cussedness, the look of relief on Jeri's face was so obvious that he didn't pursue them again. The footlocker was against and the medals hung on the darkest wall, furthest from the light of the small window which had been installed here in what had been the boy's room. The footlocker had been brought up here the day it was shipped home to the farm with Karl's personal possessions. His body stayed on the other side of the world in the Philippines.

After the inspection, the two men went out to the car to get their few suitcases, briefcases, and supplies, brought them back in, and unpacked and stocked the refrigerator and pantry shelves. With typical efficiency, they had brought enough to last them a couple of days without the need for a grocery run and stirring up the good folks of Phoenix's interest too quickly.

The afternoon was moving on, and the sun edged closer toward the town across the lake. Newark sat on the bottom porch step in the cool evening breeze. Their gear was long since packed away upstairs in the dressers. The supplies were stocked in the refrigerator and pantry. He felt he deserved a break before going over the dossiers on some of the townsfolk and local characters, so he sat counting the boards on the weathered barn.

The moon came up over the barn roof, and the first stars appeared in the late evening sky.

"It's beautiful country, isn't it?" Paalo asked from behind him.

"Beautiful? Man, this is just empty! Give me a city skyline for beauty. Where's the sound of kids playing in empty lots? Where's the traffic? This isn't beautiful, it's incomplete! Man, whatever they got planned for this place is all right by me."

"Sounds like you're making a judgment call on our orders, Newark. You know I don't want to hear about it even if you think you're right. You start deciding right or wrong, it just slows you down. Thinking about orders makes for a bad partner. Job to do? Do it. That's it."

Newark leaned forward, picked up a rock and threw it against the barn wall. He turned with half-closed eyes against the fading glare from the west to look at Paalo for a moment.

"You and I put in a lot of time together, John. We'll probably put in a lot more. You know how I work, and you know my head is straight. I don't want a lecture from you again, right?"

"Hey, no offense meant, partner. Standard Shop talk, but you know I'm right."

Newark watched his partner a moment longer. "None taken," he said at last.

"Look, it's getting dark," Paalo said. "Let's see if that thing the real estate agent called a stove really works and do up some dinner. I'll do the cooking tonight. Steaks sound good? And we've got nothing big on the agenda tonight, right? Why don't you make up a pitcher of drinks? Break in this job right."

With that, Paalo turned without a word and went back to the kitchen.

After a moment, Newark took one last look at the moon over the barn, shook his head and stood up. He made a quick sweep of the landscape, picking out vantage points from training and habit, and then followed his partner through the door.

The two men worked with quiet efficiency from years of practice. They hadn't voluntarily teamed up. The Shop had done that with its usual attention to the characters of prospective partners, and this team worked well. They had little in common except a mutual devotion to work, whatever that might be at any given time.

An hour later the meal was finished and Newark poured the last of the drink shaker into their glasses, hitting Paalo's first. The team was back together, and the earlier conversation was filed. They took out the dossiers on the people they planned to check out tomorrow and went over them for hours, talking them over, brainstorming approaches and figuring angles to use.

At 10:46 p.m., they went upstairs to their respective rooms and were both asleep by 11:15.

Neither slept well.

Paalo dreamed of a progression of people entering his room one by one. Each stood for a moment at the foot of his bed and then turned and walked back out. Even in his dream, Paalo found himself thinking they should have at least opened the door first before walking in.

Three men walked in, one after the other. Each looked enough alike to be related, but one wore his head at a funny angle. Looking at it almost clinically, Paalo wondered if it had something to do with the piece of rope wrapped around his neck. It was too dark for him to see the chest stains on the other two, but somehow he knew they were there.

The last of these three was followed by an old, somewhat nervous looking, shy woman. She smiled hesitantly at Paalo and kept glancing nervously at the small window in the room. Before leaving, she straightened the covers at the foot of the bed and tentatively tapped him on the ankle. Paalo's leg went oddly cold.

That was partially why he at first didn't see the kid who came in next. He stood there for a while before Paalo noticed him. He giggled silently with both hands covering his mouth. When he was sure he had been seen, he turned to run from the room but faded within a couple of steps.

Paalo wasn't really sure if the next one was really there, or was just the suggestion of a person—and it was hard to even say what it was that suggested it was a human. It was more a nebulous ball of light that floated through the door, pirouetted at the foot of the bed, drifted toward the small window and took on a slightly more human form as it poured through the window and then plunged toward the ground.

I wonder what's next, he thought, calmly secure in the knowledge that this was a dream. *Probably just the start of a new case and I'm wondering who we'll meet.* He was a little surprised to find he was now sitting up in the bed. *Must be a part of the dream,* he thought.

The last two, two men, almost identical, very tall, very thin, and very pale, entered together. They had wispy beards, long blond hair, and the longest fingers Paalo had ever seen. There was an almost oriental cast mismatched to the color of their pale blue eyes. Their clothes, made of hide of some sort, seemed to be reversed matching outfits of blues and browns. Both wore hats bearing points for the four cardinal directions, made of the same material as their pants and shirts. Long boots of leather with fur at the top and silver bells on the toes completed their ensembles.

Paalo thought it a little odd that he could see the colors about them so well when his other visitors, except the lightning ball, had been shadows in the dark, but then he realized there was a faint glow about these two. He realized the glow was coming from them, and in his present state that made it quite all right.

He watched as they approached, almost in step, to the foot of his bed. The one on the left made a slight bow, with overtones of sarcasm. The brother on the right—for that was how Paalo almost immediately pegged them—smiled at his sibling's respects, but did not emulate them.

As they stood there, their clothes shimmered and changed. It was as if they had become windows to another world. The seasons and settings shifted as the men moved. Paalo saw pines on a barren landscape in winter, lakesides in a summer's evening glow, starlit snowfields giving way to fields of wildflowers—some flowers unlike any others Paalo had ever seen—and all was changing from moment to moment.

They looked at Paalo curiously, as if sizing him up from a great well of self-confidence. He found himself feeling lesser, more diminished than his usual persona ever revealed. He felt somehow wanting, but there was no condemnation in their eyes, just a slight judgment from Brother Left and amused concern from Brother Right.

Then they, too, took their leave, but instead of turning toward the door or window, they slowly sank from view through the floor. As they left, a scent of cedar and a slight sprinkle of snow swept through the room from where they had stood, but it quickly melted on the wooden floor. A hint of small, light bells sounded.

Paalo slumped back down into the bed, rolled over, and slept the rest of the night away soundly, without moving. Somehow he knew his visits were over, at least for now.

Newark wasn't quite as lucky. About an hour after he fell asleep he rolled over and came up against somebody in bed with him. He sat bolt upright, threw his covers off, and reached for his bedmate from instinct.

His hands met a temporary resistance—could that have been warm flesh?—and then sank through to the sheets.

He sat shaking his head to clear it from sleep. He had almost called out but stopped himself in time. *What would Paalo have to say about nightmares spooking me,* he thought. *Just a damn dream.* He was quite aware, however, that he almost never dreamed and couldn't remember his last real nightmare.

Looking around, he realized there was a light on the wall behind him about a foot away from his own head. It was a glowing spot that slowly, as he watched, took on the form of a human face laughing silently. It was a strikingly unpleasant human face as most of the features seemed somehow rearranged, perhaps with something blunt and heavy.

Before he could act—by either attacking or fleeing—it disappeared.

He swung his feet over the edge of the bed, planted them solidly on the floor, and sat there with his hands on his knees. He was more shaken than he had been since waking in a tent in a jungle and finding a sapper moving from the corpse of Newark's tent mate toward himself. He had been able to kill the sapper.

Something was moving across the floor of his room. One part of him thought, *Rat,* and he found himself incongruously planning a complaint to Gibson about their accommodations. Just as he realized how odd a thought that was given the face he had just seen on the wall, the moving patch of dark lifted itself up and morphed into the figure of an old woman, who hurried toward him while looking back over her own shoulder. She climbed in over the footboard and scurried toward him on hands and knees. Just as he leaped to his feet, a fraction of a second before she could touch him, she disappeared.

The mattress sprang up as if a heavy weight had just been removed.

Newark walked over to the dresser, picked up the holster and gun he had set there earlier that night, pulled the pistol and automatically checked the breach for a bullet and turned back to the bed.

There were two men in the few feet between the bed and Newark. Both were tall, bearded, long-haired and nearly identical. He took in the colors of their clothes without debating how he could see so well in the darkened room, and raised his gun.

The one on the left made a lunge as if to dive in attack.

Newark pulled the trigger and fired.

There was no recoil, no sound, and no effect.

The lunging man straightened up and the two men stood there smiling. The "attacker" was quite enamored of his joke, the other brother was standing cross-armed and amused.

They moved away from the bed, and as they did, Newark, his gun at ready, automatically stepped towards it. He began to climb back into bed before he realized what he was doing and tried to bolt upright again, but the man on the right waved his hand in a slow, sweeping gesture, and Newark sat in the bed with his back against the headboard and the gun resting loosely on his lap.

He watched the two of them as they watched him appraisingly. Newark could feel some disapproval directed toward his recent actions despite the humor his visitors seemed to draw from the situation, and when he realized the ridiculousness of his sitting in bed with two intruders standing before him, he felt out-and-out embarrassed.

As he watched, their clothes began to flow into patterns of landscapes that appeared and faded, giving way to an ever-changing view of lands and seasons.

Not a word was spoken.

Finally the two men seemed to grow shorter.

Newark realized they were flowing down through the floor. He shivered as a cold breeze swept through the room and a spray of snow landed on his blankets. Then they were gone.

He rocked his head back against the headboard and closed his eyes, but suddenly leaped forward when he remembered the face he had seen back there minutes before. He looked at the wall behind—bare—and was relieved.

"What the fuck," he muttered as he looked at his watch. "Three a.m."

An audible giggle came from across the room near the large window. A small boy stood there, his hands trying to stifle his mirth. Though the window behind the boy Newark saw a ball of light gently floating, rocking slightly from side to side. *It's smiling at me,* Newark thought. *The goddamn thing is smiling at me, and it doesn't even have a mouth.*

Then it floated through the window, passed the boy, and came toward Newark. He started to raise his gun again but the ball changed direction, hung for a moment above the footlocker, and then, turning almost as if to give Newark a last look, it settled to the floor and rolled through the closed door.

He turned back to the boy, but there was nobody there.

Slowly he got out of bed, got back to his feet, and walked across the room towards the window. He hit a cold patch where the two men had slid through the floor and jumped off it quickly.

At the window he lifted the nearly transparent cloth curtain and looked across the moonlit yard towardsthe barn. He saw movement in the apple orchard next to the barn, and for just a moment he thought he saw three men among the trees looking back toward his window. The impression was fleeting, but there seemed to be something off about one of them, and he was sure they were not the men who had been in his room.

He swore softly, "I must have been dreaming. I must have been fucking dreaming."

He walked quietly to the door of Paalo's room and listened. He could hear his partner softly snoring.

At least someone is asleep around here, he thought. *This damn place is busy as all get out once the sun goes down.*

He got back into bed, pulled the covers up, and tried to calm down. Later, once more on the verge of sleep, he rolled over, but opened his eyes.

The old white woman was back in bed with him. She smiled shyly.

Newark leaped from the bed and backed up against the wall. Suddenly there was a hand, from behind, on his shoulder, and he heard a soft laugh in his ear. He turned to look, but, of course, there was nothing there. When he turned back to the bed the old woman was gone, too.

He stood there for several minutes, simply breathing and trying to calm down. Slowly, as the world appeared to become more real around him, he settled to one knee, and then sat on the floor. Almost as a passing thought, he realized he had wet himself for the first time since early childhood.

He stayed there a long time before getting back up. He walked over to the wooden chair and sat down heavily. The dampness in his shorts was getting colder.

* * *

Newark was still sitting there until the morning light began brightening outside the window. Occasionally it occurred to him to wonder why he hadn't, finally, called out to Paalo, how his gun didn't work and why, and what the shit he had just gone through. He had no answers.

When he heard Paalo begin to move in the next room, he got up, stripped, toweled off with the sheet, wrapped himself in a bed robe, and walked downstairs to shower.

"Hey, partner, there's work to do!" he heard Paalo say as he walked back up the stairs after his shower. Paalo was already getting breakfast ready.

Newark dressed, straightened the bed, and looked for any proof of last night's activities. As he strapped on his shoulder holster he began to feel almost normal.

Paalo was putting two plates loaded with bacon and eggs next to the coffee cups on the table as Newark walked through the room towards the porch door. "Hey, got your breakfast right here," he said.

"Yeah, smells great, but I want a quick breath of fresh air," Newark said as he walked through the porch, opened the outside door, and froze.

"Man," Paalo called from the kitchen, "this country living agrees with me, Newark. I slept like a baby last night. Dreamed a little, maybe, but I slept for sure."

He heard a strangled sound from the porch and rushed to his partner's side. "What's wrong, Newark?"

"We sat here last night—yesterday evening—out on these porch steps, right? Watched the moon come up over the barn?"

"Yeah," agreed Paalo, looking at his partner's now ashen complexion. "We did. What's the big deal?"

"I threw a rock and hit the barn, right?"

"Yeah, so?"

Newark pointed, "So? So? Then where's the fucking barn, partner? Where's the goddamn barn that was there last night?"

Paalo's jaw dropped as he saw the empty space where the barn had been last night.

The two stood there for quite some time while the eggs grew cold in the kitchen.

Twelve

L ATER THAT DAY, Newark was uncharacteristically not driving on the way to the Houghton County Sheriff's Department. It was interdepartmental courtesy, even if Paalo and Newark couldn't tell the sheriff exactly who they worked for. They had learned from experience that if they were planning to travel county roads late at night—especially armed—they should go through the motions of understanding local law keepers' concerns.

"I don't know what it was, Paalo. They just kept coming at me, and I've never lived through anything like that before," Newark said. "I've had three friends die in my arms and a hell of a lot more around me, friend and foe alike. I've killed people before and after I joined the Shop, shit, you know I have, yet I've never had a problem with sleep or dreams. I sleep like a baby. Until last night . . . I just don't know."

"Look, like I told you, I dreamed, too. Some of it was . . . you know, like real. It even sounds like some of the characters were the same. But you don't see me falling apart. It's this new assignment and what we were talking about before dinner last night. This job is different. Neither of us is used to being in a position like this, but at least I remember something like it from my folks' camping trips back when I was a kid."

Paalo continued, trying to come up with an explanation for the previous night's events. "You? You got nothing like this in your past. This is hitting you differently. So you dreamed. One nightmare in fifteen years isn't bad." Paalo didn't look away from the road as he drove, but Newark still felt his eyes upon him. "We both walked into something new yesterday. Today's another day. Tonight it'll be different."

Paalo took a deep breath. "Look, I don't usually say things like this. You're the best partner I've ever had, and I'm not nervous about you. Why should you be? Still, if you're ready to bolt, to cut and run, then let them send in someone else and let's get out of here. Nothing's worth taking what it sounds like you think you took."

Newark thought for a moment before replying. "Look, Paalo," he said, "I know what you're doing, but it's more than just dreams or what I think. What about the barn? What about a goddamn disappearing building? We were both awake for that one. I mean, shit, I could have counted the boards on that mother, and you saw it, too! What about the damn barn?"

"I've told you already. It was almost dark when you went out there to sit. It was even darker when I went out to join you. We were arguing and feelings were high. I never actually heard you *mention* the building, and I don't really remember seeing it at all. We're on a farm, right? There's supposed to be a barn. We imagined it because it should have been there. I don't think it was really there." Paalo did have to take his eyes off the road and look away for this one.

Newark looked up at the roof of the car and rolled his eyes. "Are you really going to sit there and tell me that you didn't see it? That I didn't see it either? Is that really where you're coming from on this one? If it is, maybe I ought to be the one looking for a new partner."

They drove along in silence for awhile. Not the usual thinking silence of the two men working on the same problem together, but a silence that came from not knowing, or not wanting to know, what should be said next.

Finally Paalo said, "Look, I'm not trying to say it wasn't there. But it isn't there now and that's all we need to know. Like

I said, this is a new job in an unfamiliar area. We're strung out. We had some drinks after a god-awful long drive . . . I'm just saying, maybe we were mistaken. Hell, I don't know—a trick of the light, a mirage—I don't know. But we still have a job to do. I want to do it, and nothing should be getting in the way, let alone nightmares and a disappearing barn, for Christ's sake. They wouldn't break us up or give us a rest for this one. They'd hang us out to dry. They'd nail our asses to the wall.

"I was in the Air Force, right, Newark? I never saw any, but I know what happened to officers who reported UFOs. They never commanded again. They shipped 'em off to bases in the Aleutians where everybody sees that kind of shit, and they stayed there until retirement if they were tough enough to stick it out. Usually they left the service—some just a couple of years from retirement. I don't want that happening to us. Besides, I know the Shop doesn't send their head cases to the Aleutians."

Newark turned quickly, almost savagely. "Is that what I am? A head case? Is that what you are? Shit, man, I know what I saw! I just don't know how or why. Look, if it'll make you feel any better, I won't say anything, but I know what I saw. But you're right; we've got a job to do. Let's do it."

Paalo turned in his seat to look at Newark. "That's what I've been waiting to hear. Let's just get the job done and get the hell out of here."

Thirteen

SHEA WALKED UP THE STAIRS of the aptly named High Steps Tavern and through the doorway. He waved to Pete at the end of the bar where he was being handed a beer by Joe Smitty, the bartender, and Shea started threading his way through the regulars. It had been chilly outside and the breeze had caught the back of his neck, but inside the heat, smell, and feel of the woodstove enveloped him. It felt like home in a number of ways.

He passed Red O'Hanahan and Hank Jacoby engaged in their usual style of debate with undernourished beer glasses before them and paused to listen.

". . . yeah, well, I still say they're all assholes, you know? You ever heard tell of a cop who wasn't? I figure it's got to be a part of their training—Assholism 101 or something like that."

"I don't know, Red. I figure it's just that new ticket you got last night. Look, you haven't met all the cops in the world, right?"

"Yeah, yeah, right, of course."

Jacoby raised his finger to eye level in front of Red. It was the usual sign that he thought he was about to nail a point. "Then how do you know they're all assholes? Maybe there's some out there who are real decent fellows—you know, hunters, fisherman, and the like. Maybe some of them are real good fellows."

Red sat back, partially to remove himself from the finger Jacoby was sticking in his face. His hand went through his thinning hair as he digested this new thought. Then he reached for what was left of the beer in the glass in front of him, raised it to his lips, and drained the glass.

With the glass still at his lips he looked over the rim at Jacoby and said, "All right, Hank, I'll give you that one."

But then he brought the glass and his other hand to slam down on the bar and said, "But you can't argue with this: All the cops I've ever met are assholes!"

The usual head shaking and approving laughter came from the others seated at the bar as they acknowledged the end of this particular round. Red ordered fresh brews for himself and Jacoby while Hank got up to "hit the head," as he called it from his Navy days.

After Smitty handed him a Stroh's without asking, Shea took the stool next to Pete. "Sounds like the boys are in their usual form tonight," he said in greeting. One night Shea had endeared himself to the two by pointing out the verbal fencing they'd been up to on that particular evening was more like a battle of wits between unarmed opponents. Both Jacoby and Ed acknowledged they'd been off their oats that day, and so no offense was taken.

Hank got back from the men's room and called out to Smitty, "Once more, my congrats and admiration, Joe. That has to be the cleanest pissoir I've ever had the pleasure to relieve what ails in."

"It is clean, Hank, but it's indoors. I prefer to express my nature out in nature, so to speak," said Pete.

"Myself, I love an outhouse," added Shea. "There's something so basic about them. Know what I mean?"

"Yeah, I know, but I still prefer a farting post and squatting like a moose if it needs to be done."

"'If needs be done, then 'tis best it were done quickly'" quoted Darren Olson from the other side of Pete.

"No, don't you see? That's part of the problem," said Shea. "Too quickly—no aesthetics. Gets the job done, but there's no style or grace."

"Same with sex," rejoined Pete.

"Wait a minute, Shea, if I get you right you're arguing with Pete over the aesthetics of an outhouse?" asked Olson.

"Well, we haven't actually started arguing yet. That comes later, but I guess aesthetics is the right term, right, Pete?"

Pete waved a hand distractedly over his beer. The gesture was general and vague enough to include everything or nothing. He had one false start complicated by an unintentional swallow from his glass, followed immediately by an intentional one, and finally declared, "They're dangerous."

"Dangerous?" asked Olson.

"This you have to explain," Shea said. "What do you mean dangerous? Splinters?"

"No, no . . . not that. You just have to watch those things. I ever explain to you about my uncle?"

Shea leaned back and smiled. Olson said no.

"Yeah, well he could explain about outhouses to you." Pete took another pull at his beer and then continued with an arch look. "Yep, uncles and outhouses. And groundhogs."

Olson had a bad moment figuring out how uncles, groundhogs, and outhouses went together. He tried a couple of different views in his mind, mulled them over briefly, and then rejected each in turn as being unpleasant if not completely distasteful.

"As I was saying then—my uncle, right? He was visiting—no, he was being visited by his brother-in-law. Never did like the man. Uncle Brent, I mean, didn't like him. I never got to meet the man before the divorce and all. I do put a lot of faith in Brent's opinions, though.

"Anyway, Brent had this sister and she had this husband then—hey, how about another beer, Olson? Good, get one for me, too—anyway, they were up visiting the farm the way they did. Far too often in Brent's opinion. He really didn't like this guy. So he always started in on every chore that needed doing on the farm just as soon as he saw their car pull up.

"One of the chores that needed doing was to get rid of this groundhog that was eating up the garden. He tried everything! Traps were sprung empty, poison was seemingly gobbled up, and dogs ran and hid when they saw it coming—nothing was working. Brent even took to sitting out on the porch steps every morning and evening with that old single shot .22 he had, trying for a shot.

"He'd take a shot, that old woodchuck would sit up as if to say 'What the hey?' and take another bite from whatever it was munching before strolling over to its hole by the buildings out back and making an exit."

"One of these buildings was an outhouse, right, Pete?" asked Roy.

"Right, Shea. This was an outhouse, but it wasn't any ordinary shitter. This was deluxe. It was actually one of three buildings all linked together out there in back of the farm. Ten foot of the length was outhouse, and that was divided into two stalls—one a two-seater and the other a three. Remember, Brent had a whole flock of kids and room seemed to be real important to that family. I've heard tell that he and his wife used to head out there when they wanted a little time to talk. I mean, they'd long since added indoor plumbing, but the outhouse was still there and occasionally used for old time's sake.

"Anyway, another part of the complex was a grain bin, and the third was a storage shed full of tools, bags of quick lime and cement, and paint cans. Rolls of barbed wire sat next to old bikes. You know, the whole place was full of stuff no one used anymore."

"What about that woodchuck, Pete? Where's he fit in?"

"Yeah, well, Brent, he decided to blow it up."

"Blow it up?" asked Olson with a little skepticism.

"Yep, that's what he decided on," Pete said with a grin. "So, with the help of his brother-in-law—help begrudged but given—he emptied out a gas tank that he hadn't used regularly since he caught his youngest dumping gravel and leaves down the pipe. They poured a bunch of it off into three five-gallon pails and then, after running thirty feet of hose down that groundhog hole, they dumped that gas on in.

"Brent had been blowing stumps that spring as usual, so he had some fuse left. If he would have had any dynamite left he would have used that, but all he had left was fuse.

"Anyway, he ran the hose and poured the gas, but about that time the brother-in-law—Phil, I think his name was—felt the call and headed for the outhouse to answer nature. That was more than all right with Brent. He'd just as soon not have Phil around."

Pete took another pull of his beer to lubricate the talking glands, and Shea took the opportunity to break in. "We were talking about the dangers of an outhouse, right?"

"Damn straight, Shea. Hadn't I told you the brother-in-law went off to take a leak?

"Well, Brent touched off that fuse and it went sputtering toward the hole. All of that gasoline, at least fifteen gallons of it, was just pooling and fuming in that hole, waiting. When the flare from that fuse hit the fumes in that hole, everything went straight up. The ground around it actually lifted.

"And a split second later, the ground around the other holes that chuck had dug—all interconnected, but unnoticed by Brent, went up too!

"One of 'em must have come out inside the outhouse where Phil had been standing. Suddenly there's a quick sheet of flame, and then he's knocked back about three feet through the door and out there into the yard with his pride in his hands and his eyebrows burned flat. Then the whole wall decided it had been standing too long and came down on him. That was followed by a cloud of mostly atomized crap. Most of that settled on Phil, too.

"Brent had watched the building and a goodly portion of the backyard blow from the safety of fifty yards from the fuse hole. He saw Phil flying out with a number of small fires about his person, his fly open, and his dick gripped.

"Turned out, after it was all over, that one of the blazes was in Phil's pubes. That's the one Ed always referred to as a scrub fire in later years."

"He actually blew his brother-in-law up?" laughed Olson.

Shea and the others were laughing too hard to ask questions of their own yet.

"Yeah, he blew him up—well, actually he blew him down, too. According to Brent's sister it was about three months before Phil calmed down enough to get it up again. Marnie, that was his sister's name, always did hold that against him. But outside of that and a few small burns and bruises, there really wasn't much physical damage done."

"When everything settled down, Brent must have kicked his own ass, no?" asked Shea.

"Well, not really. It did tee him off that the buildings went," said Pete, "but the outhouse stalls were in pretty good shape yet so he just rebuilt the walls on that part. As for the grain and junk shed, well, he moved what little feed he still needed into a new plastic bin, and losing the junk shed gave him an excuse to get rid of the junk.

"Some other good came out of it, too. Excepting for his own, Phil never completely trusted another bathroom—inside or out—again. He had to do his business at home. Whenever he showed up, Brent would force a couple of beers on him in quick succession, and the next thing you know, he's headed for home. Brent never had a problem with him again."

The crew laughed appreciatively. They all had in-laws. Some were present, some were ex, but they all had them.

"Oh, and by the way," added Pete, "the chuck was back the very next day.

Shea laughed and shook his head with the others. He liked it here.

Fourteen

YOU HAD TO BE CAREFUL, THOUGH. Last winter a downstate couple had wandered in either by accident or looking for local color. Their arrival brought a general hush that grew deeper when they ordered martinis.

Even though his idea of a cocktail was a boilermaker, Smitty mixed them the drinks and actually came out from behind the bar to deliver them over as the level of conversation returned to normal.

That night, Jacoby and Red had started in on tourists they had known over the years.

"Remember those two tenderfoots from Detroit come in here last year, Red? The ones so green to winter driving they parked their Buick halfway out in the street and then had the nerve to complain when Tommy scraped the ass end and took the bumper off with the blade of his Snow Commander?"

"Sure, I remember, but what do you expect from folks like that? Must be the air down there—one-half exhaust fumes, one-half factory smoke, and the rest the sweat of too damn many people. Why in hell would anyone want to live like that?"

"Beats the hell out of me, but then I really don't understand why they ever leave it, either. They just bring the same thing with them wherever they go."

"Is the clientele here usually like this?" asked the husband gin drinker.

"Like what?" Smitty asked with an earnestly questioning look.

"You know, rude. Loud and boorish? Talking like the very concept of hospitality is foreign to them?"

This last line was delivered while looking straight at Red and Jacoby, who had turned from the bar the moment he started to speak.

"Well, I just don't know. Sometimes, I guess. But you know, at least they don't insult my friends and my usual customers while ordering pansy drinks that show they don't know what a real bar is for," said Smitty, making a sweep of the bar in front of him with his rag. "And if they're assholes, well, at least they're assholes in their own backyard."

The couple finished their drinks in silence and left without their change.

"Hey, Smitty, don't you know how to handle customers anymore? I'm afraid you drove those nice folks right out of here."

"Damn straight, Red. Have another," the bartender replied.

But that had been awhile ago and Shea saw only regulars here tonight. Smitty served him another, and Shea dropped a dollar on the bar.

He did like this place. The oval bar was a holdover from the old days when you put people across from each other so that even when you were alone you wouldn't have to stare at your own reflection in the mirror. The woodwork was all dark mahogany, and the barstools were solid wood. Chrome and naugahyde captains' chairs hadn't found their way to the High Steps.

Just like Hank Jacoby's assessment of the men's room, the rest of the place was polished and spotless. Oh, here and there along the foot rail in front of the bar were grooves from regular customer use over the last ninety years, but Smitty liked to think that added character, a touch of history, and Shea agreed.

It was a comfortable bar with its own standards of behavior well-known among the regulars, and among locals it was a landmark.

And there were a lot of bars to choose from, too. In most of the towns scattered across the Keweenaw Peninsula, churches and bars had vied to be the most numerous buildings in town. A mining town tradition had built up around each one as each ethnic group moved in, brought their drinking habits with them, and established neighborhood taverns.

The High Steps had escaped becoming just another ethnic bar because of its location next to the theatre. It had been a "safe" area, unclaimed by any one group where Finns, Croatians, Italians, French, Cornish, Irish, and even the occasional real American slumming it could be found elbow-to-elbow. They might not be speaking to each other, but here they could at least share space.

Some, like the Cornish, came to work the mines; some, like the English and Germans, to run them; some, like the French and Irish, came to work in the stamp mills; and some, like the Finns, came to work in company logging divisions—but all had made their ways here and, often as not, established a lifestyle as close to that as they had left behind in the old country.

Roy's home town of Phoenix had grown up around one of the mill sites where the ore was smelted down and formed so it could be shipped elsewhere. Once towns liked this had thrived and spread throughout the U.P., but with the mines and mills closing their doors in the 1960s, most had shrunk down upon themselves, and a few had disappeared completely.

Phoenix's location on Linden Lake had given it a slight edge up. Although many of the sons and daughters of the stamp mills had been forced to move on and follow the mines to the southwest or wearily give in and move south to take their place on the assembly lines in Detroit, enough had managed to find jobs in nearby towns like Houghton and hang on, and the lake attracted retirees and the wealthy looking for cheap summer homes.

There were enough families who made the transition from the strike fund to unemployment to the winter dole of seasonal workers. These were the guys who supplemented summer constructions jobs with hunting —during the days when season was on and at night during the rest of the year—fishing, and snowmobiling the winters away on machines bought on credit.

But nonetheless, the town of Phoenix had been growing backwards over the years. Once a town several sizes larger than the present population of two thousand, it had been slowly folding in on itself with the surrounding fields and woods reclaiming much that had been cleared in the town's heyday.

In direct contrast to the town, the Traprock Valley and Bootjack were being parceled out and more heavily settled. As farming, always an iffy business, became less and less a money making concern, local farmers were dividing their holdings into lots which they sold to those who could afford them. In many cases these were out-of-towners who picked up the property for summer homes, retirement estates, or just plain investments.

The local farmers who had sold parts of their property, then feeling flush with cash, would again attempt farming on a smaller scale. In accordance with natural law, they again lost their collective shirts and once more had to sell off additional parcels. In this fashion, the traditional landowners were rapidly disappearing and farmhouses that had once had their nearest neighbors miles away found themselves surrounded by ranch style pre-fabs and the occasional log kit cabin.

The process had been at work on Shea's own family and circumstances. His family had been one of the ones to hang on. His father had worked the auto plants down south as a young man, and then managed to move north and buy a farm. The farm was meant to be a going concern, which says something about best laid plans of livestock and men.

First there were the dairy cattle, cows with a total disregard for fencing and boundaries. They were as apt to be on the main road, visiting at the neighbors, or looking to get a little action from the beef cattle raised by the neighboring farmer two miles back through the woods as the crow flies and the cow on a mission walks.

Through the summer they broke fences and got into grain fields and gardens. In the winter they kicked through from their side of the barn to the stored hay and ate and ate until they were damn near exploding. Yet they were always hungry when the regular feeding times came as well.

In return, they provided milk when they felt like it, but not on the regular schedule that the cattle owned by real farmers seemed to be on throughout the year.

When there was milk, the dairies were always late in payment. Shea's dad finally saw the writing on the barn wall. He and his family were not meant to be dairy farmers.

What next then? Beef cattle! That was the answer. Less care, a looser schedule—it sounded like a great idea. You let them forage throughout the summer with a minimum of feed input from the hay supply. Sell off those ready in the fall, barn the rest throughout the winter, and collect the money and repeat next season.

Except every farmer in the U.P. seemed to decide to do the same that year. The spring and summer were beautiful, the crop of calves numerous and healthy, and everyone raised exceptional cattle.

And, of course, with that many cattle available, the price of pound per head tanked, and just when everyone, including Shea's dad expected to rake in the cash, they ended up damn near giving them away to the meat processors. By the end of the winter everyone was tired of eating their own steaks.

Of course, there were the fowl as well. Chickens, ducks, geese—all among the most moronic animals God ever invented with His infinite wisdom and a huge wink. They all had their various ways to make the raising of feathered stock a hopeless venture.

Chickens would go insane running into the jaws of fox, mink, and farm dogs. Chicks would drown themselves in water tanks like fanatical lemmings. Roosters would insist a leader's place was outside of the chicken yard and get run over on the road, nailed by hawks of every description, or consumed by the aforementioned carnivores.

When geese weren't busy attacking everyone who walked out into the yard, turning the lawn into one immense guano slide, or honking up a storm making so much goddamn noise that Shea's dad would go a little crazy and massacre the lot of them, they and the ducks would catch the sound of their wild cousins flying north in the spring and south in the fall, and with their capacity for flight hampered by domesticity, find their way off the property and hitchhike north or south, depending on the season, until run over or consumed by every predator faster than they were, which was just about them all. Even with all the feathers there was no hope.

Then there were the rabbits there never really was a market for, which a fast-talking farm agent persuaded Shea's dad into buying for "easy breeding, care, and profit making." It quickly became apparent that the whole idea was flawed.

In a territory like the Keweenaw, anyone who wanted to eat rabbit either raised them themselves or hunted the critters in the wild form. Additionally, because Shea and his younger siblings gave the new "pets" names and soon treated them like miniature versions of the family dogs, no one in the family wanted to eat them. Shea's mom had a hard time cooking the first batch herself for the same reason. Shea's dad tried reason, shouting, and bribery, but all to no avail. The rabbits had become freeloaders. Finally, tired of feeding and cleaning up after the little shit factories, Shea's dad opened the pens, set all the long-eared fur balls to fend for themselves, and they all promptly moved into the hay barn.

For the next two years, anyone grabbing a hay bale and hefting it against the expected weight would fall flat on his ass because the rabbits chewed through the binder twine on every damn bale in the whole hay barn as they made their urban "burrows" in the bales.

The gardens were repeatedly raided by the voracious former pets, and most of the family couldn't bring themselves to shoot or otherwise eradicate Mr. Bun, Princess Flop, and the rest of their brood. Even the farm dogs had been trained to stay away from the rabbits when they were kept in the hutches, and they thought the proscription still applied even though the former hutch inhabitants were now in the lettuce and cabbage.

For those same two years, every night was split by the eerily baby-like screams of rabbits being taken by the aforementioned mink as well as owls, fox, coyotes, and bobcats that swarmed into the area surrounding the farm as soon as the "Free eats: rabbits!" word got out to the predator community. Even the barn cats gave up their usual diet of mice and rats in favor of the greater game and reward of stalking once-domestic rabbits.

Next Shea's dad tried to raise mink. A "friend" of the family sold him a dozen. The idea was to let them breed, reach luxuriously furred adulthood, and then harvest them for profit. The problem was, of course, that all twelve of the mink purchased—at no small price—for this enterprise eventually proved to be all males. There was no breeding, not even of the "don't ask; don't tell" variety. The mink all consumed vast quantities of food, and then, just before "harvest," disappeared into the night after a spectacular break-out that Shea always felt had been engineered by his sister, who wanted to see her little friends keep their hides. The mink moved into the woods by the farm and proceeded to eat chickens from the pen.

Finally, it became a fish farm. They dug ponds and stocked them with fish—trout for the pleasure of having them, and suckers to be sold as bait to local fishermen. The trout grew fat on fish pellets, mosquitoes (the U.P. state bird) and flies.

Soon everyone in the district who could walk, crawl, or hobble around by night was fishing the ponds and taking everything from minnows on up illegally. In the dark a few even took suckers when they hit the bait.

Realizing he was supporting a new type of shit factory and providing meals for every poacher in the community, Shea's dad finally stopped feeding the trout and allowed them to dwindle (ha!) naturally.

The suckers lasted longer. Each year they were netted from local streams when they ran in the spring during spawning season, were transported to the farm in tubs carried in the back of the pick-up, and then, one by one, were counted and hand delivered to the ponds.

Suckers are bottom feeding fish and considered by most U.P. residents to be an ugly garbage fish. A few die-hards do smoke and eat them, but it's in general agreement that their greatest purpose in life is to become bait to help to catch other fish that are eaten and appreciated. They are a tenacious fish that, like early twentieth century Russians, came in two main varieties, white and red. Also like the Russians, the white was the more desirable of the two.

At any rate, there was an incredible amount of work in catching, transporting, and maintaining them in the ponds from where they were sold for a buck and a quarter a piece to fishermen who cut them up for lake trout or pike bait.

The problem with this was that they had to keep fishermen's hours. It was nothing unusual to hear a knock on the door at five in the morning to find some avid fisherman with lake trout on his mind looking for suckers. Especially appreciated by the family were the sportsmen who called the house phone between the hours of twelve and six a.m. to make sure Shea's dad would have bait for them "first thing in the morning." Coincidently, these were the also the only ones who ever seemed to oversleep, get a late start on the day, and show up around noon with the scent of the previous night's pre-fishing beer about them.

Shea's family had been driven to taking the phone off the hook after nine and instituting an "honor system" where the sportsman was to net his own suckers from a tank and leave the appropriate fee in a can in the fish shack. The "honor system" proved to be a slang term for robbery. The money left by those fishermen honest enough to actually leave close to the right amount in the can was simply stolen by the rest and most numerous of the clients.

Eventually they stopped restocking the ponds, especially after two years in a row when the suckers simply didn't seem to run at all. The bait fish simply ran out, and after abusive phone calls and early morning wake alerts ended with disappointed fishermen, the sign at the bottom of the drive came down (Shea wasn't disappointed—he had always felt a little funny telling people when giving directions, "You can't miss my place. It's the one with the 'Sucker' sign by the mailbox"), and aquaculture in Traprock ended.

Except for vegetables for family use, that was the last agriculture the "farm" ever saw. Shea's dad went back to working construction at regular hours for irregular pay. Occasionally the idea of getting a few head of cattle surfaced, but the idea proved theoretical rather than real and the farm remained livestockless, except for dogs and cats. Like most of the farms in the Keweenaw, Shea's family home became just another place where people lived in the country that used to be a farm.

Although the Keweenaw had once been home to many farmers, they were for the most part gone now. The milk truck still stopped for pick-up here or there, but the stops were fewer and far between. Some local potato farmers still plied their trade, praying for just the right amount of rain. Too little and the crop never took, and one drop over that magic amount and the potatoes rotted in the fields before they could be harvested. On the years when just the right amount of rain fell, the potatoes thrived, bumper crops were raised, and the price fell with the overabundance, leading to truck loads of potatoes being hauled off and dumped in deer yards in an attempt that usually didn't work to artificially control the supply and price.

When Shea was growing up, his bus run was all farm kids, but now most of the farms simply weren't used for farming anymore. Families that had eked out a living off the land for generations found themselves forced to take jobs off the farm, and when those dried up, as the invariably did, they found themselves hardpressed to pay off the mortgages that had been a staple of trying to make it in the farming days. Piece by piece, acreage was sold off in an attempt to hang on to the farmhouse itself. Rural country became a string of duplexes along the highway.

Fifteen

SHEA WAS AT THE TOP of the ladder in the back of the house when he heard a car pull up in front. At first he thought it was just the neighbors across the street making another of their innumerable comings and goings. One thing about living on this street, everyone here was constantly in the process of leaving or arriving. For a dead end street it had more than its share of traffic.

The ladder was braced in the peak of his eaves, and Shea wasn't fond of heights. It took a lot to get him to make the first step up on a ladder, and rather than coming down to see who it was, he figured he's give a call down if he heard a knock on the door, and they could walk around to the back. He was a little surprised when Newark and Paalo came around the corner.

"Mr. Shea?" Newark called up. "May we talk to you for a moment?"

"Jehovah's Witnesses or Mormons?" was Shea's response. When neither of the two men smiled, he felt a trifle embarrassed. He also felt a slight knot in his stomach—the usual warning that something unusual might be up.

"No, seriously," he went on. "You can see I've got my hands full up here right now, and I've got to keep at it before this caulk hardens on me again."

"We can agree that you've certainly been busy, and your hands are certainly full . . . but we think you might want to talk to us. This may be a little more important than window caulk."

75

"Well, you guys certainly aren't from around here now, are you?"

"No, Mr. Shea, we're not."

As Newark had been talking, Paalo had moved to the base of the ladder, and now he was leaning in, braced at the bottom, making the aluminum flex slightly in and out away from the house.

"You know, Mr. Shea, working alone in the back of a house like this on a ladder can be dangerous. Especially when no one else seems to be home and your neighbors are either not home or able to see you from their homes. What would happen if the ladder were to shift and you were to lose your grip? Or what if it buckled and collapsed? That's quite a fall. You might lie here for a long time, maybe something broken or worse before anyone found you or heard you calling out. If you could call out, that is. Maybe it's a good thing we happened along. Maybe it's lucky for us."

Shea hated ladders, and characters like this weren't helping any. He set the caulk jar down on the open window's sill and began to come down the ladder. Usually each step down made him feel a little more secure, but that wasn't necessarily true with the two men waiting below for him.

Paalo stepped back just enough to let Shea step off the ladder. It was Shea who had to immediately and clumsily step back once he was on the ground to regain his comfort space.

He shook his head and decided to make nice.

"Now, what can I do for you gentlemen? Have we ever been introduced? You seem to know me, and that puts me at a distinct disadvantage."

"Yes. We do know all about you, Mr. Roy Shea. We're here to do something for you, though, rather than the other way around. We've read your letter to the paper and have heard some scuttlebutt from some of your acquaintances and associates. You know, a lot of the questions you've raised—perhaps *opinions you've expressed* might be better—really don't make you sound like a good citizen, a team player, but more the kind of thing where people are just trying to make trouble. That has some people, my associate and me, for example, a little worried about you."

"What are your names?" Shea asked. The pit of his stomach had been tightening with each of Newark's words. He had little idea about what they were getting at, but it didn't sound good for him.

"I didn't say, Mr. Shea. But as I was saying, do you think you ought to be asking questions that could upset people? Do you really think it's good for anybody up here if people get upset? After all, in a few days it's become obvious to us that you folks living up here already have enough problems. We don't think you should be adding to them."

"I'm afraid you've lost me. You sure you got the right guy?"

"Oh, I'm sure, Mr. Shea. But we haven't 'got you' yet," Newark smiled. "But we could at any time."

Shea's guts did another couple of convolutions.

"Look, I don't know what this is all—"

"Oh, think now, Mr. Shea. We think you know exactly what this is all about. I'm afraid we—and the men we work for—don't like what you've been doing, and we're a little concerned that you might be thinking of continuing to do it. Quite a few of your friends and neighbors are concerned, too. That's not good for a family man, even one like you, Mr. Shea." This, Shea knew, was as close to a real threat as he had ever gotten close to in his lifetime. Well, this and the ladder-shaking a few moments previously.

"In fact, some people are asking what we're going to do about it all. Some are asking, 'What are we going to do about Roy Shea?' And I don't think you want to know what some of the suggestions have been. It's not 'environmental concerns' you should be worried about. This is what you ought to be concerned about.

"Now why don't you think over what we've said and see if you can come to some kind of a conclusion. I'm betting you can find your way through to what's right. I'm sure you can see our point."

Point? thought Shea. But then it hit.

"This is about the company land, isn't it?"

"Smart, Shea. I figured you had it in you. Now, you just do like we've suggested and give it some thought. Doing the right thing would be good for everybody, including you and yours."

With that both men turned and walked away.

Shea leaned back against the ladder rungs, and for a moment he thought he was going to be sick on the spot. He shook— he *was* shook—both inside and out. *What the fuck,* was the only conscious thought he could muster.

Distractedly, he heard their car start, so he actually jumped when Newark stuck his head back around the corner and said with a mocking grin, "We'll be in touch." Then he turned and left again.

As Shea simply stared at the spot where Newark had been, he heard the car pull out and drive off down the street. An unmistakable urge to run for the john struck him, and he barely made it in time.

As he sat there, shaken and drained, he still had to half laugh at himself. *Here, I've just been threatened—undeniably threatened—I'm not completely sure by whom or about what— and all I can do is shit!*

The day wasn't going to be a good one.

* * *

NEWARK, ON THE OTHER HAND, felt good as he and Paalo drove down the street from Shea's place. "I'd say job done. That's one scared mother back there. He's probably shitting his pants right now. If that's all we're up against in this town, the whole project can go through without another hitch. Did you see him when you grabbed that ladder?"

"Yeah, I saw him. What do you expect? He doesn't know us from Adam, there was no one else around, he wasn't expecting it, and we had him by the short hairs. How else would he act? He's got nothing in his background as far as we can tell that would prepare him for us. I don't know though, I got this feeling. You know, like we should have handled this one a little differently. Just a feeling."

"Yeah, I know you and your feelings, but I think we just did all that needs doing. He won't be able to talk to anyone except his wife about this, and he won't want to scare her. He sure isn't going to call the cops—make that *cop*—in this burg. They'd probably ticket him for being a public nuisance. What more do you want, Paalo?"

"I don't know. Maybe you're right. I just don't know. But I have the feeling we haven't heard the last from him."

"Or him from us, if it comes to that. He'll be thinking about it and wondering what just happened, and what could happen to him. There aren't too many want to see their world change around them quick like that. One moment he's Johnny Handyman up on that ladder, the next the whole world is shaking. He'll calm down and play nice. You just wait and see."

"I hope you're right, Newark. I don't want anything that'll keep us here longer than necessary. I sure don't like this place enough to want to hang around."

Newark calmed down himself in a hurry and the thought about where they were driving back to hit him in a hurry.

"I know what you mean, man. Nothing could make me stay out in that place longer than necessary." He wasn't smiling now. "Absolutely nothing, man."

Sixteen

SHEA WAS STILL A LITTLE SHAKEN when he met with Pete for a drink at "The 600" later that night. Ostensibly they were meeting to discuss the upcoming canoe race on the mighty, majestic Traprock River, but that was really the last thing on Roy's mind right now. He couldn't figure out a way to tell Pete any more than he had been able to tell Jeri about his earlier visitors. He had been reticent, but Pete had worked at him and at least got him griping about, if not sharing, the day's adventure.

"I have to admit, Pete, there's a real question in my mind about all this sometimes. I mean, I hear a lot of people talking about the good things that have happened to them. Now, yeah, I remember the good times as being just that, but I don't really remember how it felt . . . you know what I mean? I can remember being happy that something good happened, glad that it happened, but I don't really remember how it felt to be happy at the time. That's the way it always is for the good things that happened to me." Roy paused, taking a sip of his drink.

"But the bad, now that I remember! All I have to do is recall an incident or have someone mention one, and I'm right back at the moment. I know exactly how I felt, and what's more, I feel that way again. I mean, exactly! The pain, the embarrassment—whatever—I'm right back there again. Sometimes I lay awake at night and just quiver remembering some bonehead, assholic thing I've done that I can never do anything about, but can't let go."

Pete leaned forward on the bar top, drained his glass, and turned to face Shea. "It's because you're a naturally guilty guy. You're one of those people who naturally take the blame, whether you admit it or not. I've known that about you for more than twenty years now, and I don't doubt that quite a few others, including Jeri, have noticed that about you, too. You're guilty whether you really are or not."

"You want to run that one by me again?"

"Look, you're telling me that you can remember the good times, but only as something good, right? But you put yourself right smack dab in the bad scenes immediately. That's because you never actually leave the bad scenes.

"You're always in them because that's the way you see life, your life at any rate. It's just a series of mistakes and errors you've made, and the good times are only occasional coincidental breaks in the world around you. They're mysteries to you. You might like them, but you don't understand them, and you sure as hell don't expect them. They happen and become a vague memory. Get it?

Shea sat there for a moment and then took another sip from his beer. "Yeah, I guess I get it.

"You know, for a likeable guy, you sure are a pseudo-psychological son of a bitch. I suppose I'll get the bill in the mail for shrink services rendered?"

"Hell no, you get the bill right now. It's your turn to pick up the next round."

Murphy had already come over and was setting down the fresh glasses.

"Besides, Shea," said Pete, "although taking on the sins of the world may not be a particularly popular trait, someone's got to do it, and it might as well be you. Anyway, it's nothing to feel guilty about."

"According to you, that doesn't matter to me at all."

Both men laughed and raised their glasses in an almost straight toast, clinked glasses, and drank.

One would never know what Murphy, the bartender, thought about all this. He was never the type to offer advice or listen sympathetically to some drunk's rambling tale of lost fish, fortunes, jobs, or wives. Instead, he just kept the glasses filled—an admirable trait—got matches or pretzels when needed, and gave the impression of being there to serve, not consult.

Oh, he could have blackmailed the entire town if he wanted to. He had heard things said in his bar that would have made for great gossip or even a jail term, but he never passed anything along. He was just there.

But when he closed up at the end of each night and climbed the stairs to his home above the bar, he remembered every word that was spoken in his establishment that day and mulled over all of his customers' problems and came up with solutions to their ills, which he pronounced out loud.

Only his fish ever heard, but, oh, the stories they could have told.

On the night Pete and Roy had been talking about Shea's universal guilt, Murphy saved most of their conversation for his report to his fish.

"For a change someone said something intelligent, boys and girls. It is a tough job, and somebody does have to do it. It might as well be Shea."

Murphy approved. It wasn't as certain what the fish thought.

Seventeen

THAT SAME NIGHT, Newark sat out on the stairs at the farm again. He stared at the place where he had seen the barn before. He did nothing else, just stared.

One of the first things he had done when they had gotten back from town on their first full day was to walk over the whole area, looking for any sign or trace of a building or something that might have reflected off something else to give the impression of a building.

But there was nothing there. The grass he walked through was up over his knees and closer to a hayfield than a lawn, even though it was still early fall. There were no marks where a foundation had been. Then again, Newark didn't know if most barns even had foundations.

Off to his right across a series of fields, maybe a mile, mile and a half off, there was another farm with a large barn, but that was simply impossibly far off, and, for that matter, too different of a style from the one he had seen to have caused any confusion.

It bothered him. All loose details bothered him, and this was one of the worse he had ever come across.

He hadn't gotten out of Roxbury and to where he was today by not paying attention to details or letting things distract him. It had been a long, hard climb, and some of the short cuts he had taken along the way weren't too pretty. He had simply worked it with determination and natural ability.

Now he seldom, if ever, sat back to try to figure out exactly how the world worked or the morality of his climb, but he was proud that he had made his own way in the world.

The Shop had been good to him in its own way. Sure he had to work, and work hard for them, but it was work he took to naturally. He had had to do a lot of things that could be considered crimes, if not outright evil, by others, but it was always on Shop orders. He had done them and done them well. He was a good team player.

He even liked Paalo, in a way. They worked well together, and he could always count on him to do his bit. He, like Newark himself, saw himself as having a job to do, and he never backed down from orders no matter what.

But Newark knew that Paalo was wondering about him right now, and that didn't sit well. He knew how he'd feel if the positions were reversed. He knew he'd question his partner's fitness for this assignment after what he claimed to have seen and its effect on him, and he knew he'd have good cause.

It bothered him.

But not as much as this place itself was bothering him. It was getting to him a lot even after weeks had gone by with no return of the nightmares—or night disturbances.

Again, he almost envied Paalo's ability to shrug the whole thing off as a dream or some type of basically harmless hallucination. To Paalo, it wasn't a problem because it couldn't have happened.

But Newark couldn't do that. He had spent too many years relying on his powers of observation, judgment, and sense of reality to be able to simply dispense with his experiences now. He couldn't just ignore it because it didn't fit in.

He didn't fit in either. The Shop seemed to have made a mistake, and that bothered him, too. In town yesterday there were people staring at him as he got out of the car. He wondered why until he was hit again with the realization. *I don't see another black anywhere. I haven't for the past four weeks. They're staring because they can't believe I'm here!*

It was a sort of half-ass logical mistake, he supposed. After all, this was Michigan, once home of Motown and the 1968 riots. The people here were dirt poor and the area economically disadvantaged. He supposed certain assumptions could have been made.

But this was northern Michigan, the U.P. Outside of a scattering in air and coast guard bases, his people had simply never made it here. When the migration to the north came during the war, the jobs here were already taken. Afterward, the area had already started folding and there was no reason to attract a new crew of immigrants, if not nationality. There was nothing to draw them here.

The Shop had, for a change, fucked up. He and Paalo had been sent on the premise that they could fit right in, each touching base with a part of the community the other couldn't. But his part of the community was missing, and he stuck out like a sore thumb.

When he pointed it out to Paalo, his only reaction was a smile and the comment, "At least it's not winter yet." Newark had to laugh at that in spite of himself.

It seemed to be a sign of how things were going, however. He hoped they would take care of business, get it all over with, and get out of Dodge. There was no real sign of outright hostility, and there was probably no real potential for any to develop, but it didn't feel good to be the most likely target on a job, and that was precisely how he was starting to feel. It didn't help to know he was the wrong man for this job, and then, of course, there was the other shit.

So he sat here on the steps and stared at where a barn wasn't, but had to be if his eyes had been working the other night. He sat and stared into the evening until he heard someone walk out on the porch behind him.

"Let it go, will you, Newark? Just let it go. You're getting caught up in this thing, and it's starting to make me nervous. Let's just do the job, and the hell with this other thing."

He didn't even bother to turn around to answer. "I'm doing the job, Paalo. You know I am. There's no question about that, is there? But I also know what I saw. I also know there have been mistakes made, and I don't want to ignore anything that may lead to another mistake being made, and you should understand that. I'll let it go when the time comes to leave, whether that's in ten minutes or ten days. I haven't let you down yet, and I don't intend to now."

Newark heard his partner turn around and walk back into the house without a word. He sat for a few minutes longer and was just about to go back in himself when the door behind him opened again. He turned around to face Paalo, and then froze.

It wasn't Paalo. Behind Newark stood an old woman in a worn blue housedress. She looked ancient, her face deeply lined by work in the fields, her pendulous breasts hanging loose beneath the worn cloth. In her hands she held two knitting needles.

She looked at Newark and smiled. For a moment he had the impression of the bluest eyes he had ever seen.

She pointed behind him with one of the needles, and he knew even before he turned and looked that the barn was back.

And then, just as quickly, he knew that when he looked back to her, she'd be gone.

She was.

He almost giggled when he realized she was the same woman who had visited him the first night weeks ago, and when he turned back to the barn and saw only a field of knee high hay, he laughed out loud.

He laughed until tears came to his eyes, and he couldn't stop even after Paalo came out, his questioning smile becoming a look of concern for his partner.

Eighteen

LTHOUGH THEY MAY HAVE BEEN surprised to learn so, Shea was more than familiar with the farm Newark and Paalo were renting. He had played in the house, the surrounding fields, and the barn and out buildings all through his childhood. It had been the farm his mother was raised on, and the farm that set the model when his own father bought the property in the valley.

The orchard, sheds, and barn had all since been leveled by later owners, but if Shea closed his eyes he could see it all clearly.

But not all the memories were pleasant.

His grandfather, his mother's father, had bought the place after his first house had burned down in 1923. The new place was old and rundown after being abandoned for at least seven years, but because of its condition it was cheap, and having come from Finland in 1903 at the age of seventeen, a move of less than ten miles to a new homestead with better land was no big chore.

They had heard the stories. The original family had lost two children, both young girls, at the Italian Hall tragedy. The wife of the house, despite having other children, never recovered. One December night she simply disappeared, to be found days later under the ice of a nearby frozen pond. She had entered through the thinner ice by the crick inlet to the pond and apparently drifted further in despite the iron, bricks, and horseshoes she had placed in the burlap sack tied around her waist. It was her oldest son who had seen his mother through the ice. Years later, the widower father killed his sons, shooting them where they were arguing with him in the orchard before he hung himself in the barn. Everyone in the Finnish community knew the story.

But that had been years before Shea's grandfather, Carl, his wife Amanda, and the first three of their eight children had made the move and rapidly made the new place their own. There was a lot of work to do that first spring, what with getting the fields that had been allowed to lie fallow for several years back into shape, planting potatoes and rye, pruning and tending the orchard, restringing the barbed wire on the pastures for the cows, building a new tool shed, repairing an abandoned root cellar, and enlarging the house with the addition of the wood room. They hadn't had a chance to sit back and drink the place in.

It was during the first winter that they began to realize what they had walked into.

Although Shea had heard few stories directly from him, it was his grandfather who was the first to pick up on the strangeness, the wrongness of the place. He had been working in the apple orchard, pruning away the dead branches, when he heard the voices.

They sounded like they came from a long way off, yet they were clear. Two or three men were arguing, the voices rising and falling in sequence with growing emotion driving them on. He turned to try to locate the source when he realized it was very close by, and then he hit the cold spot. Despite being warmly bundled against the winter chill, shivers—unrelated to the temperature—ran up and down his spine.

The rise and fall of the voices continued as he stood there, and then the voices grew louder and louder, becoming more distinct until he heard the sound of shots in rapid succession. A full minute later, another followed.

Then silence.

All thoughts of the apple trees gone, he stood there for a moment, and then realized it was starting again. He stood there frozen in place until the argument ran through its full cycle, followed by the shots that now sounded inevitable.

He muttered a quick prayer in Finnish and then went on to work elsewhere on the farm.

He would hear the arguing voices in the orchard again at other times. Other family members and visitors did as well over the years, but no one really talked about them as Shea was growing up, although once or twice he walked in on whispered conversations between his mother and grandmother, conversations quickly cut off when the children came into the room.

Shea heard them himself two or three times over the years while playing among the apple trees with cousins. They would stop whatever they were doing, listen while staring at each other, and with the last reverberations of the shots, move on elsewhere. By mutual, unspoken consent, they never discussed what they had heard.

Besides, there was plenty else to talk about. The first winter everyone, including the kids old enough to notice, heard the sound of a door opening and people walking into the house. The curious feature of these arrivals was that the sound came from where a door had once been, but had long since been blocked and covered over to produce a closet.

Footsteps were heard going up and down the stairs at irregular intervals when no one in the family was heading either up nor down. Figures were seen in hallways and rooms by all the living residents. Voices and cold spots were common enough to be taken in stride by family members although a definite number of visitors were nonplussed—perhaps more by the blasé reaction from the family than the phenomenon itself.

One corner of the barn was seemingly off limits despite the rest of the building being a natural magnet for playing children. Although as a child Shea hadn't realized the cause, there was a definite unwelcome feeling on a ladder leading to the beams of the barn that led he and his cousins to avoid what logically should have been a draw to their games.

Life, it seemed, was so precious that some refused to give it up, even if it seemed there were no choice. Even if they had seemed to throw it away while alive.

While growing up, Shea had plenty of exposure to various phantom roomers at the farm, but the one thing drummed into all of the kids ever associated with the family was, "They can't never hurt you so just let 'em be." This was what he would tell his own children, Erin and Sean, if it ever became necessary or appropriate.

Still, he had never really cared for the farmhouse where his grandparents lived, choosing instead to spend most of his time there as a child outside in the fields beyond the orchard and barn or playing in the crick that ran through the gully between the last of his grandfather's fields and the nearest neighbor. When his grandmother died of a long illness, Shea's grandfather had come to live with them at the valley farm. Seldom did anyone in the family go back to the old homestead except to make hay. No one ever spent more than a night or two there.

After his grandfather's death and when the farm was finally sold, no one was really broken up about the loss of the farm, but they had kept up a slight interest in the place and occasionally ran into the new owners. The older couple who had bought the farm for its location rather than to actually farm would smile knowingly when asked how it was going. "It's noisy," they would say, "and seems a little crowded sometimes." They seemed to like it even so, but it wasn't too many years before they bulldozed the apple orchard and took down the barn. "The trees weren't really healthy," they'd say. "And we really didn't have a use for the barn. It just attracted rats." And then they'd smile.

When the couple in their turn finally sold the place to others, who in turn came and went until it reached Pershing and he turned it into a long-term rental, it only briefly caught Shea's interest. It was just a part of family folklore now.

Pershing had heard the stories about the place before he bought it. He considered checking out the tales and tried to figure some angle where ghosts could be a selling point, but after the first two sets of renters left shortly after moving in—the second set telling him to screw the lease and demanding their money back—he decided to pass management along to the realtor, Ben Gibson, and the arrangement had stayed in place until Paalo and Newark showed up.

Gibson had chalked them up as officious and patronizing on their first meeting. He decided they deserved the place.

Maybe it deserved them.

Nineteen

THE PARK WAS UNBELIEVABLY packed with people. Few could remember such a homecoming for the Phoenix Fall Festival. Every fall, the chickens came home to roost for a few days as the town celebrated, and this year's usual crush was augmented by the centennial of the local high school and an all-class school reunion.

People not seen on the streets of Phoenix for decades were in town today. The cars parked on the streets offered a variety of license plates from nearly every state and most of the Canadian provinces. Traffic was backed up throughout the town and for nearly a mile out of town in either direction. Stores, restaurants, and bars were filled to capacity, and a sense of carnival (partially enhanced by the real carnival set up out on the sands outside of town) filled the air.

The exiles had come home.

From the early morning hours the sound had built up until it was a constant dull roar that those in town finally came to ignore. Voices raised in greeting, backslapping, and hugging were the orders of the day.

Shea made his way through the crowded lakeshore park. He watched out for familiar faces to greet or hunt down later, but somehow he didn't feel like a part of this crowd at all even as he walked through the thick of them. He realized after a bit that he wasn't seeing many —hardly any —of the people who still lived in Phoenix. To all intents and purposes it really was a crowd made up of the town's wild geese who had left, and in many cases, returned for the first time today. Since he had stayed here, or at least had come back more than ten years before, he really didn't feel like he belonged here with these out-of-towners even though many were former students or old acquaintances.

He wondered about that for a while while threading through the crowd. *Why are they all here? What's the draw?* he thought while distractedly returning the occasional greeting from someone who recognized him.

Perhaps it was a small scale reaction like the ones of the old ethnic groups that ended up here, hanging onto their memories of the old country even though they had left it to find something better. It was this nostalgia that led to forming Italian and French fraternal organizations throughout Copper Country, holding St. Patrick's Day parades in Hancock, and joining Kalevala societies among the Finns.

They were all people who had left a place, yet retained a tenuous tie to where they had been.

Maybe that was why Shea didn't feel a part of it all. He lived here again. He knew what it was like, and when all the hoorah was over, when all the former residents (now turned tourist) went back home, he would still be here.

He stopped for a moment as this sank in, turned, and by the shortest possible route made his way out of the crowd and walked home.

Half an hour later he was working on the sandstone steps leading to the back terraces on the hillside behind his home. He could still hear the crowd and the music at the park blocks away, but it no longer truly registered. Piece by piece he had removed blocks of sandstone from the crumbling foundation of a house that had once stood on a lot next to theirs, which Shea had purchased from the village. He hacked and dug out notches to set the blocks in upon the hillside and built a new staircase to another plateau on his property.

It was satisfying work. Unlike teaching, results were immediate. Lug and place a step, and you could stand on it. Each one brought him higher up the hillside and somehow increased the volume of the background park sounds. When the strains of the old school song wafted in, Shea unconsciously hummed along.

Shea hadn't been the only one at the park who didn't quite fit in. Paalo and Newark were there, too, but it didn't take Newark long to find the attention to his presence a bit too much to take, so he left Paalo alone after a quick consultation and plans to meet later. He started to make his own way out of the park, planning to skirt the crowd rather than cut completely through the middle of it.

Paalo didn't have the same problem. Carrying a brat and a beer in a plastic cup purchased from a vender, time and time again he was "recognized" by perfect strangers in the crowd who put some name to his face as a long-lost friend. In each and every case he went along as best he could, learning more about the lives of these strangers and growing nostalgic for his own past.

Newark came out of the park near the shoreline of the lake. His original plan was to circle around outside of the crowd, but once he saw the lake he decided on a slight change of plans. Sitting on one of the many slabs of concrete left over from the mill buildings that once stood there, Newark lit one of his rare cigarettes. It was a vice he very occasionally indulged in, but he thought it sometimes helped to clear his mind. After the cacophony in the crowd, that didn't sound like too bad of an idea.

His back toward the park, he allowed the noise behind him to fade into a background din and concentrated on the shoreline ahead of him. Eventually he was attracted by muffled sounds ahead of him.

Slightly surprised that others had forsaken the park for the relative quiet of the lakeshore, he set off quietly to investigate.

The sounds were human, but not conversational. He quickly traced their source to a thicker copse of trees some twenty feet ahead of where he had been sitting.

As he quietly parted the branches enough to allow him to see, he realized even before the first sighting what was going on.

They were in their early thirties, he figured. Her sun dress was pushed up over her waist and his hands were up in under at her breasts. His shorts were wrapped down around one ankle, and Newark noted there was no underwear in evidence for either. They were obviously not concerned with anything the rest of the world was up to at the moment.

With an eye for detail Newark noticed that she wore a wedding ring. He couldn't see one on her partner, but from their placement in the trees, if he did have one Newark assumed it wouldn't match hers.

He quietly backed away from their rhythmic coupling and left them alone. He wished them well. This was something human he understood although he did feel their sense of time and discretion could use some work. Still . . .

He hadn't moved more than twenty feet when he heard more giggles and voices through the trees. This time his reconnaissance brought him into sight of a small knot of people passing around a couple of joints. All were in their late teens or early twenties, and again, he wasn't surprised. Despite the vast amount of alcohol openly being consumed in the park, it was only natural that some would rather take their intoxication in a different form.

He wondered momentarily what the crowd in the park would think about these young people in the trees, but then he shrugged and figured it would run the gamut from amused tolerance to shocked horror, like it would anywhere else. Grass was definitely a part of the American scene despite "just say no." The Shop even took advantage of that fact. During Newark's earlier work against some young activist groups, pot use among the members had led to the occasional mistake or arrest that made the job easier.

Again, Newark backed off and out of the way. He smiled briefly, wondering how the group would take his walking out of the woods with his gun and one of the sets of ID he carried, but it was only a passing thought and he really didn't care about the group one way or the other.

He realized in an odd way that he did like the people he had met up here despite their surprise at his presence. They weren't his folks, but they weren't all that different, either. He had to admit to himself that it made him a little nostalgic for the small Ohio town he had worked in a while for the Shop. He had been there long enough to make friends with some folks on the lower edge of small town society before he had completed the job and moved on. On reflection, he thought that the differences among people might blur a little more in a small town.

He had walked back to the concrete slab and was sitting again when three men carrying on a conversation walked out of the bushes along a foot trail that went past the slab. At sight of Newark they momentarily stopped and hushed up, but then they continued towards him.

"Hell of a time back there, ain't it?" asked one, a blocky blonde guy, with a nod towards the park.

"First time in town?" asked the second, who was slightly less stocky. "It must give you a pretty weird view of the town to be here today, hey?"

"I don't know," said Newark. I've been here four, five weeks. Seems like a friendly enough place."

"Yeah, that it is. Today. Good weather, a crowd of party goers and the beer's flowing. Have one?" All three carried open cans of beer, and the speaker drew a can of Stroh's from the plastic ring of the six pack he carried and passed it to Newark.

Newark accepted without hesitation. "Thanks. You're right about the day, too," he added. "It's beautiful. Nice country you folks have up here. Nice place to live. Lots of fresh air."

"Lots of sun today, too. Looks like you already got one hell of a tan." All three laughed.

Newark, after waiting to see if there was anything else in the comment joined in. "Yeah, that's never been a problem for me."

"Kind of funny when you think about it, huh?" said the third man. "There's all this . . . unpleasantness, at times. Yet look at all the money spent on browning lotion and sun parlors . . . Yep, kind of makes you think."

Newark felt himself tightening up. There hadn't been any overt hostility, at least not yet, but the potential was there. These three were all good sized men. Momentarily, Newark wished he hadn't left Paalo behind or that he hadn't left town when he walked out of the park.

He took a long drink from the beer can and said, "Seems like you have a lot of folks from out of town here today. You people really go out of your way to celebrate."

"Yeah, I guess we do overdo it a bit. Most of the folks in the park are from around here originally. It's the high school centennial, there's a flock of people here for the reunion, and it's a holiday all at once. Lot of faces I haven't seen in years."

"What about you three? Just back visiting as well?"

"Nah, Tom here moved in from Wisconsin about seven years back. Me and Bill? Just plain locals. Never left, guess we probably never will. Construction work—we come by our rednecks honestly." With a look to his buddies, the man said, "What do you say, Tom? Shall we wander our tails back through that mess and go fishing like we talked?"

"Yeah, guess we should. About that time."

"That what you're doing up here?" the first man asked Newak. "Doing a little fishing?"

"Matter of fact, yes," Newark lied. "I heard about the Lake Superior fishing down in Chicago and decided to come on up to try my luck. How's it been going this year?"

"Could be better, could be worse," said Phil. "I guess you could say it's about the same. We're mostly fishing for pike, though. Big lake's mostly salmon and trout."

After a brief silence, Bob spoke up. "Well, good talking to you. Have a good time. Be sure to talk up our town. We need those tourist dollars, you know."

All four men smiled at that one.

"Thanks for the beer. Here, you need the can back?"

"Dime's a dime, I guess," said Tom, taking the can and threading it back into the plastic ring. "Since the deposit law this has become Michigan's second currency."

As the three walked away they were discussing the best spot for fishing.

Newark sat there and let the recently passed conversation run through his head. He certainly hadn't expected to end up drinking beer and discussing skin tone and fishing with three—Yoopers, they called them up here—when he woke up that morning, but yeah, he was starting to like these people.

The music and voices from the park reached a fevered pitch. Although he had never heard it before, Newark realized they were bellowing an old school fight song. He stood up to leave.

Just then a flurry of small rocks came out of the bushes off to his left. None hit him, and in seconds he was moving fast and crouching low through the thicket.

"Get him! Get him!" he heard from behind him as he headed toward the crowded park. A volley of stones was thrown blindly at the sound he made moving through the branches. One hit a branch ahead of him and glanced off his arm as it dropped to earth. He squatted low behind a larger sapling to catch a glimpse of his attackers.

At first he thought his "drinking buddies" had had a change of heart, but while he watched five young kids came lumbering through the underbrush.

He pegged them as junior high or high school students. Two carried bottles of beer, and another carried a bottle of pop wine. All five still carried a rock as well. They were throwing in about every direction but his.

Only kids, thought Newark. *Still, kids grow up to be men. And rocks are still rocks.*

Drunk, too. Not a good combination.

He watched them wander off, back the way they had come.

98

I wonder if they would have thrown anything without the booze, he thought as he stood up. "Hard to say," he said out loud.

This time he followed his original plan and skirted the park on his way back to the car. He kept an eye out for his attackers, but they had clearly gone back into the trees for other adventures.

Finally he located Paalo holding a half-full plastic cup and talking with a group by one of the beer concessions. Newark caught his eye, pointed toward where the car was parked, and continued on his way.

Paalo excused himself from his newfound old friends with at least one backslap and a hug from a pretty red head. He made his way out after Newark.

Three blocks down the street away from the park when the people thinned out, Paalo caught up with Newark.

"Hell of a party going on back there, hey?" he asked by way of greeting. Paalo drained the glass he still carried and dropped it into a nearby garbage can. "Those are friendly people. Hospitable, too. I must have turned down a dozen beers from various "old classmates" who haven't seen me "since when.""

"Real good memories, too, Paalo," Newark remarked. "Remember a man they never met."

Paalo looked at Newark and asked more seriously, "How'd it go with you?"

Paalo actually smiled when Newark filled him in on the details of his past hour or so.

"Hell, those kids didn't mean anything by it. You might as well have been Chinese, or a Martian."

"And they'd have still lobbed stones my way, right?"

"Shit, you know what I'm saying, Newark. They were just drunk! What would have happened to me in *your* old neighborhood?"

"'Your old neighborhood!' What have you done, Paalo? Adopted these fine folk?"

Paalo turned with a grin. "I didn't have to. They adopted me! It's amazing how many of these strangers think I was the kid who sat behind them in algebra or played left tackle to their quarterbacking. One guy even remembered how pissed I was senior year when I missed the photo session for the team picture 'cause I had a detention for flipping off Mr. Phelps! He pointed out that at least I got into some of the action shots! And that red head! You don't want to know what memory she whispered to me!"

Both men laughed.

Newark had to admit that, despite the kids, he really didn't feel any different about the town. "Ah, I guess I understand. Some folks just aren't raised right in any community."

"Most of these people remind me of the folks I left back home, Newark. I'm getting downright homesick. I like these people."

"Not enough to interfere in the job, I hope."

"Hell, you know me better than that. Nothing gets in the way. I'm only saying I had such a good time I had to remind myself why I left my home in the first place."

They walked in silence for a moment before Paalo remarked, almost as an afterthought, "Say, did you happen to run into Shea down there? I saw him from a couple of feet away, but made sure he didn't see me. I thought he might start asking questions if he had. Seemed to have his head in the clouds, and then he turned and headed, I assume, for home."

"No, I didn't see him. I didn't stick around the crowd, remember? I sure as shit know there isn't an old picture of me in their yearbooks," Newark said with a grin. "You sure you did the right thing not letting Shea see you, though? Little bastard might have filled his pants knowing you were around."

"What? And have him and his buddies lobbing rocks at *me*? No thank you. He didn't seem in a talking mood anyway, just kind of wandering through, a word or two to a couple of people. Then he had a beer and left. I wonder if he was thinking about our little talk the other day."

"Do you think he was saying anything about us to anyone?"

"Well, Newark, I didn't follow him around like a puppy dog, you know, but I doubt it. I don't think anyone would make too much of it anyway. Most of the people in that park are just like I said, good old boys. I don't think too much could ever get started with a bunch like that. Still, your rock throwers show what's just under the surface. Scratch a crowd and you've got a mob.

"But I'm feeling pretty good about the way things are going right now. I don't think he'll be causing us any trouble. Most of the folks I talked to are intent on making house payments, holding onto a job, playing with their kids, getting a little every now and then—there's enough on their plates to care about than some local crazy raving about secret deep, dark plots." He paused a moment. "No, I feel pretty good about everything."

When they reached their car, the first thing Newark saw was the broken aerial. "Shit, Paalo, someone's left us a calling card," he said.

"Take a look around you, Newark. Don't go getting all paranoid on me. The damn kids broke the aerials on everybody's car on this block. You want to do the paper work filing a report? I don't think we ought to bother talking to the local cops about it. Someone else will. Besides, it's a holiday."

He unlocked the car door, got in, and leaned over to unlock Newark's door.

Starting the car as his partner climbed in, Paalo added, "Besides, look at the bright side. If it was the same kids and you were sitting in it, they would have broken the windshield or burned the fucking car down."

He smiled as Newark flipped him off, and then he pulled away from the curb.

Twenty

HALF AN HOUR BEFORE, Shea had finished the yard project and walked down the street the couple of blocks to Pete's to bum a beer.

Neither Paalo or Newark noticed him sitting in the screen porch at his friend's house, but he saw them as they drove by and hustled down the steps to check out their license plate as they turned the corner.

"Those were the two guys I told you about, Pete, the characters who stopped by when I was up the ladder in the back."

"You were really serious about that then, were you? I thought you were leading up to some kind of punch line, to be perfectly honest."

"Hell, no. I was serious. They were, too. I don't mind admitting—they scared the crap out of me. I have their license number now, but what am I supposed to do with it?"

"Here, let me take that and call a friend of mine up at the state police post. Maybe he can trace it. Owes me a favor, anyway."

"You've got a friend who's a cop?"

"Hell, I've got all kinds of friends. Aren't you sitting here on my porch drinking one of my beers? Besides, he's not really a cop. He's the dispatcher up there, and I had to work on their hardware a while ago. Let me see if he can turn something up."

"Sure, sounds like a good idea. Point well taken about friends, by the way. Except shouldn't I be sitting here drinking another one of your beers?"

When Pete came back with the fresh long necks, Shea went on, "What do you think those bastards want with me, Pete?"

"Got me scratching, Shea. I know people can get annoyed with you, but this seems out of the local league. You been involved in anything out of the ordinary these days? Running for office? Running drugs? Running off at the mouth? Who'd you piss off lately?"

"No one I can think of, man. You know me—even-tempered, dutiful, kind to all and a natural gentleman . . ."

"Yeah, a natural gentleman, that's you." Pete punctuated the sentence with a massive beer fart.

Twenty-One

Back home, Shea sat at his typewriter. He had intended to write a couple of letters to friends whom he hadn't heard from in awhile, some of the exiles who hadn't made it home for the reunion, but the words weren't flowing.

Jeri was out on the porch with the kids. Erin was in the porch swing, and Sean, with graham crackers firmly clutched in both hands, was cruising the former church pew that made up the bulk of the seating on their porch. Jeri was pushing Erin's swing and making sure the crackers were the only thing Sean put in his mouth.

Roy stared at the blank sheet of paper in front of him, then instead of typing a salutation he typed the words "environmental concerns" and "Lake Superior." Below that he added, "Seafarer/ELF." He continued the list with "water quality," "nuclear dumping," "fish tumors," "unemployment," "PBB," "dioxin," and, finally, "two visitors—one white, one black."

He had that uneasy feeling coming back again.

He got up and walked over to the sound system. Jeri had the radio going through both the inside and outside speakers while she was on the porch, but that didn't really register as he dug out an old David Crosby CD from the rack and slipped it in to the player. He changed the selector from FM to CD, and as the first notes of "What Are Their Names?" began, he walked back to his desk.

Jeri turned in her chair on the porch and called out through the screen door to Roy. "What's this? The wife has no say in what gets listened to today? Where does it say husband listens to twelve-year-old hippie music and replaces exciting radio mix of Men at Work and Def Leppard?" She was smiling through the questions.

But most of it, as was sometimes the case when he was distracted, was completely lost on Roy.

"Say what, dear?" he asked distractedly.

"Oh, I was just saying John and Barb's house across the street was burning down and Sean ate a lizard."

"Yeah, that's fine, hon. Anything you want."

Jeri got up and came through the doorway and walked over to the desk.

"Where's your head at?" she asked. "You're either going deaf or crazy. What are you writing that's got you on cloud nine?"

As she read the typewritten list over her shoulder she added, "Definitely crazy, then. You left out famine, plague and divorce. What's this all about?"

So, for the first time, Roy told her about the two men who had visited him while she had been out with the kids earlier that week. He downplayed his unease, partially out of concern for her and partially out of ego, but he basically presented things the way they had occurred.

"I really think they were going out of their way to scare me, Jeri. I don't really know why, but I'm thinking maybe this has something to do with it. What do you think?"

"Do you think you ought to call the police, Roy? And why am I only hearing about this now?"

"I didn't want to get you worked up until I had some time to try to think this thing through. I mean, what's the point of getting you upset unless you can think of some way to make sense out of it all?"

"I don't know. Do you think it's about that letter you wrote to the *Gazette* about United? You know, the one where Pete and I both accused you of being paranoid after we read it."

Shea looked up at her. "You know, I hadn't even thought of that. My one time in newspaper print and I actually forgot all about it. Sure, that could be it. Somebody might have actually read it. But who reads the letters in the paper? How could that get someone on my case?"

"You sent a copy to United, too, to bitch at them directly. Remember? I told you to wait until you calmed down before you mailed that thing. Of course, I was mostly concerned with you doing a rewrite so you wouldn't sound quite so much like a raving lunatic when they read it. Even *I* was surprised when the paper printed it."

"Thanks for the loving support and understanding, dear, but I do think you might be on to something."

Shea opened the drawer of the desk and started rumbling through it. "You have any idea where I might have put that carbon I kept?"

"It's probably in the right-hand drawer where you keep your stories, no?"

"Yeah, you're right. Here it is."

Shea reread his own words again:

To the Editor:

Perhaps it's just me, but isn't there an odd feeling in the air? Perhaps some sense that something is not quite right in the U.P. in general and the Copper Country in particular? It's not that things have been that good all along, mind you, but this is something different, something new.

Hereditary unemployment, Seafarer or ELF or whatever it's called this week, nuclear waste disposal studies, plans to divert water from the Great Lakes, trumped up stories of possible new industries that all require geologic surveys of the area, polluted lakes and fish tumors—not to mention the traditional shafting given by industry leaders like United— the list goes on. Isn't it a bit much?

You know, sometimes it seems we must be crazy to live here, out of our minds with all of these problems. Sometimes it must seem the sensible thing to do would be to pack up and take off, no?

And perhaps that's just the idea someone wants to instill. Perhaps that's just what someone wants us to do.

Now, just to thicken the plot, think of the evacuation of places like Love Canal or even Chernobyl. You had a lot of people there who had to give up their homes, land, and possessions. They had to relocate their lives—with the help of their benevolent governments, of course.

It makes you wonder.

But what would be the point of emptying our area?

Good question.

No one wants a nuclear dump in his backyard, but what if it wasn't anyone's backyard anymore? What if, for a variety of reasons, everyone had packed up and moved away?

Wouldn't there be holdouts? Well, of course there would, but it would probably be a small enough number to forcibly convince to hit the road. There is that benevolent government, of course.

Take a drive through virtually any town north of the bridge. Pick a block at random, drive around and count the houses empty and for sale, or, for that matter, just empty. Drive down the main streets and count the empty store fronts, the closed stores and defunct restaurants. Now extend that drive to the countryside and notice the number of realtor signs on farms and vacant land.

It sure seems a lot of people are getting the signal that it's time to pull up stakes.

Now, of course, this is all just speculation and conjecture to pass the odd moment, but isn't there a peculiar feel to the air?

Perhaps it's just me.

But I don't think so.'

Perhaps it's time to do something about it all.

Sincerely,

Roy Shea

"I don't know, Jeri," Roy said after he had finished scanning over his letter. "Do you think there's enough here for someone to start something?"

"I want to believe it's just you being a curmudgeon and chowder head . . ."

"Gee, thanks."

". . . but you have to wonder, Roy. What do those two want? What about the police, Roy?"

"For all I know, Jeri, they might *be* the police."

"Do you really think—from how they acted—how could they be police?"

Roy just raised an eyebrow and laughed, "Yeah, right."

"You know what I mean, Roy. I know not all policemen are good guys, but these guys tried to scare you. They made threats."

"Yeah, I know, Jeri. Maybe I'm more worried than I ought to be, but I think we just have to wait until I know more about what's going on," he sighed. "Do you mind if I take a drive out to the old farm to clear my head? I mean, you and the kids can come, too, if you want."

"No, they're playing, and you'll think better alone. But Roy, be careful, will you?"

"No other way to be, lover. I'll be back shortly."

Twenty-Two

A S SHEA DROVE with his dog through the valley to the old family farm he found himself unconsciously counting the new houses along the road. As the towns emptied, the farmland disappeared. There were twelve new houses in the three-mile stretch from the Traprock River Bridge to the turn-off for the farm. Three of these were on land his father had once owned and which had been Shea's stomping grounds as a kid.

Driving through an area that had once been all farms sometimes depressed the daylights out of Shea. Still, he could see the humor in the new subdivisions. In more than one instance he had heard one of the valley's more recent residents complaining how "their" place in the country was being turned into large-lawned suburbia with the building of a new neighbor's home next to theirs. Fields that once held cattle and crops were rampant with the sound of dirtbikes and go-carts in the summer, snowmobiles in the winter, and hordes of children and designer dogs at any given moment.

Invariably, the newcomers, with a sense of getting back to nature, simpler lifestyles, and self-sufficiency, put in a wood-stove. Their next step, also invariably, was to defoliate their property of anything large enough to cut and split with the aid of a gasoline-powered log splitter, leaving a lack of shade and wind break they came to regret. Especially once they had to start ordering wood, delivered at a hefty fee, to continue heating in such a "self-sufficient" way.

The land had not seen such significant drop in forested area since the first loggers swept through, followed by the original farmers whose descendents now were selling the land that had finally had a chance to recover.

It seemed an unending circle.

Well, perhaps it would come to an end when the last lot parcel was sold to a retired insurance salesman from Detroit, but until that last sale occurred, it seemed the order of the day.

Still, Shea appreciated that he still had access to a bit of country that he could occasionally use as a means of clearing his head with a long walk or fishing trip.

He pulled into the empty yard and parked the truck. He and Bogart had the place to themselves, since his folks had already headed downstate with the change of seasons. The dog, Bogey, had been dancing on the seat ever since they had taken the turn out of town. He knew what lay in this direction and that he'd soon have a chance to run without a leash. He blew out of the door as soon as Shea opened it and was soon nosing about the apple trees and fence line shrubs. He barked out of sheer excitement, and Shea realized he pretty much felt like doing the same himself.

As Bogart ran from bush to bush marking his territory, Shea reached into the pick-up bed and took out the fishing pole and creel. He had planned enough time to check out the pond, but first he planned to fish the crick that ran through the gully on the farm.

Whistling for Bogart, he took his gear in hand and headed across the yard for the trail leading down to the crick and ponds. He noted, as usual, that the path was growing in from lack of use.

When he was younger and still lived with his parents, he and a variety of friends had been blade and fantasy geeks before the term existed. With Army surplus machetes and bayonets, they had kept the paths around the farm scrupulously clean while hacking at the hordes of unwashed, vicious Orcs who blocked the trails. They had also been hell on frogs, but that had been a long time ago. Now the trails and woods roads were growing in with saplings and scrub. If it weren't for himself or the other occasional walker elbowing the way through the chest-high thimbleberry and vines, the trail would have disappeared long ago.

Another bout of chronic wondering began. How long would it take for everything to grow back if somehow, for some reason, all the people just left? How long would it take to recover? Except for plastic containers and disposable diapers, Shea figured it wouldn't take much time at all.

He wished he could catch a glimpse of a world like that. He tried to get his students to see the possibility of change—how things could and did change. All was in motion.

He jumped over the stream, now in the fall running a little deeper than it usually did in summer, and Shea climbed the bank to the pond. Along the edge of the waterline grew cattails and water lilies. A trout rose up to take one of the hordes of bugs flying above the surface of the water. It left ripples where it broke water and took to the air, and then again when it returned to the pond.

A turtle slipped off the piece of wood on which it had been sunning itself and slid among the water plants, allowing only its head to break the surface. In the early summers of his years here, Shea had often watched for hours as the turtles crawled up from the water to the sandy soil of the southern exposed bank to scoop out holes in the sun-warmed sand to drop their eggs.

Bogart immediately waded out into the water, keeping pace with Shea as he walked along the shore of the pond to one of his usual spots. Of all the dogs that had been with him here over the years—all the beagles, collies, springer spaniels, black and tans, and a grand variety of assorted mutts, all the dogs that had kept him company growing up—none liked the water or fishing as much as this standard poodle did. Shea figured he had to be a throwback to his ancestral puddle dogs, or perhaps he was an Irish water spaniel left cuckoo-like in a litter of poodles. Then again, maybe it was because this one as a pup had been raised with the last, and best, of a long line of springer spaniels raised by Shea's folks.

As Bogart waded onto shore to join him, Shea kicked over a board alongside the bank, bent over, and pulled out several worms trying to pull themselves back into the ground. He slipped them into a can in his creel, and then baited his hook with one held in reserve. He added a sinker a foot higher than the hook, then threaded a bobber two feet above that, and made a shallow cast out.

Roy figured the sun was still too high to really get much trout action in the pond, so he wasn't too disappointed at the initial lack of a hit. He sat back on the bank, petting Bogart and looking out over the valley thinking about all the time he had spent here.

Then the bobber took a dive towards the bottom. Shea set the hook with a quick snap and started reeling. The fish took a jump. It looked small, but fat. He pulled out the fish, a six-inch brookie too small to keep. He wet his hands to protect the trout's sensitive skin, deftly slipped the hook from its jaw, and after a quick study of it blue, yellow, and red circular markings, he released it into the shallows.

Taking the undersized fish as a sign, he folded up the front two extensions of his pole and headed up from the pond to the crick. He could always try the pond again later.

Bogey worked the bushes ahead of Shea as they made their way up the gully. Occasionally Shea would stop and try for trout at old holes he remembered or new ones that had formed in the past spring's runoff. They slowly advanced, and Shea caught two more trout, neither of which were badly hurt so were set back in the stream.

When he reached a place where the crick cut in close to the bank, which had sloped off to form a thirty- to forty-foot cliff, he set the pole down and searched the edge above him.

Finally he spotted what could have been some rotting rope tied to a tree. Shea figured he had found the spot where Steve and he had built a fletch years ago.

The same age as Roy, Steve had been a neighbor a mile down the road, and they had grown up together in these fields and crick gullies. They had been thirteen when they commandeered the rope, nails, hammer and hatchet they had used to build the fletch—a platform made out of two logs dug into the hillside, with their outer ends crossing in a point, tied together, and supported by a rope running to the top of the hill—overlooking the crick. It had taken them one long day of work, and they were sure they were hundreds of feet higher than they truly had been. Still, it was quite a drop and a fall would probably have done damage. It was an accomplishment, and one he remembered fondly.

Momentarily he thought about calling Steve one of these days and rebuilding the thing, although now a fall from the top would probably do more damage than it would have when they were younger.

Still, it might be worth the effort.

They had spent hours up on that little poplar platform talking about the future, books they had read or would write, why things were always so screwy when it came to dealing with adults, and life in general.

But he hadn't seen Steve in years, and the reconstruction project was extraordinarily unlikely.

Maybe someday when Erin and Sean were older they could make it a family affair.

He did have a good family. That was certain, but there were a lot of old friends out of touch, and Shea had a hard time getting close to the people he met these days. There was a sense of holding back before they became close friends. He couldn't remember being like this when he was younger, or, for that matter, at any time before he and Jeri had moved back to the U.P.

It had taken a lot of thought and a long time, but he had finally come up with an answer. Ever since they had first returned, almost everyone they had been close to or folks they had befriended since their return moved away! No matter what career fields they were in, they moved off to pursue them someplace else, and usually that someplace else was far away.

When this had finally hit him, instead or providing some type of comfort or release, be became more careful and standoffish. Jeri would bring home friends whom she had met at work, sure that Roy would like them, too, only to find him acting so aloof that they seldom ever came a second time.

He realized what he was doing and tried on occasion to hold it in check, but this usually meant he went too far the other way and acted like a total moron. The usual response to this was the newcomers being put off by this pushy, extroverted mad man, and, again, they never visited again.

He hoped he'd find some solution to the whole situation one way or another before too long, because Shea had the feeling that someday he'd wake up and everyone would be gone. The houses would all be boarded up and the post office would have lists of everyone's new forwarding addresses off in Montana, Colorado, Maine, Texas, Pennsylvania and the Dakotas. The more unlucky would end up in Lower Michigan or Indiana, but they'd be gone, too.

At one time Jeri and he had been the nomads. They'd settle in a town for a year or two, make friends, become part of circles of people they felt comfortable with, and then the two of them would up and move away.

Now he knew how some of the folks they'd left behind in those towns must have felt.

Of course, some, he was sure, didn't miss them at all.

But now that they were back home and, for the Keweenaw, well established, he was the one feeling deserted.

The sight of an empty house brought the pit of his stomach up somewhere around his throat. Even when he had no idea who the past occupants had been, he still got an anxiety attack at the sight of a "For Sale" sign.

A lot of people they had known and cared about had moved. Hell, they *had* to move! There was nothing in the line of work up here for far too many, and being in what had been the poorest region of Michigan for so long, and with the whole state in the shape it was in, there was no choice. So people left, and left holes in the lives of the left behind. And with the way he'd been acting, there were damn few getting close enough to fill those gaps.

Still, there were some left, and they were damn good friends, and besides, it was a beautiful day and he'd caught fish. For a moment, Shea was overwhelmed with nostalgia and an intense love for old friends, past homes, this gully, the crick, the farm—hell, for the whole damn U.P. Occasionally he realized why he had come back and why he really hadn't had much choice, all things considered.

With a last look up at the fletch site, he picked up his pole, called for Bogey, and continued on up the gully.

Just around a bend in the gully he came to one of the few stretches of the crick that he had come to dislike. Eleven years ago he had made his way up here in the springtime to find all the saplings—*all* the saplings—along this stretch collapsed and bent toward the east. From three feet up everything was twisted off in the same direction. He had no idea then what could have caused this to hit all the trees in a stretch forty feet long and about forty feet wide through this stretch, and he still didn't know. It just didn't feel natural. Ever since that first discovery he had disliked this stretch more than the pain in the ass nature of trying to climb through all the felled saplings would seem to warrant.

Thimbleberry bushes had taken over the entire patch growing up over the bent tag alder, popular, and pine. None of the trees had ever recovered, and some of the larger saplings had yet to completely rot away and raised mounds beneath the thimbleberry.

Both Shea and Bogey skirted their way around the patch quickly. Either sensing Shea's feelings about the place or having his own canine concerns, Bogey even declined his usual leg lifting as he hustled through.

Just on the other side, however, Shea hit a stretch of stream he knew to be good fishing, and his sense of near-Nirvana returned. He dropped a wormed line into a hole at the base of a large pine growing on the bank. The worm had no sooner hit the water when a brown streak picked up on it. Shea gave a quick pull to set the hook and then had to reel madly before the fish could snarl itself in the exposed roots of the pine.

Grinning like a madman, Roy pulled a fourteen-inch brook trout out of the water. Almost as soon as it was above land the trout dropped off the line, hit the ground and bounced toward the bank. Dropping the pole, Roy literally leaped through the underbrush to grab the fish before it flopped back in.

It was a beautiful fish. He held it up to admire its markings in the mottled sunlight, and then rapped its head against a pine branch, killing it quickly. He set the fish on the bank, took out a pocket knife and quickly cut a forked branch from a nearby sapling. Removing any unnecessary branches, he inserted one of the side forks through the trout's gills and out its mouth and then ran the foot-long branch through his belt for a carrier.

This perfect fish made his day, which was now already going pretty strong. He whistled as he picked up the pole and continued upstream.

He fished more seriously now since he had a stake in turning this one keeper into a meal for four. Within a half-mile he had picked up seven more trout, five of them keepers although none as big as the first, and he was feeling pretty good.

When he reached the fence line cutting across the crick that marked his usual stopping place, he wetted down the limp fish for the walk back to the pond, returned the carrier to his belt, and with a call to Bogart made his way to a bush road that led up to the back forty, and from there across the field to another relatively clear path back to the pond.

Fishing now done and away from the stream, Shea quickly made his way back. Within a half-hour he was coming out of the tree line by the pond.

Once there, he took the stick with the fish, embedded one end in the sandy bottom of the pond to a depth where the fish would stay cool and wet, and tried the fishing there again.

Bogart lay down in the grass about six feet away and watched quietly as Shea added a bobber to his line for pond fishing. After fifteen minutes he got up and began to walk up and down, snapping at bugs and frogs in the inlet that fed the pond.

Shea picked up another couple of trout, including an eight-incher he added to the catch stick. After an hour, starting to feel lazy in the sunlight, he reeled in his line, removed and threw what was left of the worm out to the waiting fish, set the hook in the rubber of the handle, and folded the pole down to carrying size. He whistled for the dog, retrieved the fish, and headed to the path up from the pond and back to the house.

He cleaned the fish on a newspaper out on the back porch. When he was finished, he wrapped the heads and viscera in the newspaper and carried the package back to the fifty-gallon barrel turned into a garbage burner. With a stick match from his pocket, he touched off the paper, along with an old collection of garbage already there.

He brought the fish into the house to wash them off at the sink. As he was running his fingers down their spines to clear out anything he had missed outside, he worked on a tall boy Stroh's he kept stocked in the fridge.

Done with his fish cleaning, Shea nudged the cabinet door open with his elbow, carefully, so as not to drip fish water on the shelves, took a plastic bag out, and closed the cabinet in the same fashion as he had opened it. After dropping the fish in, he gave the bag a couple of twists and tied it off with the excess.

Taking a second beer from the fridge, he sat down at the kitchen table to admire his catch.

Trout fascinated him.

Seldom was he anywhere near as lucky as he had been today, and he sincerely offered up a prayer to whatever powers that may be for the fish in the bag.

Shea had always admired Richard Brautigan's passion for trout, but felt Brautigan had been a little off in comparing them to a semi-precious metal in some of his books and stories. Trout struck Shea as being some form of solidified water, or summer ice. Their markings were fluid, watery. They were of the stream, although Shea would swear he sometimes saw trout in the autumn air at night when the northern lights were particularly active.

It had been a good fishing run, but it was time to pack it in now, take the dog, and go to find out what Jeri, Erin, and Sean were up to at home. Roy drained off the last of his Stroh's, left a note thanking his folks for services rendered in their absence, and headed out the door.

The sun was sliding toward late afternoon once he got outside. Roy watched the reddening skyline while Bogart took a last few ceremonial squirts on the bushes, and then they both got in the truck. Shea closed the door, set the bag of fish on the floor of the passenger side, and started the engine. The tape deck kicked in automatically, since Shea had forgotten to pop the tape when he'd stopped, and Jerry Jeff Walker started singing about rolling wheels as Shea pulled on down the drive.

Twenty-Three

OVER A THOUSAND MILES AWAY, a gray-suited man sat behind a polished rosewood desk and studied a map of the Keweenaw Peninsula. He was thinking of profit margins and plans laid out with the ends justifying the means. He reflected on quiet meetings with hired hands, both in the government and out. He thought about how development was the key to growth in America and at the stock exchange. He thought about what the company had been, was now, and would be. He thought about the workers from the Shop and the jobs he had been the impetus for having them do. He thought of cash flow and water flow and how they could run together.

Mostly he thought about money—not what it could buy, just money.

He hadn't been fishing in years.

Twenty-Four

L
IKE OTHER BACKWATERS in the United States, the U.P. had a tendency to catch a real variety of specimens in its eddies. It was a sort of retirement home for attitudes, fads, and fashions that had long ago faded elsewhere. Ideas and ideals moved into the area, settled among the resident thoughts already there, and in a few short decades found themselves rocking on the figurative porch with earlier arrivals. The very nature of the area brought them together.

As with ideas, so with people. It was not unusual to find duck-tailed greasers, old beats, and middle-aged hippies elbow to elbow with 1920s-style socialists, love-it-or-leave-it rednecks, the remnants of mining glory, old money society, and the unemployed of three generations among retired miners, farmers, loggers, fishermen, and workers returned from downstate factories finding common ground in some of the local watering holes. In a state of undeclared truce they could shoot the shit about the old days the way they had never happened.

And the jukeboxes in these dives! They were among the most eclectic in the world. Roy Orbison could be followed by Glen Miller. Mingus could be the lead for George Jones. Don Ho and Rick James could be side by side. Etta James and Johnny Cash, Robert Johnson and Roger Miller, Dylan and Rudee Valli might exchange licks.

They all had their own listeners, and given the proper conditions that could only exist in such bars, they all won converts from the various camps over time. They seemed to blend and blur. Some sort of sonic evolution seemed to take place until all boundaries disappeared. Shea even swore he had heard Frank Sinatra do "Madame George" one night in the High Steps. Given a pocket full of quarters—and, miracle of miracle, most of the machines were still quarter driven—you could take a journey through the past and into the future of popular music, and if there was a song you really wanted to hear, traveling among the bars would allow you to hear it.

It was on one such musical odyssey when Shea first met Spirit Tooth. Shea had walked into one of his irregulars, the Cliff View. At first Shea thought the place was empty except for Mickey, the bartender, but then he spotted another patron and wondered how he could have missed him at first. Over by the jukebox was a mountainous shadow. In its bear-sized paw was one of the largest mugs he had ever seen (Shea later learned that Spirit Tooth carried it with him in his pack). Shea got the sense of sheer size and strength swaddled in furs, from the badger hat on his head down to the furred boots.

He made his way back to his table and sat down as the jukebox kicked in with a Bessie Smith number. On the table in front of him were two pitchers, one empty and one half-full, and he hunched over the table with his nose almost pressing against the porcelain top.

Wouldn't want to meet that in the woods alone, was the first thought running through Shea's mind. Shea settled at the bar and ordered a glass of draft Leinies while he watched the apparition in the bar mirror.

"Bartender!" rumbled what was possibly the deepest voice Shea had ever heard. "I mean, Mickey! Get yourself another and set the moose up with one on me!"

Shea watched Mickey fill himself a glass on the stranger, and then he watched intently as Mickey filled another glass and carried it over to the shelf immediately beneath a stuffed moose head. Mickey had to remove an empty mug already sitting there.

"Can't forget our animal friends, you know. Ol' Spirit Tooth here, I remember. I and my furry friend thank you for your service."

When Mickey came near again Shea asked, "Spirit?"

"Spirit Tooth," corrected Mickey. "William B. 'Spirit Tooth' Mundy, to be exact. A local legend in his own time. Very local."

"Afraid I haven't heard it. Care to fill me in, Mick?"

Mickey pulled up his bartender stool and lifted his own beer. After a satisfactory pause, he began.

"Spirit Tooth's been up on the cliff for as long as anyone accurately remembers. Never seems to get older; never seems to change. Once in a blue moon, usually when you're about to wonder if you'll ever see him again, he wanders in. Plays the box, drinks a few pitchers, but never gets drunk. I still haven't decided if he's good or bad for business."

"Never gets drunk? Then what's the bit with the moose?"

Mickey grinned, "You just came in. Wait a while and ask me again.

"At any rate, he's always been around. I've had this bar for—what is it—twelve years now? I got back from the war and bought it with back pay and the G.I. bill. He's comes in and orders two pitchers on the first day. What in the hell is this, I figure, a talking bear? He's got on the same coat you see tonight, the whole mountain man outfit, and it was sixty-five degrees outside that night.

"I bring the beer and he brings out this mug I find he always carries with him. Huge. Since he usually has his hand wrapped around it you may not notice, but there's this design on it—looks like silver. Looks Masonic to me. One time I asked him why, given the size of the mug, he just doesn't drink it out of the pitcher. 'Wouldn't be civilized,' he says.

"Anyhow, he pours it full then downs it off. He always does the same with the first one. Then he settles into drinking more slowly back there in the corner. At least more slowly for him. A couple of times he gets up and puts what I swear are nickels into the quarter-only jukebox and plays songs I never knew was on there. One night I swear it was 'Finlandia' by Sibelius! I've given up looking for some of the stuff he plays on the playlist, and I'm the one that sets 'em up!

"He's here two, maybe three hours. Usually doesn't say much, but once in a while he starts in with these stories about Two Ravens or Coyote. Tells 'em like he knows the characters personally. Funny as hell, and they can get out and out dirty, too. Always tells 'em like the gospel truth from a firsthand account.

"Anyhow, that first night, about the time I figure he'll be falling all over himself and I'm wondering how to lift him when he falls, he gets up slow, and just like a bear ambles on over to me and says, 'Thanks, but you better think about getting that moose back up. He's not too happy back there.'"

Mick took another swallow of his beer, and then went on. "It's the first day this bar was reopened in what, five years it had been closed? I get to asking myself how he knows I had taken down an old moose head and hauled it to an upstairs storage room. So I tell him maybe I'll think about it.He grins and walks out, sober as a judge, without saying anything more."

Shea looked at Spirit Tooth in the mirror and could see he was watching Mickey and himself at the bar and smiling.

"Anyway, a couple of days later I go back in the storage room, and that moose is just sitting there, looking at me. I could feel that doggone thing working some kind of a moose mojo on me. So, I decided to put it back up.

"It took me near an hour and a hernia to get it down off the wall and hauled back up into storage in the first place, and here I am now putting it back! But the weird thing was that now it's light as a feather and it only takes fifteen minutes to get it back up on the wall, and when I get it there, I just feel good. I mean, I can feel the moose smiling at me. It made my day. It's been up there ever since."

Mickey took another break with his beer before he continued. "The next day that old fart," Mickey said, pointing to

Spirit Tooth, who sat there grinning, "comes in, takes one look at the moose and breaks out laughing. Quiet laugh for a big guy, by the by, but it sure carries.

"'Hi, Buddy!' he yells to the moose. 'I knew you wouldn't have to wait up in that room too long.' Then he orders a pitcher for himself and a mug for the moose. I figure he's crazy, but what the heck, it's his money. That's how it's been since then."

Spirit Tooth spoke up for the first time since ordering. "I tell you, Mickey, I know what my friends like. Let me tell you, little buddy, me and that moose there go back a long time. We remember when there were gaslights in this place and when that little cubbyhole in the back where Mickey keeps his safe held the best little shine still in the Keweenaw. And the girls upstairs! Let me tell you!"

"That's another thing," Mickey broke in. "Spirit's never been in the back since I've been here, not upstairs, either, yet he knows where everything is."

"Not everything, Mick. Just what the moose and the others see," Spirit Tooth laughed. "Thing about this place is bartenders come and go—there's been four in the last sixty years alone—but me and my friend there are more constant. We know where the secrets are because we've been in on them longer."

"Why the name 'Spirit Tooth?'" asked Shea. "How come they hung that handle on you?"

"No one's hung nothing on me, laddie. That's my name and that's my place. I live on Spirit Tooth Mountain. Always have. Besides," he said as he raised his upper lip, "what do you see?"

Shea took a look and saw there was a gap from his upper, left front tooth to the left canine.

"You're missing a couple there."

"All kinds of reasons for things if you look close enough. Of course, can't be seen don't mean they're lost, son."

"Besides, you ought to see him eat," piped in Mickey.

"I've never heard of a Spirit Tooth Mountain—you did say 'mountain,' didn't you? Is it around here?" Shea asked.

Mickey answered first. "You won't find it unless you look at an old, and I do mean *old* map. It's straight back there on the cliffs, but no one knows how it got the name and damn few remember it's there at all. Personally, I think it's named after him."

"That's what I like about you, Mick, you're quicker than most. Time in the jungle must have taught you something." Spirit Tooth looked out from under a red thatch of hair. "You're not far from wrong, but it's time to trundle off."

He drained his mug, put it back in his leather pack, and hefted that onto his back. He left a handful of what looked to Shea like silver dollars on the table and headed for the door. Pausing on the threshold, he waved back to the moose. "Take it easy, buddy. Be seeing you. Maybe Shea there will buy you another.

"And Shea? Say 'howdy' to the twins, Piiku and Kookas, for me when you see them, will you?" With that, he walked out into the night.

Shea turned to Mickey. "Is he always like that? And what's this Piiku and Kookas bit?"

"Pretty near. I don't know what he meant by the twins. Sometimes, like I told you, he tells stories, but mostly he *is* the story."

"Well, I guess it takes all—wait a minute! I never said my name, did I? You didn't either."

"Nope," Mickey said with a smile. "If you figure out the bit about the twins, though, let me know."

Shea was staring over at the moose. "I'll be damned," he muttered.

Mickey took a glance over and said, "Yep, it's empty. Always is unless you sit staring at it."

"But no one went near it," Shea said, still staring at the empty mug in front of the moose. "That's it. I've had enough. How much I owe you, Mickey?"

"Six bucks."

"Here's a ten. Set a mug up for the moose."

With a final wave to Mickey, Shea wrapped himself in his coat and left the building. On the top of the stairs he paused and thought, *Mine was the only car in the lot. There're no houses for miles. How'd Spirit Tooth get here? And where did he go?*

Looking down in the parking lot he saw a set of widely spaced tracks in the early fall snow heading straight across to the woods, illuminated by a nearly full moon.

"Well, I'll be damned," he whispered aloud.

Twenty-Five

THE DAY DAWNED CLEAR and cold. The first real snow of fall had been coming down off and on for the last three days. The waters of the Traprock would be getting higher. It was already 9:00 a.m. when Pete and Roy turned off Valley Road onto the old graveled Park Road to the Traprock River Bridge. They pulled in at Hosking's and parked among the cars, station wagons, and pick-ups that had beat them to the starting point of the race. People were off-loading canoes from many of them, and Roy and Pete got out of Pete's truck to do the same.

"Looks like we got a good day for it, Pete."

"Yeah, looks like there's a little snow on the banks, but at least it's not coming down today. They're calling for more later this week, though."

This year the Great Traprock River Canoe Race, the Fifth Annual, actually, had more entrants than ever before. The race was an annual late fall event and attracted more and more people each year. The confusion of the parking lot and the staging area increased exponentially with each additional canoe team.

Roy and Pete, although Pete had been one of the founding members of the race and Shea had only participated with a different partner last year for the first time, were partnering up this year. They were of a similar mind about this year's race and planned to ride unofficial sweep, in other words, come in last. Their only effort to win was over the Prize Lunch competition, to be held at the halfway point on the river.

The canoes which had already been unloaded were either being carried to or were at the places assigned to them—by luck of the draw or underhanded finagling—for the LeMans style start. Pete and Roy found their spot, as far away from the river as a starting place could be. They set down their canoe, the *Curmudgeon*, and went to join the throng for the opening ceremony and the blessing of the fleet by "Father" Harold Kraft.

After the crowd was treated to a stunning—literally—rendition of "Shall We Gather By the River" performed by a motley collection of voices, nose flutes, kazoos, accordions, and mixed wind instruments, Harold, wearing a black cassock and a life vest, stood on the bridge overlooking the staging area and motioned for silence. As the noise level began to fall he looked skyward and began to intone:

"Dear God or gods as the case may be (and please stay off our case if you would be so kind) in heaven, we come to you today to beseech your blessings upon this race and the racers involved, not to mention lunch. We ask you that we be not sent up this creek without a paddle, but be allowed to flow downstream with your blessings until we come to the lunch, and thereafter verily to the end of the race.

"May you support the deserving among us and smite the heathen who might hinder your chosen, and by heathen I mean you, Pete, and may you grant peaceful waters and a passing thereof as necessary.

"If our canoe rather than our cup runneth—make that turneth—over, may we not lose our brew. But if some other team should tilt, may their unopened brews flow to us. May our cigarettes not get damp despite the dumping, and may fresh snow hold off until the end.

"And may we, at the end of our journey, cold, wet, and tired beyond all measure, find comfort in the arms of our loved ones waiting for us or hot babes of loose morals and little apparel.

"In short—"

"Way too late for that, Harold!" someone shouted from the crowd.

"—we wish to go with your flow and ask you to cast your bread upon our waters. Amen."

"The ass has ended! Thanks be to God!" someone shouted and a roar of approval arose.

Before anyone realized what was going on, a gunshot barely heard above the hubbub announced the start of the race and there was a mad dash among the racers to reach their canoes and run for the river. Many of the crowd were already, despite the early hour, somewhat intoxicated, and immediately there were collisions, crashes, and tipped canoes. Laughter and obscenities flew with equal abandon as the race got underway. In the hours that followed the canoe crews would make their way past the snowy river banks, occasionally helping or hindering others, more interested in survival and fun than winning.

In most cases, that is. There were always a couple of teams who actually did try to win. It was almost as if they were in a separate race that coincidently started at the same time. These crews invariably were driven to come in first at the lunch break and race's end, arriving hours before the last stragglers arrived. Flushed with victory, they would begin to wonder at the total disregard for their winning or the lack of anguish for defeat on the part of the other crews. Then they would rant and rave as the rules committee, as effective a band of ballot box stuffers as ever existed, rescinded their victory on the basis of some technicality or rule that hadn't existed until spoken by the committee.

Year after year, such crews failed to see the humor in the situation, always were the most upset at dumping, and had far less fun than anyone else. Frequently they stayed sober, too.

But now the race was on. Already there were at least three teams, canoes dumped and spirits doused, sodden and struggling in the shallows.

Despite their sincere intentions to bring up the rear, Shea and Pete found themselves on the river and underway, ahead of at least a dozen other canoes.

"All right already!" Pete directed. "Slow down and let the guys coming up on our left—"

"That's 'port' to you!" Shea shouted.

"—On our left, you lubber, pass. They look like they've dumped already and have nothing else to lose."

"Aye, aye, my little, stinking captain! I respond to you in my best Bluebottle voice."

The river was choked with struggling canoes ahead of them. Words, threats mostly, and water were flying liberally around. "What do you say, Pete? Want to head toward those three trees on the bank? Looks like there's no one heading that way, so we can let this pack pass."

"No, I think we better keep going for a bit, Roy. We have to fight the river, too, besides these idiots, and I don't want to get hung up on the bank and spun around. Let's just try to stay behind the guys ahead and ahead of the guys behind for awhile."

"Whatever you say, skipper."

As they took the next bend in the river they caught sight of two of the canoes ahead floundering against each other in a tangle of fallen cedar blocking about half of the river. This would be a fairly typical sight throughout the race as the thirty-some canoes jockeyed for position in a stream that was only thirty-eight feet wide on average and much more narrow where the current ran the strongest. Branches, deadheads, fallen trees and sandbars were constant. Besides the natural objects, there were the occasional shoal of old tires and other manmade hazards, dumped for decades from farms and camps along the river. With luck and a little judicial portaging, a single canoe or maybe even two could make fairly good time down the Traprock without getting hung up, but it called for greater care or sheer insanity to make any time while moving through a herd of this many canoes.

Pete and Roy managed to shoot past the hung up, near capsizing canoes while their straining, swearing crews hurled imprecations at each other. They got onto a straightaway, passed another jam of colliding canoes, and actually found themselves catching up to the three lead boats.

John Garland, in the stern of the boat immediately ahead, turned to shout back at Pete and Shea.

"Hey, Pete! What are you guys doing behind me? I thought you vets of this race knew how to run this river."

"We sure do, Garland. That's why we're back here. By the way, look out for that branch."

Garland turned around in time to only lose his hat to a cedar bough hanging low over the river, but as he shifted position, his partner, Mark Stravis, still paddling hellbent for leather, drove them straight into the bank.

The stern of their canoe caught the current and immediately swung out into the path of the *Curmudgeon*. It was all Pete and Roy could do to stop from running right through them or overturning themselves. Stravis had grabbed a branch when he plowed into the shore, effectively anchoring the bow as the stern completed its 180-degree swing, before he lost his grip and they once more headed downstream, backwards, alongside Pete and Roy.

John tried to swing the canoe back around by dragging paddle while Mark simply sat there in a state of confusion. John might have succeeded, too, if while halfway through the swing their canoe wouldn't have hit a submerged sandbank. The canoe leaned heavily downstream, crosswise in the current. With a flailing of arms and paddles, Garland and Stravis overcompensated, leaned too far upstream, and dropped the gunnels until the water poured in and they capsized.

Pete and Roy just managed to snake past the two men now trying to hang onto their canoe and paddles in the deceptively strong current.

"Careful, Garland! I hear banjos!" Pete shouted as they rapidly drew away from the cussing crew.

"Hey, Roy, does it look like they're going to be all right?" he added more quietly.

Just before they turned a corner Roy looked back as three more canoes all went aground on the same sandbar and created a true nautical cluster fubar. It looked like all were able to stand up, though.

Laughing, Shea told him, "They're wet, mixed up with at least three other boats, but it looks like they're all safe. Well, as safe as you can be standing in water this temperature."

He shouted a question, "Hey, commander! What *does* give? Where's the rush? I thought you knew how to run this river sanely! We're almost in the lead! I thought we were supposed to stay dry this year."

"That's the plan, man. I just didn't plan on everyone else being so incompetent. We can slow down a little, but I don't want the rest of this pack catching up and trying to pass on the next patch of river. We're almost to that stretch of little rapids. That's what got me last year."

Although they had been lucky so far, both Roy and Pete had soaked themselves down in past trips on the river. They knew how cold it could be.

But neither man had a lot of time to think about it. Roy pulled the bow to the left almost frantically as they came into a tight bend in the stream. They managed to make it without incident, but almost immediately the river took another turn, this time to the right followed by a quick left.

They passed a paddle worked into the roots along the bank as they came around the last of the series of bends and saw a canoe, complete with dripping crew, drawn up on the bank ahead.

"You guys all right?" Pete shouted.

"Yeah, just wet is all. We lost a paddle when we tipped, though."

"It's about twenty feet back in the roots on that bend. You can probably reach it from shore."

The stream ahead demanded their attention, however, as they saw a downed pine completely blocking the river .

"Left! Pull left, Roy! We're going to have to portage this one."

"Yeah, you can see where the others have pulled up. Can we get the hell over there?"

They hit a low spot on the bank and grabbed for bushes. Roy got out over the bow and pulled the canoe partway up before holding it steady for Pete, who leaped into ankle-deep water and grabbed the stern. Together they carried the canoe up the bank and around the tree, and then they launched back into the river from the shallows on the other side of the blocking pine.

"If we can get 'em all like that, we're okay, hey?"

"Yeah, Roy, but do you remember that tree being down when you and I took that practice run two weeks ago? I remember a few down past the swimming hole, but not up this high."

"You know, you're right. I don't remember that fall. It might have come down in that wind we had last week, or maybe there's kids screwing around again. Remember all the canoes those damn Parvolaa kids got two years ago?"

"Remember? Hell, I was in one of them. I was running the river with Jack then, remember? We came around a bend by their place, and just as we started to swing back out into the middle, they pushed that pole into our gunnels and over we went. I wanted to kill all three of them."

"Well that's understandable, but Ralph said he took a stroll down looking for traps, but didn't see anything."

"It's probably a natural fall then."

They had to get back to the business at hand as they hit a stretch of small rapids that took all their attention.

But the tree hadn't fallen on its own, and it wasn't kids, either.

When the *Curmudgeon* reached the first break spot, Pete and Roy were amazed to discover they were only the third boat in. They pulled the canoe out and up the nearest bank to make room for others. When everyone finally checked in there would be a replay of the starting madness in a slightly lower key. Each boat was assigned a number as they pulled in. When the numbers were called out they'd take off one by one in reverse order from how they landed. Usually the numbers were called out quickly enough to create mayhem on the shore.

Most of the participants cracked a beer as they landed, and depending upon time, downed more than one. There was no rule against sobriety during the race, but it certainly wasn't encouraged. People drank.

It made the successive starts and stops more interesting.

A number of spectators, most also nursing brews, were at the stop. Some followed the route from start to finish, cheering or jeering as the spirit moved them. Shea expected to see Jeri along with Pete's wife at the lunch stop. A number of people called to Roy and Pete, walked on over, and made a receptive audience for the crew of the *Curmudgeon's* recap of the race.

Two of the spectators made pains to be sure Shea didn't see them, however. Newark and Paalo stuck around the edge of the group at the landing just long enough to see Pete and Roy pull in, and then headed downstream on foot through the trees. Dressed in L.L. Bean outwear, they disappeared quickly, carrying small packs into the woods.

Eventually the last load of dripping canoeists and the official sweep boat pulled in to shore. The greetings and catcalls went on as they struggled up the bank to cold beers, handshakes, and a raging bonfire to warm the blood. The break for the late-comers wouldn't last long, and all exchanged their tales of disaster or triumph until the officials, under the almost constant nagging of the "real" racers, announced the start of the second leg of the race.

The numbers were called, crews rushed to gain the river, and again the race was on.

Shea and Pete, toward the back of the new line up, took on a little water when they cast off, but all in all they were still remarkably dry. More from a sense of safety than ambition, they actually tried for speed for a while as the massed pack thinned.

So there weren't many canoes in front of them as they came around another of the ever-present bends and saw at least four canoes and crews either already or nearly capsized in what looked like an easy stretch of water. Pete and Roy headed straight toward the bank furthest from the mess to figure out what was going on.

"There's a goddamned cable just under the surface here. Watch out, you guys!" Frank Muljo, whose own canoe was already pulled up on the opposite shore, shouted. "Some asshole stretched it across just under the surface and hung a few branches up in it. We didn't see it until the canoe got hung up and swung around, and then Tilden hit us broadside, dumped over himself, and took us with him."

"A cable?" shouted Pete.

Yeah, a bona fide, metal cable! Must be someone's idea of a joke."

As they watched, one of the canoes still afloat made it over while the crews dumped in the river made it to shore. People were annoyed and drenched and some gear was lost, but no one was seriously hurt.

"What do you think, Frank? Where's the best place to get across or do we have to portage?" Pete asked.

"Just aim for the middle. I think we've dropped it a little so you can shoot across. Joe and Ed and their partners got across. Apparently they didn't have as much draw below the surface as we did. I'll warn the others coming, and we'll try to cut this damn thing before we continue. Better hurry, though, there's a bunch right behind you, and I don't think you want to mix it up like we did."

"Thanks, Frank. We'll buy you a beer!" Roy called as they made their way across the line. Their keel scraped slightly, but they got over and made their way downriver.

"Plan on making it three, all right?" Frank called after them.

"You got it, buddy! See you at the lunch."

Although the two men were both thinking about who could have set the trap, the river kept Roy and Pete too busy to talk about it as they swung around the bends below from bank to bank.

When they finally hit a long, straight, slow stretch, they saw only two canoes ahead of them, and when Roy looked back he just saw the empty river. Apparently the main body was still hung up at the cable crossing.

"You still think that tree had come down by itself back there?" Roy asked.

"Well, I never positively believed it hadn't, Roy, but after that cable I admit I'm wondering. Sounds like too much work for it to be kids."

"Yeah, well let's keep our eyes open." They turned their attention back to the river as the straight stretch gave way to another series or turns and twists.

Shortly after hitting another straightaway, Roy heard Pete say, "There's three or four canoes catching up behind us now. Let's slow down and let 'em pass."

"Sounds like a plan," Roy replied.

In a few minutes he heard Pete talking to John Sheer.

"Pete, you must have seen that mess back there," John said as he pulled alongside.

"Yeah, John. Did everybody make it through okay?"

"Yeah, thanks to Frank. He warned folks, slowed them down, and it looked like they were going to be able to get the cable down completely just as we were finally passing through. Whoever did that one sure put some work into it. That cable was thick! Ron almost got caught up in it when he and Frank turned over. Good thing no one drowned."

"Least not yet," Roy called back. "We better keep our eyes open today."

"We'll, Roy and me are taking it easy anyway," Pete added. "You guys still pushing?"

"Yeah, I'm thinking maybe it's a good idea to finish this race quickly today. Besides, George and Lucky are right behind us. They're out to win again, and it pisses me off to think of them taking the lead again, even though the race is just supposed to be for grins."

"Well, we'll let you by, then," Roy heard Pete say as they pulled toward the left bank.

In just a minute Sheer's and two other canoes, including George and Lucky's, passed the *Curmudgeon.*

"Sounds like John's got the race bug after all," Roy said after they had been passed. "I thought that was just for assholes."

"What do you mean, Roy? Both of us have had it before."

"Yeah, well, what did I say about assholes?"

"Curve ahead. Let's take it on the right." For the next mile and a half it was all work.

No one else passed them until they arrived at the swimming hole, where the lunch would take place, again far higher up in the ranks than they would ever have anticipated.

They pulled their canoe out and scanned the crowd. Jeri and Pete's wife Joyce were supposed to be waiting with food and a fresh supply of brew. It was just a second before Roy saw the two women waving them over to a blanket spread near a bonfire.

"What's up, Roy?" Jeri asked when they joined them. "You guys still look mostly dry. Doesn't look like too many can say that today."

"Yeah, you got it there, Jer," Shea said as he hugged his wife. "You hear about the cable some turkey put back there?"

"Yes," said Joyce. "Sounds like whoever did it has the undying love of all of you guys. Harris and Andy said that someone had got it down, though."

Pete was leaning over, slipping off his boots to empty what water they had picked up. "Frank said he was going to try to cut it," he said, "but it sure looked thick." He scanned the arriving canoes. "Did Frank make it back yet?"

"That's him just pulling in now," said Shea. "From looking at him, I hope he never gets that angry with me."

"Let's go give him a hand in."

Carrying a partial six-pack, Roy and Pete walked down to the water's edge with Jeri and Joyce right behind them.

Pete took a bow line Frank tossed him and pulled the canoe in. Shea helped steady it once it was on shore as the crew climbed out.

"Thanks, guys," said Frank, standing and stretching on the sand. "I tell you, I really don't feel like getting any wetter today."

"Yeah, it looks like you got your share of the river today."

"Well, I never claimed to have ever made it down dry before, but this is the first time I've really been pissed about getting dumped. Not only was there a cable, but we found some netting attached to concrete blocks that looks like it had been tied to the cable before breaking loose. In water that deep it could really have caused some trouble. If I ever find out who's responsible, I think I'll take a length of rail line, duct tape it to 'em, and give 'em free swimming instructions out on the lake."

"Let me know if you do, Frank, and Roy and I will help out, okay? Thanks again for the help back there," Pete said.

"Sure thing. You know, I'm beginning to wonder if this thing is getting out of hand."

"I don't think there's any question," said Jeri. "Did you see how many strangers are in the race this year? Some of the college kids showed up looking too drunk to walk, let alone canoe."

"Maybe next year," said Pete, "we should send out invitations with four separate dates on them."

"Come on, Pete. You guys in charge already did that once by mistake, and look what that got you."

"A smart-ass partner, that's what it's got me," grinned Pete.

"Come on, Roy, let's see what the girls brought for lunch. Thanks again, Frank. See you later, and I'm even remembering about the beer. Here's a down payment."

Frank popped the top, took a pull, and finally said, "Thanks," after stopping to take a breath.

As they walked back over to the blanket Joyce said, "You know, I've been wondering how fair this all is. You guys come down to play in the river all day while we get to stay with the family, prepare this grand repast, and then have to lug it down here to you."

"It's a man's life, remember, Joyce? Besides we're sharing it with you," Pete said as he dodged a swat from his wife.

"Speaking of family, where are the kids, Jeri?" asked Roy.

"Marion's watching them next door so Joyce and I could come down. It was nice of Marion to take them for a while. She's got her guys, too, of course. I hope they all don't drive her crazy."

"Enough small talk!" Pete demanded when they reached the blanket. "Food! What's on the menu?"

"Oh, just the usual prisoner's gruel," said Jeri. "Actually, Roy made up a batch of that seafood bisque you guys have had at our place before. He made it last night, so all I had to do was heat and thermos it."

"And I remembered to stop by the store for the bread, cheese, and caviar," added Joyce. "And, a little window dressing . . . Voila!" she said as she lifted the cover off a silver platter of steak tatare. "Oh, and if you beer swillers can handle it, there's wine, too."

"You did just great," Pete said with a bow. "It almost makes me guilty to eat it."

"Don't feel guilty, Pete. Joyce paid for everything at the store," Jeri said.

"Besides that, you're the captain today," added Roy.

"He's my captain every day," said Joyce. She poured a glass of wine and offered it to Pete. "Your mead, my lord?"

"Loyal servants and a dedicated crew," Pete announced in a grand manner. "What more could—"

He was interrupted to dodge an empty tossed by Roy.

"Dedicated to staying dry, Captain, and that's about it!"

"You're forgetting dedicated to creature comforts, too. Now eat," added Jeri.

Armed with plastic dinnerware, they tucked into the food and drink. Conversation was sketchy during the initial attack on the provisions.

Finally Roy looked up from his cup of bisque. "You know, I forget how hungry I get running this river. And with food this good, this annual exercise may be worth it after all."

"Or how thirsty," Jeri said. "If you don't slow down, you might not finish this race."

"Antifreeze, my dear missus. That water gets cold—this is the secret of our success."

"The success must be secret, too! I haven't seen much sign of any success."

""That's coming, Jeri," said Pete. "Your husband and I are doing great so far. Besides," he added, raising his glass, "it's for courage. To us men who go down to the sea in—"

"Or up the crick," Roy called.

"Down to the sea," Pete pontificated, "in ships. We need our courage."

"Especially this year, it would seem," said Joyce. "Sounds like someone's out to get you guys."

"Probably just kids, Joyce. They've pulled stunts on us before, remember?" asked Pete.

"What I remember is last year," Roy said. "Remember when I found out that two of my students had been plotting to live trap a skunk so they could drop it on us from the bridge? If they hadn't gotten sprayed themselves trying to drive one toward the cage that would have really been the mother of all stunts."

Jeri looked serious though when she said, "Still, you two better be careful out there. I've got this nagging feeling. Besides that, if anyone gets to damage you two, it should be us!"

"Spoken like a true spouse, Jeri. I appreciate the sentiment, m'damn wife." But then Shea took her hand. "Don't worry. We're going to try to be the slowest, right? We're riding sweep this leg, and the motto is high and dry. Right, Comrade Captain?" he added, turning to Pete.

"'High and dry'—I'm partially there already, Comrade Crew. Comrade *Curmudgeon* promises to deliver us safely or die trying."

"None of this 'die' stuff, Petroff. Just high and dry."

"And a nubile young thing on a wet man's chest, too, no, Roy?"

"Come on, dreamer," said Joyce, "it's almost time to start again, so eat up."

Twenty-Six

TWO MILES BELOW THE LUNCH SITE, Paalo and Newark stood in a stand of poplar whips on a rise above the river. Just below where they stood a bend in the Traprock opened up into the only real stretch of fast-moving rapids on the river's course.

Newark kept an eye on the river while Paalo unpacked the parts and put together a black-metaled rifle.

"You do think this will do the trick, don't you, Newark? From the look we've had, I say this is the best place. The sound of the rapids will cover the shot, and they ought to go right in ass over tea kettle. What do you say?" he asked without looking up from his work.

"The spot's fine, but it's the whole plan I have my doubts about. I don't know, Paalo. Trees and cables, yeah, but this? There's so many things that can wrong with a rifle."

"We're not pulling a Lee Harvey here, Newark. It's just the canoe I'm taking out, and not even that if there's a chance others can see. If they come through in a pack we leave it up to native incompetence. The other traps we set will incline anyone to think this was another by persons unknown if anyone does hear the shot or get suspicious. And this idea has been cleared. You know how fast the water's moving down there. If they get dropped in the river at the top of all that, their chances of making it through are slim at best. That would be an end—an approved end—to this whole thing.

"For whatever reason, Shea's got them nervous. I personally think they're far too nervous, if you want to know the truth. This guy is just a small town nothing on the ass of the world. But they're the ones calling the shots, so I make the shot. You know what they want. I know what they want. I figure this is the way to give it to them." He looked up at his partner. "It's not up to us to ask questions."

"So why ask me what I think, then? All right, it might work, and that'll be that. I'll just be happy when it's all done with and we head back out of here. The last thing I want is getting chased through the woods by crazed rednecks like we're surrounded by right now. You saw the pick-ups parked down there. Three-quarters of them have gun racks, complete with rifles in the cab. There're more guns down there than in some countries!"

"So no one's going to think anything about hearing a shot, right? These yokels are shooting all the time. Don't get so worked up, Newark. Keep it up and I'll start worrying, too."

"I told you before, Paalo, don't worry about me. I don't give a rat's ass about Shea or the plan. It's just this whole thing has gotten blown out of proportion, and it's our bosses who are doing so. We're the ones on the line here, and I'm ready for it all to end."

Both men silently turned to look down into the river valley.

Twenty-Seven

THE THIRD AND FINAL LEG of the race once more started in reverse order, although this time there were two less canoes. By the time they had pulled it out after dumping at the cable, Tilden's canoe was too badly bent out of shape for his partner and him to trust it. A couple of the first timers had dropped out, too, but that was more from intoxication than common sense.

After they had made their goodbyes to their respective wives—who had pointed out that now they had to clean up while the men folk went back to play—Roy and Pete had hustled down the bank when their start was called and took off.

Again they managed to avoid the worst of the jam at take off, and soon found themselves somewhere between the front runners and the rest of the pack that was now obviously slowing down.

There wasn't much time to talk on this stretch. The river kept turning back on itself and the current grew faster as the Traprock began to narrow. They were forced to pay attention if they didn't want to get wet.

About a mile downriver they heard assorted yells and screams from behind them. Even though they were out of sight, it was obvious a slew of canoes had gone over in a batch.

"Sounds like they were caught on that last corner, Pete."

"Yup, that's what it sounds like. Narrow enough, too, that it'll probably take them awhile to untangle. Just keep pulling us in on the corners like you've been doing, and maybe we won't join them."

"Will try, Captain! Looks like we're going to be alone for a while."

Except for the occasional cry of consternation at the sight of an obstacle or a yip of elation as they passed one by, the partners were quiet as they concentrated on the stream ahead.

Then Pete yelled up to Shea, "Roy, we're coming to that stretch of white water. Make sure you hug the left bank as we go into that corner above it."

"Right!" Roy called back, and then they were into the turn.

They were headed in at just the angle they wanted when the bow of the canoe seemed to jump to the left. Shea had a quick glimpse of metal shards and water pouring in through a breach, and then they were in the river as the bow plunged down and the current threw the stern up.

Roy heard Pete yell, "Shit!" Then he had to pay too much attention to breathing as he went below the surface. He grabbed for the canoe from sheer instinct as the water closed over him, and he felt the current pull it and him away and into the rapids. He broke surface long enough for a quick breath and then he was pulled under again.

When he came up a second time he was facing upriver. He caught a quick glimpse of Pete bobbing along behind him. Pete was shouting, but Roy couldn't make out the words.

As he went down again he tried to twist to see what was coming, but then the canoe jerked to a halt so abruptly his hold on it was almost broken, though he managed to hang on. A branch from shore had caught under the front seat, momentarily stopping the canoe, and now, with the help of the current, the bow lifted out of the water, carrying Roy with it.

Pete grabbed onto the gunnel before he could flow by, and both men pulled themselves along the canoe, now pointing toward and close to the bank.

So much in unison it almost seemed planned, Pete and Roy grabbed branches and released their hold on the canoe just as it broke loose from the branch and the river carried it back out into midstream. It appeared to fold in on itself when it hit a large rock, and then the *Curmudgeon* disappeared into the froth.

Pete and Roy held onto the branches. Hand by hand, despite the pull of the current, they managed to pull themselves higher into the riverside thicket. Once there, they managed to get out of the pull of the river and shimmied up over the bank, where they lay panting and shaking.

Roy heard Pete mutter, "Shit." He looked up to see Pete looking downriver, where one end of the *Curmudgeon* broke surface in the whitewater for an instant before disappearing again. One of the cushions and a paddle appeared briefly riding a crest before they, too, were washed out of sight.

"What the hell happened, Roy? Just what the hell happened? I thought we were right on target and out of the rocks."

"Don't know, Pete. By the way, you all right?"

Both men began to laugh. There was an edge of panicked relief in the sound.

"The bow just seemed to kick in front of me," Roy went on. "It jerked somehow to the left, and then we were in the river. There were pieces of the sidewall swirling in the water, so we must have hit something, or something hit us."

Pete ran his hands over his head as he said, "No shit, Sherlock. 'We must have hit something' the genius tells me."

"I don't know how we could have there, though, Pete. We weren't to the rocks yet, and anything floating in the river would have been moving as quickly as we were downstream. There should have been no way we'd get pushed over like that."

Pete was going through the pockets of his jacket. "On top of everything else—my matches are wet and I lost my cigars. I'm going to have to buy another."

"You're going to have to go buy another canoe, man. The *Curmudgeon* is, I believe, history.

"But all is not lost, mon capitán," added Shea as he pulled a plastic-wrapped package out from his coat pocket. "I came prepared for everything this year—well, not everything. I didn't prepare for that swim. Nevertheless . . ." he said, handing Pete a dry cigar and a package of matches, before he lit one up himself.

"You're a good crew, Crew," said Pete around the lighting of his cigar. He put the match out on his wet jacket. "Isn't this one of the things we're supposed to laugh about on some unspecified later date?"

"I think we've already started to."

As they sat quietly smoking, two canoes passed them and went down the whitewater of the rapids. The men in the first didn't even see them on the bank as they concentrated on the river. Someone in the second yelled something to Roy and Pete, but it was lost in the sound of the river.

"Let's get up on the bank proper and walk back to see if what we hit was a deadhead, Pete," said Roy. As he was getting up another canoe passed and he could see a number more approaching the bend.

They saw Frank wave at them before he and his partner went around the curve.

They walked back to where they had gone over.

"I don't see anything, Roy. What did you say happened? I thought I heard something just before we went over."

"Like I said, Pete, the bow just gave a kick and down we went. I think the bottom gave in at the waterline, but it was over so quickly I really can't be sure. Maybe we caught the end of a hung-up log and forced it out and down?"

"I don't know, partner. I didn't see anything but water."

Pete looked back down the river. "She was a good little canoe."

Back up above Shea and Pete, hidden by the scrub, Paalo and Newark had moved away from the river almost immediately after firing. Paalo began to break the rifle down as they moved through the saplings.

"Well, they went over. Unless they're exceptionally lucky, they went down those rapids in a big way," said Paalo as they walked.

"We'll have to go down to the end of the race, but that always attracts a crowd, according to what I've heard. We'll just have to blend in," said Newark. "I sure would like to know if we're done here."

He looked back over his shoulder.

Don't worry, Newark, there's no posse—" Paalo froze.

On the hillside behind them stood two men. One raised his hand and waved before they turned and disappeared into the woods.

"Son of a bitch! There was someone there! Do you think they saw anything, Newark?"

"I don't know, and I'm not sure I want to find out. Let's get out of here."

They both hustled away.

By the time Shea and Pete had walked down the river to the finish line, everyone knew about the end of the *Curmudgeon*. Their canoe had ended up wrapped around a tree about three-quarters of a mile below where they'd dumped. Shea and Pete had saluted it from the opposite bank when they passed its remnants.

From the sightings of them by other teams, everyone including Joyce and Jeri knew they were okay, so they had all just waited for their arrival. Pete was carrying one of his seat pads that they had found hung up on branches downstream from where the canoe had ended up.

Frank and Harris walked down to meet them as they approached the landing site.

"Game called on account of rain, boys?" Harris asked as they came near.

"Tough break, guys," said Frank. "She looked pretty beat up when we passed by her there in the bushes."

"Yeah," said Pete, "we got a pretty good look at her from the other bank when we walked here. She's had the course."

The crowd when they joined it was basically sympathetic, rowdy and somewhat crude, perhaps, but basically sympathetic.

Shea and Pete accepted beers from friends and a couple of guys they didn't know returned a paddle and another seat cushion they had found to Pete.

"I don't know, Pete," said Roy, eying the cushions and paddle, "you think this is enough to run the race with next year?" He watched Pete carefully for a response. "After all, you're the captain."

"That's right, I am. You're the crew. You carry this shit," he said and passed it off to Shea. "And as to having enough to continue, I've had enough. Let's hit up someone for a ride back to the start to get my truck and go find the girls."

The man in a new wool plaid shirt just milled around in the background. Not truly noticeable, no one got the impression that he was eavesdropping intently.

As Pete and Shea began moving up the bank toward the parked cars, Paalo turned and waved in the same general direction. He watched the two men get into the back of a pick-up truck driven by another local. He looked very disappointed as the truck headed down the road, and then he, too, walked up to the parked vehicles, got in the car with his partner, and they drove off.

Twenty-Eight

THE NEXT DAY, now dry, warm, and rested from the circus of yesterday's race, Shea watched the tea settle to the bottom of the glass five-gallon jug from the caddy lowered into the bottle. The sun had skipped behind clouds, but there was enough solar energy to get the jug brewing.

There was something about the process that Roy really liked. It seemed like such a passive form of creation—simply putting things together and settling down to await the end product.

Shea wondered if God had felt that way when He sat watching the primeval ooze he had created on Earth become life.

He had a hard time with the idea that God had just sculpted man from the clay of the Earth. After all, Roy had a lot of respect for human sculptors, but it was a lot to ask to get a sculpture to sit up, no less to create towns and families and war. The trick God pulled off must have been more like this. Mix all the ingredients, provide the right setting, then sit back to wait.

It gave him a nice contact buzz with the Big Man upstairs, or, he thought, should that be the Big Person upstairs? The Big Girl, even?

Either way, he felt good. For then.

But later in the day after thinking about the traps in the river and the destruction of the *Curmudgeon*, Shea began to get worked up again. It all seemed so damn deliberate, and so nasty.

He vented to Pete. "I want to see the people in this town stop being people that things just happen to. I want to see them— hell, I want to see *us*—just stop taking what's served and start taking a little control over our lives! We're the ones who have to live here—the ones who *want* to live here. Don't you think we ought to be the ones who get to say what happens here?"

"All right, now do you have any suggestions on how we get that to happen? It's easy to say, isn't it? But how do you get it to actually happen?"

"I don't know, Pete. I wish I did, but I don't. But someone's got to know how to get it going. Someone's got to have enough sense, and enough sense of purpose, if nothing else, to get it rolling."

"Forget someone else, Roy. No one's going to step up to the plate and do it for us, but you seem to be able to get the ball rolling. You seem to have some sense of purpose, as you put it. Why not you?"

Roy shook his head. "I'm not a leader, Pete. You know that. I'm not some wide-eyed radical with a plan. I'm not the sort of person who raises flags high enough to be seen by the crowd. I'm just a hayseed from a backwater burg. It's just that I'm smart enough or leery enough to see that something's going down, and it's not something good for us. That's all I am."

"Maybe that's all we need right now, Roy. Maybe that's all that anyone ever needs—someone who sees something going down and is at least loud enough to point it out to a few other people."

Shea leaned against the table and stared out the window. Outside, an early winter squall was kicking up and snow was blowing across the yard. Shea watched it dance across his view.

For a moment it took shape. There were two men standing there now in the snow. They were dressed in blues, browns, and grays. For just a moment they were there smiling at Shea. Maybe they were trying to tell him that Pete was right. Maybe he was all that was needed right now.

One raised his hand and waved, and then they both disappeared into the flowing white.

Shea shook his head and slumped down in his chair.

"Great, now I'm hallucinating."

"Not the first time, is it?" asked Pete.

"No, I'm serious, Pete. I swear I just saw two guys—no, not those two from the ladder—outside the window. I don't know what the fuck is going on. You know, I'm getting tired of saying that."

They were quiet for a minute, and then Shea turned to Pete and asked, "Why didn't you tell me earlier?"

"You have to, maybe had to, decide that for yourself. You want another beer?"

"Yeah, why not?" He sighed. "You ever notice how good we are at that? Having another beer, I mean? Maybe that's part of the problem. We're all good at having another beer, or another cigarette, sandwich, whatever. But we're not as good at doing anything else. How many times has there been something else that needs doing, but having another whatever got in the way?"

Pete popped the top on a long neck and passed it over. "One, or having another one, doesn't mean that something else doesn't get done. I mean, it doesn't have to. That part's up to us," he said.

"Are you so sure of that?"

"Yeah, I guess so."

"Then," said Shea, "why is everything geared to having more? More of this, more of that. Why do we, why does anyone, for that matter, have another?"

"Where are you going with this? I take it you think there's a connection?"

"Damn straight there is! Of course there's a connection! How do you keep people down? By telling them that there's more that they need to have, and can have, by playing by your rules. That's how. The Man is keeping us down!"

"'Just because you're paranoid . . . ?'"

"Right! 'It doesn't mean they're not out to get you!'"

"Right, I can see that."

"Drink up, you dissident bastard."

They drank up. Decisions, of a sort, had been reached.

Twenty-Nine

OUTSIDE OF PHOENIX, Newark and Paalo hustled through the snow from the farmhouse to their car. The sun was already below the horizon, and Newark took care not to look over to where the barn might or might not be.

They had reached a conclusion.

Now's the time, Newark thought as he climbed into the front seat. *One way or another, it's going to be over.*

Goddamn snow, was the only thing going through Paalo's mind as he got in.

The two partners had changed a little on this assignment.

Pulling out of the yard, the car slipped a little before the positive traction took grip and they rolled down the driveway to the road.

They were watched as they left. Others knew it was time, too.

Thirty

"I BETTER GET HOME, PETE. Looks like it's really starting to blow out there—don't you love fall in the U.P.? I want to be home when Jeri and the kids get there."

"All right. Look, take it easy and let me know what you decide."

"You mean you think there's something left to decide that doesn't seem to have been decided for me?" asked Shea as he put on his winter coat. "You must have a better handle on things than I do.

"See you later."

"Right, later."

Outside of Pete's place, the snow as well as the wind were really picking up. The five-block walk back home was a lot more unpleasant than the walk to Pete's had been, but somehow it refreshed Shea and made him feel more alive, infused.

Damn! I feel a sense of purpose growing, thought Shea, smiling. *Maybe I ought to go back and tell Pete.* He stopped and stood there for a moment, but finally he bent over, scooped up a double handful of snow with his gloveless hands, and made a snowball. After pressing it to the desired consistency, he continued on his way home. Half a block down he chose a stop sign as his target, took aim, and let fly. At first it seemed to be going wide, but then it hesitated before passing the sign. The wind, or whatever, caught it and flew it straight to the center of the sign.

Shea stopped cold.

I'll be damned! he thought. *Maybe there's some hope and help in this whole game after all.*

The house was still dark as he walked up his slippery steps. Just as he opened the door, the phone began to ring.

"Hello?"

"Hi, Roy, it's me."

"Yeah, hi, hon, what's up?"

"I don't know what it's like back home, but over here in Hancock it's really getting bad. Have you been listening to the radio?"

"No, I was down having a beer and talking to Pete at his place. It was snowing pretty good as I was walking home, though."

"Well, they're warning folks to stay off the road and they've pulled the plows. I guess winter is coming to stick around early this year. Anyhow, I was wondering whether I should be on the roads with the kids. My folks asked us to stay for supper and the night if it keeps getting worse. If it's all the same to you, I'm going to stick around, for a while at least."

"Yeah, Jer, that makes sense. I'll dig myself up a sandwich or leftovers or something. Like I said, I did just walk home, and I really don't want you driving in this stuff is you can help it. Maybe you should just all stay there for the night."

"Well, I don't know if it's that bad, but we'll see. At the very least I'll be here a couple of hours and then decide. One way or the other, I'll call, Roy."

"Sounds like a plan. I'll be sticking around here waiting for your call. It is nasty out there."

Okay, we'll see you then. Love you!"

"Love you, too."

"Oh, yeah, and take it easy on the beer and brandy."

"I do love you despite that. Night, Jeri."

Shea hung up and walked over to turn on the TV. Almost immediately he turned it off in favor of the stereo. He looked through the record trunk for something to go with snowstorms.

He almost chose some Bill Evans, but went for some Jimmy Buffet instead just for the incongruity involved.

As the first notes of "Who's Going to Steal the Peanut Butter" came on, he lowered the lid on the turntable, tossed the album cover bearing a white-coated Buffet back into the trunk, and turned to the kitchen.

He was rummaging around the lower shelves of the fridge after fishing out and opening a beer. He was still thinking about what Pete had said.

Maybe he's right. Maybe it's time to quit waiting for someone else to do something and start in on my own. Someone's got to be the village idiot, and I guess I'm fit for the job. But there is the question: What am I supposed to do?

Thirty-One

PAALO AND NEWARK WERE NOW in a four-wheel drive pick-up carrying a snowmobile they had picked up from Pershing at the police post.

"I don't know what you guys are going to do with this in the storm out there, but I guess you Shop guys know your stuff," Pershing had said.

"Don't worry, Pershing. We do. You remember to forget all about this, right?"

"Forget what, Mr. Paalo? These things get impounded all the time—mostly being driven drunk. And if you need it, who's to say where it went, right?"

"That's right. By the way," said Newark as he had climbed into the cab of the truck, "the Shop likes people who can be quiet. Treats them just like their own. Don't be surprised if you get a call once things quiet down."

"Hey, that would be just fine, gentlemen. Always happy to help out others on the job, so to speak."

As if he had ever had any dealings with folks like Newark and Paalo before.

"You remember what we said, right?"

"Oh, I will. I will," purred Pershing as Paalo rolled up his window and started the engine. "Just remember to tell them they can count on me," Pershing called as the truck began to pull away.

Paalo turned to Newark and said, "Count on him to be an asshole. Guys like him would sell their own daughter into whoredom for a chance to move up into ops. If I had to work with people like him all the time, I'd quit."

"Imagine how I feel," Newark replied, "I've got to work with you."

Both men laughed, but not as fluently as they would have five weeks ago. They turned back towards Phoenix.

"So you think we have the right idea here?" Newark asked.

"Well, it's the best of those we discussed. There's just enough ice out there to make it believable, and Shea's not noted for being the most practical guy in the world. This is just the sort of dumb ass thing people around here would believe of him. Get drunk, blow off some steam, wind up dead. We've got to do this before he begins making even more noise. Everyone's getting nervous about how long it's taking, which means their customers are getting nervous, and that makes me nervous."

"Yeah, well, I wish I felt a little better about it."

"'Felt?' We better get this job done. This place is starting to get to you, Newark. Tell you what . . . we'll finish this tonight, stick around a couple of days to watch the fireworks and make sure Pershing behaves, and then it's back home to report and then? I'd recommend a vacation. You better go see your family and get your head together."

"If this works, my head *will* be together, man."

They lapsed back into silence, the wind and snow outside making the only sound outside of the engine.

Paalo reached over and turned on the radio. It came to life with a blast of country whining.

"That's another thing," Newark said, "I can't wait to get away from this country shit."

Paalo didn't even bother to reply. He just hummed along.

When they got back down the hill to Phoenix, they avoided the streetlamp-lit main street and took the edges of town onto the last dead end leading to the old quarry. Newark killed the engine and both men got out.

The quarry pit looked like an irregularly shaped field the size of several football fields, but below its ice were roughly two hundred feet of water filling the hole where sandstone had been harvested for several decades in the late 1800s and early 1900s. Once operations had halted, the pit was allowed to fill for recreation and as a source of water in case of fire.

Paalo and Newark walked over to the edge.

"Looks like there's just enough ice on it, Newark. The middle was open when I checked two days ago, but with this cold snap and storm it looks covered. Ought to hold up for the first fifty feet or so, and then it'll go right through."

"The snow ought to kill our tracks, too. Maybe even his for a while. It would be handy if he went missing for a couple of days, but I wouldn't count on it. We can't ask for everything."

"No, I wouldn't count on it either, but this ought to fill the bill."

"Let's go get him."

They walked back to the truck, got in, and Newark threw it into reverse and swung around until they were aiming at their own track in. He put it in forward and pulled out.

Shea was just finishing his second sandwich when he heard the knock on the back door. As he opened it, Paalo and Newark pushed past him and walked into the kitchen.

"Good evening, Mr. Shea. We've stopped by to pick you up for a ride."

Shea was actually angry rather than his usual nervous self in the face of surprise. "What are you two doing here? Who asked you in? My wife and kids will be here in a minute and I want you gone by then."

"Now you know that's not true, Mr. Shea. It's handy that your family has a port in this storm at Jeri's parents' tonight. That's a good thing. It's handy that they're not here. Let's go."

"I'm going for a ride with you two? At night? In a storm? Hell if—"

Shea saw the gun in Newark's hand and stopped talking.

"Yes, Mr. Shea, we are taking you for a ride," Paalo laughed at the unplanned gangster cliché, "and you are in a hurry to go with us, so grab your coat and come on."

"What is this? I haven't done—"

"It's not what you've done, it's what you might do that bothers us, Mr. Shea. Now shut up, and let's go."

Newark handed Shea his hat and coat. "You better take the hat, too. It's cold out there tonight, and we don't want you becoming ill."

"Wait a minute! Just put the damn gun down and let's talk about this. You guys can't pull off something like this—just waltz in with a gun and start giving orders. Not even a warrant? Even cops can't do this."

"Ah, but we're not the cops, and we *can* do it. Let's go."

Shea looked from man to man, then at the gun, and shrugged into his jacket. He thought about asking to leave Jeri a note, and then thought about the ridiculousness of the request in this situation. When he put on his hat, Paalo took his arm and led him out the door.

"Lock it behind us, Newark. Shea usually locks doors when he leaves."

"Right. Remember Shea, I'm right behind you with the gun. Right to the pick-up."

When they reached the parked truck Paalo opened the door, hustled Roy into the middle seat, and climbed in beside him as Newark got in the other side with his gun still trained on Shea.

"Just sit back and enjoy the ride, Mr. Shea. Remember, there's two of us and one of you, and we have the guns. No theatrics. All we want to do is go somewhere undisturbed to have a little talk."

As they pulled away from Shea's home the wind was kicking up even more than before, and the visibility was bad even on Shea's somewhat sheltered street.

Snow day tomorrow, Shea thought, and then smiled in spite of everything.

They drove to the edge of town and pulled up the hill leading to Quarry Road outside of town.

Newark reached into the glove box of the truck and pulled out the bottle they'd placed there earlier in the day.

"Drink some of this, Mr. Shea. I think we've got your brand, and knowing you, it's probably following the beers you've already had."

Shea took the fifth and looked at the label. Hartley's brandy—it was his brand. He looked at the gun in Newark's hand and took a quick drink.

"Have another, Mr. Shea. You see, it's all for you."

Shea drank.

Two miles up the road they pulled into the quarry. Paalo stopped the truck and got out while Newark kept the gun on Shea. "Have another drink," Newark said. "No point in being shy."

The brandy and, he had to admit, the earlier beers were going straight to Shea's head. He heard Paalo unfolding the ramp from the back of the truck, starting the snowmobile engine, and backing down the ramp.

He came around to the door of the truck cab, opened it, and said, "Time to take a little ride, Shea."

"Another ride?" asked Roy. "What's this all about?" He was slurring a little.

"Guess it won't hurt to tell him now, hey, Newark?"

"Look, Shea, it's lesson time. You live in the worst shithole excuse for a piece of the country that I've ever seen. No one in his right mind would want to live here except for you and a crew of drop outs from the world at large. But a group of people who we work for have been hired by some other folks who actually have a use for this place. You crackers have been driving it into the ground for years, but these people can actually turn it to good use, and they don't need some loud mouth asshole dropping letters and organizing at the first sign of progress this place has seen in decades. They don't want someone asking a bunch of questions about shit he doesn't understand.

"And that's what you've been doing, Mr. Shea. You're even asking questions that go against national security. This country is for more than just the people who live here—surely even you should be able to understand that."

"Do you want me to shut up? Is that what this is about? Scaring the shit out of me so I shut up? Well, you got it. I'm quiet! I'm just as quiet as you want me to be."

"We don't think so, Shea," added Paalo. "Besides, it's a little too late to get laryngitis now. That might get some other people asking questions. No, you just climb out of this truck and walk over to the snow machine."

Still carrying the bottle, Shea climbed from the cab. As he walked to the snowmobile he could feel the gun aimed at his shoulder blades. He also felt something else, something besides fear, something he couldn't identify at first.

Then it hit him. *I'm right! I'm not paranoid. This time I was just completely right!*

Somehow it didn't comfort him a lot.

"Now," said Paalo, "let me make this clear to you. You're going to get on this machine here and drive straight across the quarry pond to the other side, got it?"

"What are you talking about? There's not enough ice yet to hold this thing up all the way across. You're trying to kill me!"

"Hey, we're betting men, Shea. There's a chance you'll make it. I doubt it, but there's a chance. Maybe you'll even make it back home to your family. Maybe we'd even give you a chance to leave town with them. I do know, however, that we'll kill you right here if you don't get on the machine, and if you try to turn, to cut across to the side bank, we'll kill you then, too. Paalo's a damn fine shot. Took out the front seam of your canoe, didn't he? You should have had the sense to drown then so you weren't taking that chance now."

He continued calm as could be, "If you didn't do what we wanted you to do right now, I couldn't guarantee the safety of your family now, either, Mr. Shea."

Shea looked from man to man, and then nodded. "I understand," he said, and he climbed onto the snowmobile.

"You know," he said, "no one is ever going to believe I came out here on my own, right? I'm one of the few adult males here who doesn't even own one of these things."

"You let us worry about that, all right? I don't think anyone around will have too much of a problem with your getting drunk and stealing a snowmobile with the key left in—particularly if there were respected witnesses like local police troopers and others. You know, you're not exactly looked on as a pillar in the community or the brightest candle on the cake."

Paalo spoke up. "Besides, look at how strange you've been acting—paranoid, writing letters to the editor about conspiracies. I even hear there's been a prescription or two called into the pharmacy in Houghton. They were picked up, too. Probably don't mix with alcohol, either, although some may be found in your system mixed with the brandy. You got problems, Mr. Shea. Maybe you're even suicidal."

The brandy was going to Shea's head. "I can't believe you'd make me do this! Come on, tell me it's a scare, just some kind of cruel half-assed joke before I drop here."

Newark gestured with the gun at the bottle. "Now you have another good pull or two of that fine brandy, and then tuck the bottle in your coat. It's time to go for your ride, all right?"

Shea looked from one man to the other, shrugged, took a long hit off the brandy and threw the bottle into the snow at Newark's feet. His head was truly spinning.

"That might be even better than taking it with you, Roy. The snow will obscure our tracks, but they ought to find the melt hole from the snowmobile idling here, figure you sat here drinking until you made up your mind, got good and ready, and then headed out."

"Look at the bright side, Mr. Shea," said Paalo, "you're doing this for the good of the country. You always wanted to be a hero, didn't you? Now remember, we've both got guns, so don't ruin your one chance, such as it is, and make us shoot you outright when you tried to get away. No one would hear the shot, and you'd just be dead more quickly. It might be slightly harder to explain, but that would be our problem, not yours, and there is the family."

Shea flipped them the bird, clutched the handlebars, and pressed on the gas to take off. The old yellow-and-red vehicle revved, the gears caught, and Shea lurched forward, almost losing his grip on the handle bars. The wind tore at his too-light clothing, and he ducked lower into the relative calm behind the windshield.

The machine was over thirty feet away from the two men in seconds. Newark kept his gun trained on Shea as the distance between them grew. Even though he was an excellent shot, he didn't want to take a chance on a miss if shooting became necessary.

Then Paalo shouted, "Shit! There's someone out on the lake there with him!"

Ahead of Shea's machine the whirling snow danced around two tall men standing somewhat to the left of Shea's path across the quarry.

Newark swung the sights of the gun from Shea to the two onlookers. "Shit," he muttered, and then he froze.

They were the men from his nightmares at the farm-house. Now he knew where he had recognized them from on the hillock above the Traprock.

Shea saw what looked like open water ahead of him and considered jumping off before he hit the patch, but then he saw the two men to his left. The closest of the two raised his hand in an expressive wave, and Shea could swear he saw the water ahead turning to ice in front of him.

All thoughts of turning gone now, without any conscious thought he actually accelerated and barreled straight on ahead. The ice kept forming like a floor before him, and he scrunched down further on the snowmobile to present a smaller target of his back as he expected to hear shots ringing out behind him at any second.

He risked a quick glimpse back, hardly making out the figures of Paalo and Newark hustling back to their truck through the falling snow.

The two agents felt their plans falling apart as soon as the two men had appeared out on the lake. Newark had shouted, "Shoot for Christ's sake, Paalo! Shea's getting away and those two fuckers saw—probably heard, too—everything."

But Newark had already tried firing. The gun had refused to go off. He had stood there, legs slightly spread and bent at the knee, the gun pointing first at the taller of the two, then the shorter, and then Shea's departing figure as he squeezed the trigger in proper fashion again and again and again, but nothing had happened. There were no reports, no kickback. It was if the hammer was falling on empty chambers. For a sickening second he had the thought that it was his fault—that he had forgotten to load his weapon, but he knew better.

He remembered the first night he had seen these two and almost wished it were his fault now.

Paalo had turned back to run to the truck to retrieve a rifle, and Newark had turned to follow him, but they both stopped short in their tracks.

Ahead of them the truck was starting up on its own. The cab and the engine lights, which they had left off, were now on and dimmed momentarily as the engine struck. The truck pulled forward on its own, narrowly missed the two agents as it accelerated by them and pulled out onto the ice of the frozen quarry.

A hole seemed to open under the vehicle, and then in an immense splash it nosedived in. In seconds it disappeared, air bubbles escaping from the cab and undercarriage marking where it had been. For a brief instant they could see the cab and headlights, but then they were shorted out by the water and disappeared as well.

Unbelieving, Paalo walked towards where the truck had been. Starting from the center of the hole where it had disappeared, the open water began to freeze. In moments even the falling snow was refusing to melt on the ice, and, indeed, seemed to be targeting the spot, covering up where it had been. If not for the tracks leading to the spot or the testimony of his own eyes, Paalo would not have believed what he had just seen.

He turned to Newark, who still stood in place, staring. He held his gun limply at his side, and to Paalo he looked unnaturally pale. Paalo turned to take a look across the quarry where the taillights from Shea's intended deathmobile were now arcing over the top of the rise on the other side. He watched Shea reach the top and then descend onto the road on the other side. In the distance he heard the sound of the snowmobile disappearing into the distance off into the night.

He looked to see where their two visitors still stood out on the lake, watching the agents' reaction to their disappearing truck. With the distance and the falling snow, Paalo couldn't see their faces clearly, but he had the distinct image of them both smiling.

Then, in unison, they both raised their hands in a farewell wave. The snow either rose to cover them or they both disappeared down into a drift, but in a second they were gone.

Paalo and Newark stood alone on the ice of the quarry.

Newark faced Paalo, and then slowly raised his gun to himself, and for just a moment Paalo thought Newark was about to shoot himself, but then Newark collapsed to his knees in the snow.

Paalo took several steps towards him and then froze as a chill made its way up and across his back.

His partner, Newark, was kneeling in the snow—and laughing hysterically.

Paalo stood there for a moment trying to get this and the last few minutes' other shocks to register, then felt something move at his feet, and, involuntarily, he jumped. As he leaped his boots literally disintegrated off his feet, and he landed in stocking feet in snow up to his knees.

Newark laughed even louder and then seemed to start to pull himself back together. "Don't say a thing, man. Yeah, and I know about the boots. It just happened to me, too. Something tells me it's going to be a long walk back to Calumet to get our car. We have to call Pershing."

As the snowmobile carried him away from the quarry, Shea, too, was laughing almost as loudly as Newark had been. For him, though, it was the sound of a man proven right. He did mean something after all. First, the two agents had told him so as they tried to kill him, and second, their plan hadn't worked! Someone had tried to stop him, and then someone else had decided he was worth helping out. Now he had to make the most that he could out of the chance they had given him.

He made the turn to head back into town when he hit the junction that would bring him home, but first, he had a couple of stops to make.

Thirty-Two

PETE, STILL HALF ASLEEP, stumbled downstairs to his ringing phone.

He figured it was a call for an emergency repair run, and he soundly cursed anyone and everything that had to do with work.

"Yeah, Pete here."

"Pete, it's me, Roy. Look, I need your help, and you're not going to believe me, so please listen.

"I need you to come meet me right now. I'll be on that road that we cut into for our skiing trail, and I'll need to be picked up. Right now I'm calling from the booth by Fall's Park. Are you listening?"

"Yeah, I'm here, Shea. What the fuck is this about?"

"I don't have time to explain over the phone, all right? You come get me and tell you the whole thing, but like I said, you aren't going to believe me."

"This had better not be—"

"No joke, Pete. Please, *please* get in your car and hustle on up there. I don't know how much time I have before they come after me again, although I'm pretty sure someone's trying to give me some breather time."

"Breather time? From what, Shea?"

"Some assholes tried to kill me tonight, all right?"

Shea sounded excited rather than drunk, as Pete had expected. Somehow he sounded convincing.

"All right, Shea. Where our ski trails meets the road, right? That's what you said?"

"That's right, and I'll owe you one, man."

"You already do, and I'll be right there."

Now wide awake, Pete hung the phone back up. He grabbed a pair of pants and a shirt hanging in the bathroom, got them on and headed for the door. He sat for a moment at a kitchen chair to put on heavy socks and his boots. He reached for his coat from the wall peg, and then paused, went to the refrigerator, grabbed a twelve-pack from the shelf, and then went for his coat.

Outside it was blowing up a blizzard. The snow was knee-deep in the driveway although it looked like the county plow had gone by not too long before.

The car didn't want to start. Pete didn't blame it. He pumped the gas twice then took his foot off the pedal altogether as he cranked the key again. This time it kicked in. Pete let it run for a minute or two, and then he pulled out. Mentally he chastised himself for forgetting to use his turn signals again, but then he realized the time, what he was up to, and what Shea had said. "Whom am I going to signal?" he muttered.

There were no other cars on the main street as he drove through to the end of town. As he hit the corner leading out of Phoenix and up to Calumet, a gust of wind carrying the snow eliminated all visibility. *It's a bitch of a night,* he thought as he drove up the hill.

The wind kept whipping and forced him to slow repeatedly as he drove the three miles out of town. "This had better be good, Shea," he said out loud as he lost sight of the road again.

He was almost past the turn-off he had to take to meet Roy before he spotted the side road, but at the last minute he caught sight of it and turned—almost spun—the car around.

No sooner had he stopped where the ski trail crossed and Shea was at the passenger door getting in.

"I owe you a whole bunch, all right?" he asked.

"Damn straight," Pete said, "Now what's this all about? Besides that, where's your car?"

"Believe it or not, I got here by snowmobile. I just parked it off in the trees to keep it out of sight. Snow ought to cover the tracks completely. Like I said on the phone, some assholes tried to kill me tonight. Remember those two guys I've been running into and told you about? The ones we saw drive by your place that time? Well, it was them."

"Now I know you rub a lot of people the wrong way, and I know you're turning paranoid in your old age, but there's got to be some kind of reason behind all this. Why do you think they're after you? By the way—you smell like a distillery, you know. Doesn't increase your perceived veracity."

"Let me tell you what happened. Maybe you'll see a reason in there somewhere, 'cause I wasn't too sure about it myself, at first. They came by and picked me up tonight.

"By the by, Jeri and the kids are out at her mom's and staying there because of the weather. I called her right after I talked to you in case she called and I wasn't home, but I didn't let her in on what's happening yet."

"*I* still don't know what's happening yet," said Pete.

"Look, I'll tell you everything, but right now how about heading for the Millwash Road? You know where my grandfather's place is?"

"You mean the place you've always claimed is haunted?"

"Yeah, that's it. I've got this feeling I really should be there right now, but I'm not quite sure why. You mind driving me out there?"

"Once more, man, this had better be good. I tossed a twelve-pack in the back. Grab me a beer and open it up. Might as well both of us smell drunk—although I have to admit, you don't sound looped. Now, what's this story?"

The road was a mess on the way back to town and the turn off towards Jacobsville. Pete kept his eyes on the road as he drove and Roy filled him in on the night's events. Occasionally he had to sneak a glimpse to make sure Shea wasn't smiling and that it wasn't a strange, twisted joke of some sort, but Shea sounded sincere, even more sincere than usual.

There was something else in the sound of his voice, too, a hint, a sound of something that could be out and out triumph. It was obvious that something was changing his friend, and Pete was withholding judgment on whether the change was for good or bad.

Self assurance, he thought. *Maybe that's what I'm hearing in Shea's voice. It sounds like he knows what he's doing for the first time in a long time. Still . . .*

He interrupted Shea's narrative to tell him, "Shea, if I find out you're making this all up, you won't need *them* to kill you."

"Hey, man, gospel, right? It all went down just like this. So after I called you and Jeri, I drove the snowmobile out to meet you just like I said."

"You just took the machine you were supposed to be killed with, made an escape from two guys straight out of central casting for a spy thriller, with the help, no less, of two supernatural dudes—"

"I'm really not sure I saw them, Pete. Even I'm sketchy on them."

"—two supernatural dudes doing a ZZ Top intervention, and after you get across a frozen lake you drive off to call and meet with me, the cavalry. Do I have that right?"

Shea grinned, "Oh, they got the snowmobile from Pershing. He must be in on it, too."

"The biggest asshole on the local force helping thugs . . . sounds about right. This is a new side of you though: Shea, the target of assassination and escape artist."

"It does sound a trifle out of character, doesn't it? But all I can tell you is it's starting to feel right for some reason. I'm obviously making someone nervous, and that feels like the right thing to do. Just like heading out here."

They were pulling past the Millwash Inn, which looked strangely deserted until the two men realized it must be pushing on two.

"Remember, this is our turn coming up, Pete."

"Yeah, I remember. Now if I could only see the damn road."

The car turned onto the side road, a gravel-covered rut at the best of times, and now a snow-covered track lost in the drifts.

A mile up they faced the drive on up to what had been Shea's grandfather's farm.

"What do you want me to do, Roy?" asked Pete.

"You've got your boots on, right? Look, I hate to ask you to do this, but how about driving past and parking beyond the next curve? We can walk up to it from there."

"'We,' Kimosabe? Well, I suppose. 'In for a pound' and all that. Weather's crap enough I can understand why you hate to ask, though."

"I also hate to ask because these guys seem to be playing for keeps. They're making threats, man, and I don't think they'd stop with just hurting me. Still, I'm asking you to walk up there with me. I don't think they'll be there, but I don't know that for sure, and if they are . . ." he let the rest of the sentence trail off.

"You say these guys have something to do with the shit that happened at the canoe race this fall, don't you, Shea?"

"Yeah, Pete, I think they do."

"Then they owe me one, too. That damn canoe was beyond repair."

Pete smiled for the first time since Shea had got in the car. "I'll be glad to take a stroll with you on such a lovely night."

Pete pulled the car off to the side as far as he could when Shea indicated the place. He killed the engine and the lights and turned to Roy.

"Now what?"

"Now we take a little walk up the back path to Grandpa's farmhouse. There was a trail up from here past where the barn used to be. Erickson's cows probably still come down here to drink out of Millwash Creek. It ought to be walkable through the trees—if we can find it."

"'Ought to be . . .' 'If we can find it.' You really know how to make a guy feel secure, you know?"

"Look, I wouldn't be asking if I didn't think I need you along for some reason. You've already done more than I could have hoped. It's up to you."

"What are you talking about? You think I'd pass up a chance to meet all those family spooks you've been talking about for all these years? Joyce would never forgive me. Not to mention Jer."

Shea grabbed his friend's arm for a moment and just stared at the snow coming down along the road and the treeline of the gully. "All right. Thanks, hey? Let's go."

"Male bonding is officially over, right?"

"Right. Say, Pete, think we should lock the doors?"

Pete just looked at him and burst out laughing. "You've got to be fucking kidding, right? You know two other assholes who would be out here wandering around looking for cars to rob? What's going to happen? You think professional auto strippers are on the Millwash Road tonight?"

Shea returned the laugh, shook his head, and waded through the snow in the ditch. With Pete right behind him he climbed over two strands of barbed wire still exposed above the snow and then turned up the hill leading to the back of the house.

Thirty-Three

I T WAS MISERABLE CLIMBING UP the side of the gully, but doable. They made their way despite the blowing snow and darkness of the night. A time or two Shea had to stop to get his bearings, but he finally found the path he had walked enough as a kid to lead them onward.

When they topped the hill they could see the farmhouse through the blowing snow. When Shea used to play here the barn would have been between them and the house, but with it gone it all seemed more open, more exposed.

There were no lights on in the place, no car in the drive, and no sign of anyone being around, but Shea still hesitated. He could feel a little of the old sensations in the pit of his stomach. He had never liked being in the farmhouse itself. That was one of the reasons the countryside and fields around the farm were so familiar. He had been avoiding sitting inside when he could. Now he thought he had reason to dislike the farmhouse even more with its present occupants out to get him, but the feel of anticipated trouble wasn't as strong as he had feared it would be.

In fact, after a couple of seconds of standing and watching the place, he actually got a feeling of welcome.

"Come on. We might as well not stand here all night," he said and started across the field.

"Spoken like a sensible loony," Pete replied and stepped in Shea's tracks heading towards the house.

They floundered through the snow and up to the front door. Shea reached for the doorknob at the top of the concrete steps and hesitated again. Then he tried to turn the knob.

It was locked.

Shea broke out laughing despite himself. "It's locked! How anticlimactic can you get?"

"You expected it to be open to all comers with the two guys staying here being the type of guys you think they are? Maybe the welcome mat ought to be out and the steps swept clear."

"Yeah, I know. You're right, but still."

He jumped from the stairs and walked to a window off to the side. "You used to be able to jimmy this window to toss in wood." He took out a pocket knife and used it to pry at the lower pane until it moved enough for him to get his fingers in to lift it higher.

"What an education you're giving me tonight, Shea. I never saw this side of you before. First trespassing and now breaking and entering."

"Just give me a boost here, will you, Pete?"

Pete cupped his hands to give Shea a leg up through the open window. Shea almost fell through rather than climbed through, but he quickly climbed to his feet.

"Let me see if I can open the door. I'll be right with you."

Roy stumbled across the dark wood room trying to remember a probably long outdated layout to anticipate objects along the way. He made it back out into the entryway with nothing more than a skinned knee and opened the outer door to let Pete in.

"Oh, Shea! I was just in the neighborhood and thought I'd drop in."

"Get in here, will you? Those guys will probably be back any time."

"Unless they've gone back to your place to await their favorite playmate," Pete suggested.

"They might have," Shea admitted, "but they knew Jer and the kids weren't at home—good thing, too, and I'll bet they expect I'm still running."

Pete shook the snow off his shoulders. "Your family's going to be all right, but we're here for a reason, right?"

"Coming up here isn't something I like to do either, though, Pete. I'm not afraid to admit I'm a little nervous. Maybe I should have run."

"What are we looking for, Roy?"

"I've got to be honest. I'm not sure, but I am sure I'll know it when I see it."

They opened the door from the entryway to the kitchen and stepped inside. Once in the kitchen proper they took a moment to look around and get their bearings. The room was faintly lit from the embers glowing through the mica window on the kitchen woodstove.

"They banked a fire to keep the place warm, Pete. They must have planned to come right back after they were done with me."

"So let's find what we're looking for and get out, right?"

"Right."

"Hey, I didn't take a flashlight, did you?"

"Now that you mention it, Shea, yeah, back in the car."

"Well, all right then. We need to see," Shea said and flipped the light switch.

The place had changed. Not enough to be unrecognizable, but enough to make it different. The sink, stove and table were in the same places, and the table itself was the metal and yellow Formica-topped one Shea remembered so well. There were French doors leading into the pantry now rather than the old curtain, but the shelving seemed untouched since his grandfather had died.

The table was bare except for a salt and pepper shaker set and a single glass.

Shea turned through the archway and walked into the living room.

Reflexively Pete turned the handle of the sink faucet to stop it from dripping and then followed Roy into the other room.

"What's one light more, right?" asked Shea as he turned the wall switch in the front room.

Everything was painted a different color and the drapes had been changed. Most of the furniture was newer replacements, although still obviously used, than what his grandparents had before, but although it wasn't his grandfather's, a wood rocker was still in the same place in front of the window.

Everything seemed changed in a way, but nothing really seemed that different.

"This is the place, hey, Roy? The place I've been hearing about? I never thought I'd get in here. From the way you talked, I never thought you'd walk back in it again."

"I never expected to be back in here either, Pete."

Shea took a look around the room. "Those guys are neat! Look. No books, magazines, clothes —nothing. They must have everything upstairs."

As he took the first step up, Shea thought he heard someone walking around above him and stopped. "Did you hear that?"

"Stop it! Right now! There's no one here but us, hear? Otherwise they would have heard us when we came in and they would have already been down to check us out."

Shea walked up the steps with Pete behind him. As he turned the corner at the top of the stairs he automatically reached for the switch on the wall plate. All three upstairs rooms were at least partially illuminated at once. There was no one around.

"There's a suitcase in there. I'll check it out. You keep an eye out through the window there on the drive in case anyone comes up, all right? If they do, hit the light, get out, and make it back down the gully. I'll be right behind you."

"Aye, aye, mon capitán! You just find what you're looking for."

But there were only clothes in the suitcase with another shirt hanging on the post of one of the beds. Nothing else outside of the usual furniture was apparent.

"Nothing in here, but I'll check the other rooms. There's got to be something here—I just know it."

The second room was the one always referred to in Roy's family as "Karl's room." That's where the uncle he had never had a chance to meet had slept. The memory of the boy who never came home hung heavy over it.

The room, however, was almost empty. It held nothing but the furniture and seemed to have been almost untouched since Shea had last been there.

The third and last room had the same lack of clutter as the first, but it also held a second suitcase at the foot of the bed. The only thing that seemed out of order was a hole—obviously from a fist—punched through the plaster wall above the head board of the bed.

Shea quickly began going through the suitcase and then the drawers of the dresser. The suitcase yielded nothing but clothes, the dresser, mothballs and bedding.

Shea ran his fingers through his hair. "Shit, there has to be something," he muttered.

He was about to look through the rooms again when he heard Pete call from over by the window. "Roy! I'm not sure, but it looks like there might be headlights on the road below the drive."

Roy ran out to the landing and looked out next to Pete. "Where?"

"Just coming up towards that straight stretch of the road below. It's just a glow, but I think something's coming. It's must just be reaching the curve below the drive."

"Let's get the hell out."

He turned off the upper lights and they pelted down the stairs.

They hustled through the living room, turning off the lights as they passed through on their way to the kitchen.

Just before he reached for the switch, Roy ran into the back of Pete, who had frozen in place on the threshold of the kitchen. Both men stood there frozen.

There on the table sat a briefcase.

Moving into action again, Shea hit the switch, grabbed the briefcase, and both men ran out the door with Shea checking behind him to make sure it was locked as they had found it.

Pete was already moving across the yard but shouted back, "Hey, man, did you close that window you'd opened?"

"Shit! No, I didn't, but I'm not going back now. Let them worry about it. They'll see our tracks anyway if they just look when they get here—if that's them on the road."

The snow was still being blown fiercely by the wind. It seemed, if anything, to have gotten wilder and darker outside. The two men made their way through the blizzard and across the field as fast as they could. Even with the wind and snow they could see the headlights and hear a car as it came up the drive. As the car topped the hill, the headlight beams fell directly upon Roy and Pete.

Thirty-Four

THE LITTLE BASTARD'S PROBABLY halfway out of the county by now, Newark. Probably left his family behind and lit out." As the car came up the drive, the house came into view. "Say, Paalo, I don't remember leaving the lights—"

The words froze as Newark saw the upstairs lights go off. There was a surge of bile in his throat. "Someone's at the house. Two will get you ten it's him."

As they topped the drive they saw the lights go off downstairs, and then as they rounded the corner the headlights caught Shea and Pete in full flight.

"This time," shouted Paalo, leaping from the not quite stopped car, "I've got him!"

Newark threw the car into park, threw open the door, and joined his partner, who was already drawing his gun.

Pete took a quick look back as the headlights hit them and shouted, "Shit, they have to see us, Roy."

"Take off, Pete. Run as fast as you can."

They were approaching the edge of the gully and the path down when they heard the car doors and the shouting.

"Keep moving!" Roy shouted.

"Shea, stop right there!" Roy heard.

He turned back to look despite the need to keep running, saw Paalo aiming his pistol and Newark standing next to their car, using the door frame as a support to take aim with his handgun.

Shea expected to feel the slug any second—when the lights went out, both men disappeared, and suddenly there was a barn between Shea and Pete and the farmhouse.

Shea stopped and just stared.

"Come on, man! You said to keep running," Pete called from the top of the path.

Shea turned to look at him, then took a final look at the impossibility providing cover behind him, and took off running with the briefcase again.

"I've got him this time, Paalo," Newark said through gritted teeth, and just before he could squeeze off a shot, the barn appeared.

"What in fucking hell . . ." Paalo swore, and then both men just stood there staring at the weather-beaten barn clearly visible in their headlights and the blowing snow. They also could clearly see the tracks of Roy and Pete disappearing directly into what looked like a solid wall.

Newark looked at his feet expectantly, but their shoes didn't disappear this time.

"Who do you have, Newark?" Paalo asked. "Just who fucking has whom?"

They didn't pursue their once more escaped quarry. Quite frankly, neither man wanted to approach the barn.

Paalo turned away from the barn first. He shut the car door on his side and began walking toward the house.

Newark finally got back in the car and drove it up to the porch. Then he doused the lights, turned off the engine, and slipped out to join Paalo. He watched as Paalo reached for the doorknob with the house key in his other hand, and then both men fell back as every light in the house blazed on.

The front door opened, and two men looking enough alike to be brothers were standing in the open doorway. Both were laughing as they waved and bowed in greeting. And then they disappeared.

After a couple of seconds Newark walked past Paalo into the house.

"Whatever you do say, Paalo," he muttered as he walked by, "just don't say 'Did you see that?'" Then he continued on into the kitchen.

Paalo finally followed him in. He joined Newark who was standing in the archway leading to the living room. All the lights were still blazing, and the rocking chair in front of the window was moving back and forth slightly, as if someone had just gotten up from it.

Newark shook his head and walked upstairs.

Paalo stood with head bowed, mulling it all over. He could hear Newark moving around upstairs, but it wasn't really registering. When he heard him coming back down the steps, he asked without looking, "Think we ought to go after him?"

When he looked, he saw Newark carrying two suitcases.

He looked at Paalo like he couldn't believe the question, muttered "Diehard," under his breath, set the suitcase down and walked into the bathroom.

Through the open door Paalo could hear him pissing followed by the flushing of the toilet, and then the sound of the sink running. When he walked back into the living room he was drying his hands on a towel.

"No way, Paalo, no way. Looks like Shea went through the suitcases, by the way—you might want to check, and the briefcase I'd hidden in the crawl space is gone. But I'm done. I'm leaving. For the first time I'm feeling like maybe, just maybe, I'm on the wrong side. Like maybe I've been on the wrong side for a very long time now, and someone's just told me it's time to go home to my family. Go home, move south—maybe to the islands—and look for another job."

He picked up his suitcase and headed to the door.

"You coming, Paalo?" he called back.

Paalo picked up his suitcase and followed his partner. He stopped at the threshold of the porch and said, "Wait a minute, Newark, the lights . . ."

The door slammed and the lights all went out.

Newark, already in the driver's seat, actually smiled.

Paalo checked to find the front door already locked against him and joined his partner in the car. The snow was letting up as they drove down the drive.

Paalo did look back, though.

From the living room window overlooking the drive, a small group of people were watching them drive away. In front of the house two men, the brothers from the doorway, shook hands. Paalo caught a glimpse of the barn before the car dipped below the hill and the farm fell out of sight.

He didn't bother to mention any of that to Newark.

Thirty-Five

AFTER THEY HAD HALF-RUN, half-slid down the hill, and after Pete had disengaged himself from the barbed wire on the bottom, Pete and Roy got into the parked car with the briefcase.

As Pete started the car, Roy asked, "Did you see it?"

"See what, man? After they started shouting I thought they'd start shooting. I didn't see anything until the lights went out and I shouted for you to run. Lucky break, the lights, hey? Must have accidently hit them getting out of the car. Why'd they stop, anyway? I figured for sure they'd chase you. Even with that sudden gust and everything getting dark I still figured they'd fire. You're damn lucky the snow kicked in when it did."

"The snow?"

"Yeah, the snow! Blew up so bad there wasn't anything visible back there."

They drove in silence for a while. Pete drove up the hill away from the farm until he reached another side track that would bring them back towards town.

Shea sat there clutching the briefcase.

Finally, he set it down on the seat, turned around over the seat, kneeled to reach the twelve-pack, and fetched two cans. He popped the top on one and handed it to Pete who silently accepted the brew, and then Shea opened his own. "You know, I think maybe we actually earned this one."

"Damn straight," said Pete after a long pull.

"You know, Roy, to my dying day I'll never know how we missed that briefcase on the first trip through the kitchen."

Shea looked at him, grinned and shook his head and said, "Yeah! Almost like it hadn't been there yet, hey?"

"Right, that was weird."

"Well, at least the ghosts didn't get us, Pete." *But I sure think they helped us tonight,* he thought as they drove on. They drank their beer as they headed back to town. The weather cleared almost instantly.

"It's getting nice, Pete. Sun ought to be up soon in a couple of hours, too."

"You know how that goes, Roy. The weather, like everything else up here, changes as quickly as a man can turn."

"Right, Pete."

"Grab another beer."

Talking it over, they decided that Paalo and Newark might be watching Shea's, but probably didn't have a handle of Pete's role yet so the plan was to bring Shea there.

When they pulled up in front of Pete's place, Shea asked, "You sure this isn't going to be a problem?"

"This is from the guy who woke me up to go breaking and entering, and you want to know if crashing at my place is all right? Come on in, Roy."

Climbing from the car Pete added, "Don't think you're going to get away without me seeing what's in that briefcase, anyway. You don't really think I endangered life, limbs, and good name to be left out now, do you? Looks like today's going to be a snow day for you, and Jeri and the kids are safe in town, so let's go in and look that stuff over."

Shea carried the briefcase, Pete scooped up the empties and what was left of the twelve-pack, and they both headed inside.

Once they had taken off their coats and kicked off their boots, they picked up their respective baggage again and padded across the living room rug to Pete's den.

Pete flopped in an easy chair and Roy settled on the floor, his back against the wall on the opposite side of the room. He opened the case and began going through the papers they found. For the next few minutes, almost nothing was said as they passed around the papers, occasionally pointing out particular passages to each other.

"It's all here, isn't it? Everything! The plans this company—"

"You mean the powers that be, don't you?"

"Well, whatever."

"'Whatever,' that's a good way to put it."

"Look, Shea, you were right. Everything you were guessing around about in the dark is here. They were—make that *are*—trying to stick it to us again."

Shea looked up at Pete. "But maybe this time we've changed the rules. This time we've got some idea about what they're up to. Maybe this time we can do something about it."

"What are you planning to do?"

"I don't know, Pete, any suggestions?"

Pete took a drink from the can next to his chair—it wasn't quite like breakfast beer if you hadn't been asleep—and said, "I don't know. I haven't had much time to mull this through. You've at least been suspecting it, but I'd say getting the word out is the next step. Maybe the papers? Maybe you should go see Cathers at the *Gazette*. He's good people, Roy. Maybe he can help."

Shea stood up and walked over to the window. Outside it was starting to get light. It was also snowing again, but not as bad as it had been when they were out last night.

He turned around and said, "That's about all I can think of, too. I mean, I have this stuff now. There has to be some way to use it."

Almost as an afterthought, Roy went on, "Say, this might sound really stupid, but you mind if I turn on the radio? I really should find out if I'm working today."

Pete laughed and got out of his chair. "Sure," he said as he tuned the radio to a local station. "I don't mind. You've only been out chasing or being chased by people all night, and you're naturally worried that you're going to miss work."

Within minutes, the local announcer reported that all area schools were closed for the day.

"Well, that should be a load off your mind," Pete laughed. "If they still manage to grab a hold of you, at least you won't have to worry about missing work."

"Thanks for the vote of confidence, Pete. But actually, what I'm thinking of right now is what to do with this stuff. It may actually be the goods on the whole program we've been getting wrapped up into."

"Wrapped up? You're the one who's getting wrapped up, not me. I'm just along for the ride. No one's after me."

"You think guys who draw up plans like these won't figure out who my companion was running across the field behind the barn last night? I know we came here because it would be safer than my place, but come on."

"Guess I never looked at it that way, Roy, but what's this you're saying about a barn?"

Shea shook his head, "Just drop it. My mistake. There's more things in heaven and earth and all that. I'll explain this, too, someday."

But, he thought, *it really had been there.* Of that he was sure—just as sure that given the right circumstances, it might be there again.

Pete, of course, wasn't following his exact train of thought, but had moved on to a more immediate problem. "I still think Cathers might not be a bad idea. I think I'd go to him without a second thought about now."

"But your thought wouldn't be sitting there because someone tried to drop you through a hole in the ice tonight, now would it? Maybe I am paranoid, but they are out to get me now, aren't they?"

Pete looked at his beer can for awhile before answering. "A couple of days ago, hell, a couple of *hours* ago I would have been sure of one of two things. One, you're pulling my strings to get a reaction , or two, you finally lost enough brain cells to make a real loony out of you."

"Yeah, and knowing me, I'd have guessed you'd go for the first. Now?"

"Now I'm sure neither of those choices is correct. There's a third. You're telling the truth, they're playing for keeps, and I'm getting—make that am—involved. The weird part is it feels good. Know what I mean? I guess, like I know that I'm doing something, that something you've done has made enough of a difference to piss someone off. Someone who plays for keeps, at that. It's not like going to work or getting in an argument in some bar. This is something that's getting a reaction. Things are going to happen because of what we're doing.

"Outside of seeing the kids being born, knowing my part in starting new lives, I can't think of anything else like it in my life. I really thought that someone was going to shoot at you—at us! And it's actually got me high. A person or two can make a difference, Shea. They can. Hell, we can."

"Even if they didn't plan to, Pete. Even if they didn't start off wanting to. No, you're not crazy. I can feel it, too."

"Then that's all the more reason to get a hold of Cathers, Roy. He wants to change things. That's what he's been trying to do for as long as I've known him, and I'm sure it started a long time before that. The man's a crusader. A time or two we've been together dismantling a beer or two, and he talks about the old days. He talks about the folks who tried to change things, to make a better world and life, and how it usually turned to shit. That's why he moved here originally—figured things up here were far enough still locked outside of the modern world that a man could make a difference. He was looking for something and some place to care about, and that's what brought him here. I think you need him."

"And I think this is starting to sound like a better idea. Well, no time like the present. What's his number? You know it, don't you?"

"Now? You're going to call this guy now? Have you looked at the time?"

"You think he'll think it's any more important if I wait until office hours? For all I or you know, our two friends have it all figured out and are on the way here right now. Or maybe they figured out where my wife and kids are. Yeah, I'm calling him now." Shea had the phone in his hand and was watching Pete with an expectant smile.

"Well, at least let me call him. He at least knows who in the hell I am, and although he'll probably still hang up after bitching about the time, at least he'll call me back when he settles down."

He dialed the number from memory, placed the receiver to his ear, and waited. After an uncommonly large, but not unexpected number of rings, Pete heard Cathers answer.

"At this hour it better be the death of someone important, a suddenly declared war, an offer for gratuitous sex, or a repayment of owed money in the works. It better not be an inquiry about sports scores or an attempt to get an answer to settle a bet, anyone calling from an after hours bar, or one of my reporters calling in sick . . . probably from a bar. Now, who is it?"

"Pete Terzel here, Terry. First, I apologize for calling so early, but I'd like to talk to you right away with a friend of mine, Roy Shea. I know it's ungodly early, I know it's an inconvenience, I know it's storming, and I know you don't know me all that well. I also know you're probably pissed, but it's important, too important to put off. We have to talk."

Pete could visualize Cathers shaking his head to clear it and trying to process the rambling of the crazy man on the other end of the line. Then he heard him say, "All right, it's important, is it? You meet me or I meet you? Is it still snowing like it was last night?"

"It's starting to let up," Pete said while nodding to Roy to let him know it was going okay, "but it's still not pleasant. Which do you prefer?"

"You still have that Scout? You do? Fine, I'll go downstairs and wait for you. But Pete, this had better be good. Oh, you have alcohol? Better question: Will this require alcohol?"

"Yes to both questions. We'll be there as soon as we can. Oh, hold it a minute."

Cupping the phone he turned to Shea. "This all right with you, Roy? I figure it's what you wanted, but I'd better ask."

"Yeah, that's more than fine. Come to think of it, we might be wise not hanging around your place too long anyway. I still don't think they'll just give up unless there's even more going on than I'm aware of."

Pete turned back to the phone. "Fine, Tony, we'll be there, and I'm sure you'll see why we're so excited after you talk to Shea. You shouted 'Stop the presses!' lately?"

"Enough clichés, Pete. No one ever shouts that for real."

"Well, maybe so, but I'd get ready to act out the cliché if I were you. Later."

He hung up the phone. "Well, I guess we're underway. What do you say? Shall we get going?"

The two men rewrapped themselves in their winter clothes, and Shea grabbed the briefcase.

"What if there are two guys freezing their asses off in the snow outside of your house, Pete? You know, keeping an eye on the place?"

"I've been watching the side street, Roy. No sign of anything moving out there. Even the birds aren't awake and watching yet. But say, when you get paranoid . . ."

"I thought we were beyond that paranoid stuff."

"I'm just not used to this cloak and dagger business, but I suppose I could get used to it."

"You mean if your life depended on it?"

"Cute, Shea. Real cute."

"Couldn't resist, partner."

"So we go," said Pete as they walked out to the Scout.

There was, as Pete had said, no sign of anybody about as Pete pulled out into the snowy street and drove down to Main before making the turn on the highway that would bring them to Houghton and Cathers's home.

Thirty-Six

ANTHONY CATHERS'S HOME was in a neighborhood that would have said old money in Phoenix, but suggested gentrification in Houghton. Again, it was a case of upper middle class people being able in a time of low property values to move into homes that were bigger than practical, but too cool to resist. The upshot was having a fine looking home that screamed old class. The downside was trying to pay the heating bills for such drafty old masterpieces in the frigid northern winters.

Pete parked the Scout in front of Cathers's home, and he and Roy walked up the steps to the glass fronted porch. Cathers himself answered their knock to let them in, and then after exchanging what passed for pleasantries between Pete and him and the shedding the winter accoutrement, he lead them into his den.

"Thanks, Tony, for seeing us. This is Roy Shea, friend of mine and Phoenix teacher. I'm sure you guys have probably crossed paths before."

"You were in the canoe race on the Traprock three years ago, weren't you, Tony?" asked Roy.

"Damn near drowned launching from the second staging area, but I have to admit it was fun until then. Haven't been able to take part since.

"Not to be rude, though, but you gentlemen did say it was important."

"I think you're going to think so, too, Tony. Roy, do you want to fill him in?"

Once more Roy launched into his story of the past weeks' events. He talked in a general way about his suspicions as well as what he thought went down on the Traprock River. He finished with the previous night's events and the finding of the briefcase.

Cathers looked at him with a half-grin. "If you walked into my office with this story, I'd either toss you out or call the authorities. Even with Pete's backing, I'm still not sure that's not the right thing to do."

"Even if I showed you this?" asked Roy as he slid the brief-case across the table. "I think maybe it's time for you to look at these."

Cathers opened the briefcase and pulled out several sheaves of papers. "What are these, Roy? Where do they come from?"

"This is the briefcase we found last night. The two agents I told you about? This was in the house they were renting. I took it with me when I ran from the house. I'm assuming they may still be looking for them, and I'm assuming they won't be too happy with anyone who reads them or passes them along. Some are directives to the agents I ran into. Some is background read-ing to fill them in on what they needed to know to carry out their mission—and they did have a mission. They were supposed to stop any interference with the plans outlined here. Some are copies or unsent field reports Newark and Paalo had written up.

"All in all, it's pretty clear. Whatever this company or firm is, they want our area. There's plans to make prison building the only going concern which requires the government to buy up more and more of the real estate here or take it by eminent domain. There're discussions of water transferrable from the Great Lakes to the Southwest. There's a white paper on containment systems— I assume nuclear waste. It looks like a blanket deal to me, covering widespread removal of the population under a number of guises and the institution of a variety of high stakes scams and programs to make somebody rich while clearing the landscape of anyone who might object. You do understand why I might want you to look at them while we're here rather than leaving them behind?"

"Pete, is this on the up and up? Is anything that Shea's saying true?"

"Tony, as far as I know it's all on the up and up. I was with Roy at the house when we found the briefcase, and although I've some real questions about how that went down, I'm not mistrusting Roy on this. I've read through them, too. In fact, I saw them at the same time as Roy did for the first time. We were chased by these men. I do think there was an attempt on Roy's life, and inadvertently on mine, on the Traprock during the race. I know how shook up he was after the ladder incident he spoke to you about. And I know how reluctant he's been to being a hero. These guys, and these papers, are, I believe, completely real. Something's going down, and that letter Roy wrote all those months ago seems to have attracted the wrong kind of attention."

"So, even if it is all true, gentlemen, why bring it to me?"

Roy looked Tony in the face and said, "I don't think half of these things can get started in the light of day if people know what's up, Tony. That's where you and the *Gazette* come in. I know we're locals going up against what looks to me like an international group, but this is our home. If people care we can stop them from getting beyond the planning stage. That's where you come in, as you know. Let people know, let them get angry, direct that anger and let them do the rest."

"You're counting on me to rouse the rabble?"

"I'm counting on you to tell the truth and to make a difference. Pete tells me that's the kind of man you are, and I'm thinking he's right.

"Look, I'm not a hero, but I don't like being jerked around, and everybody up here tends to feel the same way. Yet we keep getting the short end of the stick. Someone else makes the money from the metals, the lumber, the resources. We get the leavings and then end up abandoned until the next robber baron comes along. At least the old thieves used to live here themselves, at least for a time. They occasionally stopped ripping long enough to build. Look at Peter White, but these guys have no intention of setting foot here, and they don't really care about the area at all. They just want to use us from a distance and scrape us off their shoes when they're done.

"You can help prevent that. Look, I'd be lying if I said I wasn't scared or I didn't think I'm in danger, and maybe putting you and Pete and our families in danger, too, but I think—I'm beginning to think—I have to. Read these, and see if you agree."

Cathers looked at Roy, nodded, and started shuffling through the stacks while he read. From time to time he'd ask a question or point something out. More than once he shook his head and muttered imprecations under his breath.

"Damn it, you're right, Shea. How can people be like this? It's obvious they see something they want, therefore they feel entitled. Are people already living there? Move 'em off. Someone wants to keep their resources? Rip 'em out from underneath. Someone raising legal questions? Take away their rights. Damn, I feel like an Indian."

"The Yooper tribe. That might be a good way to think about this situation. We're the natives—even if you just moved here when you were twenty-eight. They're the pale skin interlopers."

"I don't know, Roy, both of those guys looked pretty tan to me."

"Those two are just buffalo soldiers, Pete. I'll bet the big boss is a pale skin."

"Hell, reading this, Roy, I'll bet they don't come out of their coffin until the day's up," said Tony. "All joking aside, this really pisses me off."

"How best to use it though, Tony?" asked Roy. "Pull a Pentagon Papers and just release the info and damn the consequences? Try to acquire it legally through the Freedom of Information Act when you actually already know that the papers exist? Maybe go after some of the people and organizations named?"

"Look, Roy. I need these. I know you said you didn't want to leave them behind, but I do have a copy machine in the home office. May I make copies? You can even stand there while I do to keep track if you want."

"I'll stand there, but not to check. We'll keep you company, and as long as you're making copies, how about making three more sets? One for you, one for Pete, and a back up for me so I can squirrel away the originals?"

"Definitely a plan. Come with me, gentlemen. It's upstairs. I like having a view when I can't write."

"You have a phone I can use, Tony?" asked Roy as they walked up the stairs. "It's time I should be calling Jeri. She probably thinks I've run off the deep end and disappeared."

"And she'd only be half-right," said Pete.

"And probably disappointed with what half," Tony added.

"Thanks for the vote of confidence, guys. Your concern fills me with confidence."

"I don't think there's ever been a wife who didn't wonder if life would be better if her husband disappeared. I know mine did. Then she left."

"I've always told Tony that shows brains and good taste, Roy."

"Hey, Pete, I'm taking it in stride! I don't use the voodoo doll everyday, and I don't break out into tears of rage more than once or twice a day. Anyhow, the phone's in here."

The room they walked into was spacious and warm. A large bay window overlooked the Houghton Canal and the lift bridge. Before the window was a large oak desk with an oak barrister's cabinet full of books alongside, partially closing in the workspace. Mementos and awards of various papers along with framed stories hung on the wall. Trophies and bric-a-brac filled any horizontal surface not covered with books and notebooks. A photo of a pretty woman dressed in a style more than ten years gone sat on the corner of the desk, and it looked like a mustache had been painted on the glass over her lip and then imperfectly wiped off at some point.

"The telephone's on the wall over there, Roy. You need privacy?"

"We've been married almost fifteen years, Tony. No privacy necessary."

"I don't know. I don't necessarily want witnesses when the shouting starts," Pete added.

"'Let's not talk shop' like John Prine sings, Pete."

"That's the ticket."

"Well, I'm calling early enough it should still be safe."

He dialed the number, and as he carried on a muted conversation Pete and Tony began running the packets through the copy machine.

After awhile Roy said, "I promise I'll fill you in on everything, Jer, when I get there, but in the meantime stay at your folks, take care of the kids and yourself, and if any strangers show up, please ask your folks not to let them in. Love you; kiss the kids. I'll see you soon."

"That's sweet, Shea," said Pete.

"Yeah, if I talked like that—or ever called for that matter—I might still be married, too," Tony said.

"Hey, soldiers on the line still have to think about the family back home, guys. How's it going?"

"Great copies Tony gets with this set-up. I think we ought to try money next."

"Sorry, Pete, but it only does black-and-white. Any counterfeit here would just fool the colorblind."

"Still sounds like a workable idea, Tony. Say, didn't you run a story on that a while back?"

"I can see you're a loyal reader, too. You in that 'only fit to wrap fish guts and use for kindling' crew concerning my flagship newspaper like Pete is?"

"Hey, I even sent in a letter. And I guess that's what got the target painted on me. Thanks loads for printing that, Tony."

"Look, if you hadn't written the letter and attracted their attention, we wouldn't know what we know now, would we? They'd still be operating under the surface and we'd still be chub for the sharks. All in all, I think you've done well, Roy. It's better for the knowing, and with being warned about just what kind of people we're dealing with, we might just win in the end."

"Good guys take it in and win in the final reel, hey?"

"I just hope the good guys don't take it up the end, Roy."

Thirty-Seven

LESS THEN FIVE MILES AWAY in their car in a motel parking lot, Paalo and Newark were locked in an argument. "I know we had to get out of there, but I didn't think you were serious about just giving up on the job, Newark."

"It's not so much a matter of giving up as wising up. We've got ourselves on the wrong side of this one. I can feel it. There's no way this is coming out well for us."

"'Wrong side,' did you really say that? Since when do we do more than take the pay and do the job? Since when do we start making value judgments about what we're doing? You've been my partner a long time, but, man, I just don't know who you are anymore. What's with this growing a conscience instead of a pair?"

"When the dead rise up against you, you have to be pretty dense not to know you're on the wrong side. I'm out of here. If it means I never work for these people again, well that's just fine with me. I can be a pretty determined bastard—you know that about me—but I'm not stupid. Ma Newark didn't raise a dummy. She might not like what I do for a living, but she knows I've got my smarts. This can only end badly for us, Paalo. I'm out of it, and if you have any sense, you'll be out of it, too. We've worked a long time together. I'd hate to see you go down."

"I don't know where this is coming from, Newark. You lost something out at that farm. Just what happened to you anyway?"

"Besides disappearing barns, skinny ass old white lady ghosts, and the glitter twins out on that ice? You were there, too,

Paalo. Are you going to stand there and tell me none of that happened?"

"I didn't see any ghosts."

"Hell you didn't! You saw the fucking ghost of a barn, for Christ's sake! Take your head out of your ass and face the music. There's powers here, man, and they're not on our side. You need to get bit on the ass by the boogey man again? You were out there on the ice."

"I don't know what happened out there. Fluke freeze or something making the ice thicker. Maybe we were wrong about there being an opening in the first place. It was just bad luck that little shit got away. It was a mistake on our part. It happens. Look at the canoe race: we should have had him there, too. Mistakes happen. They're not out of the ordinary."

"Where are the boots you were wearing, Paalo? You tell me that. If we didn't have spare boots in the rental car's trunk we would have been chasing those two stocking footed through the snow like we walked back to Pershing's."

Paalo stared at him a minute, then shook his head and muttered, "I don't know. That one I'll give you. I mean, I know the parts were left behind on the ice, but I can't tell you how that one happened."

"But you know why that one happened, don't you. We were . . . interfered with, or maybe we should say what we were doing was interrupted, and interrupted by someone with a lot more power than we had. We just had guns. Whoever they were had a damn sight more."

"'They,' I'm not so sure about the 'they,' Newark."

"Don't you try to pull that one. You saw them, too. Hell, you even trained a gun on them for all the good it did. You saw them again on the porch of that farm, too, just like I did. You know they were there, Paalo, so don't even try."

"Look, I know what we think we saw, but I also know it's impossible. I've a simple rule, Newark. If it's impossible, it ain't going to happen."

"I've got a simple rule, too, Paalo. If I see it, it's real. Impossible, my ass, we both know what happened."

"Well, I'm not going to argue about it with you—"

"What do you call what we're doing now?"

"—but I know I was hired to do a job. I'm still getting paid, I do the job. You were hired, too. You've always come through before. Why should this one be any different?"

"Because it is! I can feel it in my bones, Paalo. This is wrong and I want out. I'm done."

"I guess this is goodbye then, Newark. Who has to hire a new rental, you or me?"

"Doesn't matter one way or the other, but I'm gone."

"You take this one, then. Shea already knows what we've been driving. Maybe a change will actually help. Drop me off at Pershing's. Looks like I need a new partner."

"That hick asshole?"

"What other choice do I have at hand? It's not as if I can look in the Yellow Pages. Drop me there, and just leave. If you're not going to do the job, don't get in the way. And, Newark? I don't think we'll be working together again."

"Paalo, you stay here with what you're up against, I don't think there will ever be an opportunity to work together again."

Paalo gave him a long look, but Newark just drove the car out of town and along the upper road to Calumet and Pershing's office.

"I'll miss you, too, partner," Paalo said.

When they arrived at the station, Paalo got out, took his suitcase out of the trunk, and walked over to the driver's side door.

Newark rolled down the window. "Good luck, Paalo," he said.

"Good luck yourself, Newark."

Then Newark rolled the window back up and drove away.

Forty miles later he pulled off to the side of the road. *Am I doing the right thing?* he thought. *Maybe it is just that farm.*

He looked up into the rearview mirror. There were two men, close enough alike to be brothers, sitting in the seat behind him, smiling. One raised an index finger and wagged it at him in a *no, no, no* gesture.

Newark put the car back into gear and pulled out. When he looked again in the rearview mirror he saw he was alone again.

"Guess I've been told," he said out loud. He didn't stop until he needed gas over an hour and a half later, and by that time he was already in Wisconsin and well out of the U.P.

Thirty-Eight

E ARLIER, PAALO HAD INFORMED Pershing of his new call to duty. He hinted at the future help of powerful friends and perhaps a grateful, and generous, reward for his service. Pershing was only too happy to sign on.

"To be perfectly honest, I always thought that Roy Shea was a bit of a spoiled jerk, but I never figured he was smart enough or had enough balls to be dangerous to anyone," he said. "There must be someone with more hair putting him up to it."

"I've found that you never know what folks will care about," said Paalo. "You got a guy toes the line, works hard, supports his family, a model citizen—one day he'll up and shoot his neighbor over a badly trimmed hedge. There's no accounting for people, and you really see that in this line."

"And what exactly is 'this line' of work?"

"Some questions you really don't need answers to, Pershing. Just help me out, do a little running, maybe carry out an order or two without any questions, and I'll see this is all worth your while. You don't want to know too much about it though. The guys I'm working for, that you're working for now, they don't send W2s or leave records."

"Sounds like there was some kind of record in that briefcase you say you lost."

"You just help me find it and deal with Shea. That's all you need to know."

"As to that, the second guy you described must be Pete Terzil. He's about the only guy I know who's crazy enough to get wrapped up into something like this with Shea."

"Wasn't he Shea's partner in the canoe race, too?"

"Yeah, I'm sure he would have been."

"Then maybe," Paalo speculated, "they've figured something out about that day, too."

"Didn't they have some kind of accident of the river? I heard in the bar Pete's still pissed over losing his canoe."

"He'll lose more than that if he doesn't settle back down like a good boy. In fact, let's take a swing past his place. You know where it's at, right?"

"In this area I know where everything's at, Paalo. You want to take the official car or are we going more quietly?"

"Your car would be just fine. Maybe it's time the boys find out who's on the side of law and order here."

Pershing smiled, "Well then, that's just what we'll do. Those scoff laws are just going to have to realize you don't buck authority."

"Ought to be a good lesson in there somewhere," Paalo agreed. "Let's go."

On the way out the door Pershing double checked that he had his sidearm. It wouldn't do to be unprepared with this guy to impress. He patted his shoulder holster again and followed Paalo out to the car.

On the way to Pete's, Pershing acted as a native guide and filled Paalo in on the background of the men they were checking on. Paalo didn't bother to tell him he already knew all the details on Shea and could get everything there was to get on Pete with a quick call, but he was getting a local take. Pershing didn't have anything good to say about Shea or Pete, or anyone else in town or elsewhere for that matter. It didn't take long for Paalo to figure out that Pershing was a small town bully, not terribly bright, and very bitter.

While discussing Shea and Pete's wives in a snarky way, Pershing revealed he had been married twice, with both marriages ending in divorce.

How'd you ever find two women to marry you, Pershing,
Paalo thought. *You sound like a little prick. Of course, I'm enlist-*
ing you to be a worker bee and not a best friend.

". . . most folks keep their heads down where they belong,
though. Just a few jokers muddying the waters every now and
again." Pershing didn't really notice that his new "partner" wasn't
really tracking his monologue. "I keep a pretty tight rein on this
community. People respect me, with cause, I might add. I wish
it could be like the old days. If someone didn't know his place,
you were allowed to set him straight."

Right, respect you. I'll bet there's not a man, woman, or
child in this town who respects you, Lard Ass. Fear you, maybe,
and afraid of your night stick, but respect? I doubt it.

"This is the street right here. See that big house on the rise?
That's Pete's. You want to stop or just pull past? There's an alley
running behind the house, too. They keep it plowed all season to
help with garbage pick-up and what not. He's got himself some
pretty big windows. You can pretty much see what's going on at
night. Daylight, like this, of course, you're not bound to see much."

And I'll bet you're looking in every open window you can
when and if you get off your ass to drive circuit at night, Paalo
thought. *What you looking for? Women and girls in a state of*
undress? Couples doing it on the couch?

"If he were home his Scout would be parked right over
there next to the car. His wife drives the one they keep in the
garage. She's probably at work now. I'd say Pete's out."

"How about swinging past Shea's?"

"Will do. Just a hop, skip, and jump from here."

As they drove by, Pershing said, "His truck's sitting there
next to the garage. No tracks out of the garage, either. Then
again, I don't see any lights on except for the porch light, and
that might have been left on all night, or maybe they left real
early. They sure didn't take his truck though."

Paalo didn't bother telling him that they'd picked up
Shea the night before. Nor did he mention they'd seen him tear

off across a frozen lake and into the woods with Pershing's snowmobile.

"I guess I'm not surprised to find him gone. Wouldn't surprise me if his wife and kids were out, too," said Pershing. "His wife, Jeri, has her folks in Hancock. Sometimes if the weather turns or there's something going on she might hole up there. Don't blame her for not wanting to come home to him."

Bet you wish someone'd come home to you, though, you letch. "Slow down and take another turn past, Pershing," said Paalo. "Stop for a moment right outside the house."

When the car stopped Paalo jumped out and ran to the mailbox. A quick check revealed the morning mail still sitting there. It looked obvious that Shea either hadn't returned to his home or had gone right back out. His wife and kids were already out of the house last night, and he probably warned her to stay away after he escaped from them last night.

Damnedest thing I ever saw, the thought rose unbidden. *First there's the hole and the water. Next thing he's tearing across like solid ground. I know those snowmobile racers do daredevil runs across open water, but that old machine of Pershing's never would have made it.*

And it did look like there were two men standing there, and, yes, they were the same two at the river and the house. Newark wasn't crazy.

"Maybe it's me," Paalo said out loud.

"Maybe it's you what?" asked Pershing.

Paalo shook off the distraction. "It's nothing, just thinking out loud, Pershing. So if neither of our boys is at home, then where are they?"

"Can't help you on that one, Paalo. If it were a normal day Shea would be at work by now, but it's a snow day. Another perk those guys get for doing the easy job. Me? Weather don't make no never mind. I have to patrol no matter what."

"Just makes you tough, Pershing. Let's go over to the Ramada in Hancock. I'm going to check in. By the by, we're leaving the farm. Well, I am. Newark's already gone. I have to go back to make one more sweep, but I'm not spending another night out there."

"Did you guys have a problem with the place?" Pershing asked. "Seems a lot of my renters check out early."

"Something tells me you ought to be arrested for putting that damn thing up for rent, Pershing. You ever stay there yourself?"

"Why would I want to? No need, I've got a good place. Anyhow, what was wrong with the farm?"

Paalo gave him a long look. "It's noisy," he finally said. "It's just too damn noisy and busy out there."

"I don't know about you city boys. Countryside has different noises from your sirens and ambulances. I think you just can't take the silence."

"Silence my ass, Pershing. At any rate, I'm done out there. Let's go."

Thirty-Nine

"T"HE KIDS ARE OUT TO McDONALDS with Mom and Dad, Roy,"
Jeri said as she opened the door to her parents' house.
"Oh good," he answered. "I want to explain everything to
you without being interrupted."

"What's going on? I've been so worried."

"Well, I don't know if you're going to believe me, but . . ."
Roy said as he launched into his story for the third time. When
he finished, he waited for Jeri to say something.

"I don't know how much of this to tell to my folks," she finally said. "How do I tell them? I barely know what's going on
myself, and I can barely believe what I think I know."

"Yeah, I know, Jeri. It's all up in the air right now, but I really have to do this."

"That's the part that bothers me, Roy. I know you have to.
In fact, I want you to, but that doesn't mean I'm not afraid there'll
be consequences. This isn't just one of your usual rants against
authority figures. This isn't just some administrator here. These
are the guys the conspiracy nuts warn us about, but it's no wild
conspiracy theory, it's a real plan by people with no scruples.
That's what worries me. I am proud, though. You said in the letter maybe it's time someone does what needs to be done, and
here you are doing it."

Roy looked at her. "Proud? Woof!"

"Don't blow it, Roy. I said it, and I meant it. I am proud
of you. I love you, too, for that matter."

"And I love you, too, but thanks, Jeri. I know you're worried. I am, too. This doesn't even feel like my life right now. I've never really been the 'take action sort of guy,' more like a 'if a job needs doing I hope someone gets to it real soon' sort, but right now I'm convinced this is something I have to see through to the end. I'm worried about you guys, though. If anything happened to any of you because of something I've done . . ."

"We'll be safe enough here, Roy. I've got the time to take so that's no problem. I can't help feeling, though, that there's someone we should be contacting, someone who should be let in on what's been happening."

"I've been thinking about that, too, Jeri. The local cops are out. I'm sure they got the truck and snowmobile from Pershing. That little weasel's probably in on it all. The state cop post in L'anse is probably no better, and it's fifty miles away. Besides that, what could I say? No one else saw what happened at the quarry. It's their word against mine on everything else, and I did break and enter."

"Stole, too, you have their briefcase. It doesn't sound designed to instill faith, does it? The local guys would probably arrest you."

"I think the fact that they haven't arrested me means they want to keep things quiet. It wasn't arrest they had in mind out on the ice."

Roy paused a moment before continuing. "Cathers had a suggestion, though, Jer. Remember my classmate, David Reynolds, who went into the FBI? Turns out he's stationed in Marquette. I haven't seen him in years, but Tony knows him from working that extortion story a couple of years back. Says he's good people, and when he was checking into his background for the article, he was told that he was efficient, effective, and squeaky clean. Sounds like the guy I used to know in school. Anyway, Tony suggested I get in touch with him."

"Now that might be a great idea, Roy. I knew Dave, too. He used to date the sister of one of my friends. I always thought he was a straight arrow sort. Maybe he can give you some leads on this or make some suggestions."

"At the very least I might be able to get what happened on record, and maybe if I can show Dave what's in the briefcase, he might want to check into it, dig a little deeper. He hasn't lived in the Keweenaw for a long time, but his sister's still here with her husband and kids. I figure he'd be interested."

"And since he knows you—at least knew you—he just might not have you locked up on suspicion of insanity."

"God, woman, you can fill a guy with confidence."

"That's not what you're full of, but this time at least you might be on to something real."

"There's that confidence thing again. I do figure Cathers is on to something, though. I think I ought to call Dave."

"Do you know how to get ahold of him?"

"I don't, but Cathers said he has the contact info at his office, and I'll be meeting back up with him later. Maybe I shouldn't call from our house. Do you think that's too paranoid or does it seem likely we might be tapped?"

"Maybe you shouldn't even be going back to the house. I'll call Sarah down the street to let the dog out and feed him. Bogart knows her, and he's probably overdue."

"Good idea. I had let him out just before I was picked up last night, but I'll bet the floor looks like he's been locked in since then."

"A small price to pay for keeping safe, Roy, and the floor can be cleaned."

"Yeah, I know, but I'm glad you're thinking ahead. I'm glad you're on my side, too."

"'For better or worse,' right? The other side was bound to come around sooner or later."

"I won't ask you to clarify, Jeri, I'm just glad you're here, but now I have to go. Pete's probably on the way to pick me back up right now. Hug the kids for me when they get back. I'll talk to you as soon as I know what the next step's going to be."

Roy hugged Jeri and the two kissed.

"Can you count this as a down payment for later, Jer?"

"Kissing in the house when my folks are gone—reminds me of the old days. Yeah, I guess more will follow later. Just make sure you're here for it."

"I will be, hon, but . . . I do have to go."

"Go get 'em, Roy. Boy, there are some things you never expect to hear yourself say!"

"There's that confidence builder again," said Roy, and buttoning his jacket, he headed out followed by Jeri's laughter to meet Pete.

Forty

WHEN PETE AND ROY reached Cathers's office, they found him hunched over the copy stacks from the briefcase and a collection of other memos and notes.

"Greetings, gentlemen. I've been busy over here and I've got the rest of the office hopping, too. The interns are earning their stipends today."

"Find anything out, Tony?"

"Even more than I would have hoped, Roy. This company, this crew you've got on the wrong side of? They've been around for a long time, have a lot of influence, and also have their thumbs in all sorts of pies. You ever hear of Bhopal?"

"The gas deaths in India?"

"They're a stockholder in Union Carbide India, the company responsible. And here at home, does the name Camden Hollow ring a bell?"

"I remember hearing the name, but I can't put a story to it."

"It's a grim little thing that never got the attention I thought it should. It was a mining town in Minnesota. The mines had been pretty played out, but a new company—our friends—brought in a new process. The idea was to pump the ore field with solvents that leached the remaining metal out so it could be pumped in a liquid form to the surface. Opened with a lot of hoopla about saving the community economically, won a slew of awards from various business groups, and went into production."

"What happened?"

"After two years they found the solution had gotten into the aquifer for the entire community. Cases with symptoms very much like cystic fibrosis began appearing, and the rate of cancer cases skyrocketed in no time."

"I do remember hearing something about it," Pete said.

"Well, it turned out the solution in the ground water was implicated," Cathers said. "The company said they had no liability whatsoever, and their friends in Washington agreed. Remember, this was under Ronnie. EPA? Forget about any muscle."

"Wasn't there a physical tragedy there, too?"

"Yep, that's the place. The solution not only leached out metal, it destabilized the sandstone bedrock as well. There was a sinkhole, remember? It took out part of a neighborhood strip mall. Twelve people were killed, at least thirty more injured, and no one was ever held responsible.

"The company claimed that geologic surveys had shown fundamental problems long before they started operations and blamed the effect of the old mining shafts that riddled the area. It didn't stop there, either. The whole area was destabilized, and although there was almost no public awareness, the town basically had to close up shop. Forced evacuation of some neighborhoods, a strong recommendation to the rest to move along, and Camden Hollow is essentially a ghost town today.

"The company pulled up stakes, took their short term profits, wrote off the rest, and scraped the community off its shoes. Those are the guys you're playing with, Shea."

Shea looked at Cathers and Pete. No one said anything for a moment.

"I take it there's more, Tony?"

"Lots, Roy. Not all of it's this grim. These guys are successful. It's just that they've been so successful they've gotten to the point where they can do whatever they want, or at least they think they should be able to do whatever they want. They own the strings attached to the way things work."

"And now they're looking at us up here."

"Looks like a combination of things. They're quietly buying up land—both private holdings and commercial. They're investing in a number of area businesses and even more so in a whole bunch of local and state politicians. Looks like contacts with local law enforcement, too. If I had to guess, I'd say they already have a loyal crew of supporters among the powers that want to be up here. On another note, I did some checking on your story, too, Roy. You know, your family's farm has some history."

"There were always a lot of family stories, Tony, but you mean you were actually able to find something?"

"Interns in the archives, Roy, is always a good combination. I shipped Beth down as soon as I got here today, and I sent Justin over to MTU's archives as well. Both of them found haunting stories going back at least seventy years. The local papers, including ours, used to carry that type of thing regularly. Ghost stories—preferably with a good sensational murder thrown in—were circulation staples back then."

"Like gossip and innuendo today, Tony" asked Pete.

"Hey, I thought we were all on the same side here. I guess yes, though. Sometimes I think I was born too late. I would have liked working for a paper back then."

"You're doing a fine job, all joking aside, Tony," Pete said almost sheepishly. "I've said more than once the Copper Country doesn't deserve you. You turned this paper into something real."

"Thanks, Pete, that's the goal, but to get back to the farm. Here's what they found, Roy. Did you know there had been suicides and a murder-suicide on the property?"

"That's the ghost fight in the apple orchard and the hanging in the barn, right, Tony?"

"You do know about it, then."

"Yeah, us kids used to pick up on that so finally my grandfather had to come clean and tell us the tale. That was the first owner right? The guy who actually built the farm? They lost their girls in Italian Hall and his wife drowned herself, right?"

"Appears to be that way, Roy. Shot his sons and then hung himself. Is that the way you heard it?"

"That's what Isa said."

"Well, those were the first deaths there, but not the last."

"Not counting my grandmother, Mummo, I know of at least two more."

"Mummo and Isa?"

"That's what we always called my mom's mom and dad. Finnish, you know."

"They both died there?"

"Yeah, my grandmother did. They died within a few years of each other. Mummo went first. Isa left the farm and stayed with us a couple of years until he died himself. There's no ghost story about either of them, though. There is one, however, about a witchy woman who lived there between the original owners and my grandparents. She was supposed to help heal and read signs and things. Apparently my grandmother was related in some way. She and her mother were supposed to have been visiting when Mummo was just a little girl. After dark but before they started for home, a bird tapped on the window three times, and the old woman—I don't remember her name if I ever knew it; I was pretty young when Mummo told me the story—just matter-of-factly said she would die in three days like the bird foretold. She did, too, according to Mummo. Her ghost is supposed to be the one walking around the house on a regular basis.

"One of my mom's siblings died there, young, too. She apparently got a fever that couldn't be cured. Mummo used to talk to her all of her life. I mean Mummo's life. She was seeing and talking to the ghost of her dead daughter. I used to see her, too, you know."

"So you're used to these stories?"

"Why do you think no one in the family wanted to hang onto it and why I don't like being there?"

"This just keeps getting stranger, Roy."

"I know, Pete. It seems about a million miles away from the company."

"Well, Roy, how about this? I think Justin found something on your two companions on the ice."

"That's not the only place I've seen them."

"Well, they're a lot older than your family ghosts. Kookas and Piiku, old Finnish spirit types. They sound like Tricksters in the literature."

"Kookas and Piiku?"

"Big and Small in Finnish."

"'Big and Small'? They both look the same."

"I think that's part of the point. Is there such a thing as Finnish Zen?"

"I'm sure there must be, Tony. What little experience I've had with these two—yes, I'm serious, Pete—has been strictly down the rabbit hole stuff. I remember seeing them the first time when I was just a kid. My grandfather was out at the edge of the woods one evening when I went out to find him, and he was talking to these two characters. I remember that although it was getting dark, they both seemed to, well, glow. The colors were swirling around them. I think Isa made a little bow, and when they bowed back, they just seemed to fade.

"When I asked Isa who they were and where they went, he just laughed and said they were old family friends. He may have told me their names, but I was terrible with Finnish, and by that time I mostly just tuned it out. I regret that now. I've dreamed about them a time or three since. In these dreams we're having sweet, milky coffee around a kitchen table. There are leaves and snow and stuff that blow out of their jackets from time to time. They always seemed to find that hilarious, but I didn't really see them again until that night on the ice, and I'm still not sure quite what I saw."

Roy paused a moment, musing on his words. "You know, doesn't it bother anybody that we're discussing these sorts of things like we're rationally dealing with reality?" he asked.

"I think it might just be as rational as the 'real' people we're going up against, Roy", said Tony.

"Yeah," added Pete, "'more things in heaven and hell,' right, Roy? Besides being part Finn, you're Irish, too. I expect you're used to this on both sides."

"Familiar with, yes. Used to, no, Pete."

"I think it's harder to imagine real live people behaving the way we're learning they do. Speaking of which," said Tony, "we turned up something on your other two friends—what were their names? Paalo and Newark?—turns out there was a reporter, a good man by all accounts, Jim Pattersen, checking out some of these sorts of allegations after an interesting land swap took place between the company and the state of Arizona. He had followed a track all the way back twelve years through a whole string of similar deals and such. Did some small town paper articles out West when he attracted the interest of the national magazines, *Rolling Stone*, I think. Then he had an accident rock climbing outside of Tucson. In his notes they found a reference to being visited by these two men. You're not their first, Roy."

"And he was a little less lucky than you, too, Roy," said Pete. "I wonder if there were any native spirits thinking about stepping in."

"Something tells me that the native spirits there wouldn't be too thrilled about stepping in for any white man—assuming the reporter was white, right?"

"Yes, he was."

"Well, then, unless they thought he was actively defending the land or their people, they probably wouldn't step in. Here you've a case where Roy's not only defending their adopted land, but he's a part of their clan as well. Didn't you say your grandfather called them 'old family friends'? They have good reason to be on your side, Roy. Poor Pattersen didn't have that going for him."

"So you think they killed him, Tony?"

"Given what they tried to do with Shea? There's no question in my mind. What about you, Roy?"

"No question they planned for me to hit the water, and I don't think there's any question they would have shot both Pete and me if they had a chance at the farm. If it wasn't for the barn showing up . . ."

"You do know how crazy that sounds, right? Even if I actually had seen the barn on my own I don't know if I could believe in a ghost building, Roy, and I was there with you."

"'Ghost building' indeed. You know how much I'd love to see something like that? I've been to the Paulding Light. For stories I stayed nights in the Calumet Theatre and the Douglas House hotel. I've gone through the Marquette Asylum and the Luigi House in Negaunee. Nothing! I've never seen a thing anywhere! I've never felt anything odd, heard anything paranormal, or seen a hint of an apparition. I am so jealous of your experiences I think I'd risk a shooting," said Tony.

"Roy and I have talked about this before, Tony. I don't know why some people do and some people don't. Roy's got a theory, though."

"It's all in the way you're raised, Tony. Like I've told Pete, I've been running into ghosts and haunted houses since I can remember, and my folks never tried to tell me I was imagining things or anything like that. It was never too unusual to have relatives drop by even after they died. On the Irish side it's just as bad—or good, depending on how you want to look at it. Grandma Shea was never surprised by anything. Her dad used to come back and tell her what was coming. Probably helped to keep her alive for a while with the heart condition she had. No sudden shocks, you know."

"No sudden shocks! What about talking to your dead dad?"

"It's not a shock if you expect it, Tony. She did. Hell, I do, too. It's all in what you believe."

Roy went on, "When I was a kid one of my Shea cousins visiting from downstate said he didn't believe in ghosts, and my Uncle Martin overheard him. 'Come on, guys,' he said, and loaded us all into his Pontiac. He drove us out to the Baraga Plains road as the sun was setting. We were going nuts in anticipation figuring Marty was going to show us something cool. Ten miles out of town he parked the car and turned out the headlights. 'Look at that,' he told us. We looked. There was nothing but a house next to an orchard across the field. We could clearly see people moving around through the lit windows and hear a dog barking from the porch. That was it. Pretty soon we got antsy, and I was thinking the folks inside were going to notice us peeping toms, but Martin just told us to take a good last look, and then he drove back to town. Now, I always did think he was odd, but this was odder than usual. He didn't say no more about it.

"Next morning we all woke up in a tangle out on grandma's porch, where we always camped out when the cousins were up. Uncle Marty walks in after breakfast and said, 'Load up,' and drove us all back out to the Baraga Plains again.

"When he pulled off to the side we could tell we were in the same place. We could even see the tire tracks and the cig butt Martin had tossed out the night before. If you were standing there you would have also seen four boys with their faces pressed against the glass looking across the field.

"There was no house across the field. We could see the orchard, but the house simply wasn't there.

"Martin opened the car door, and then we all piled out, hopped the ditch, ducked under the fence and crossed the field. When we got closer, we could see a foundation that showed signs of charring with some rubble collapsed in the basement.

"'There was a fire,' Uncle Marty said. 'Everyone, even the dog, died. Most nights they seem to come back.' Let me tell you, I felt a chill. It was a quiet car ride back. My cousin never said he didn't believe again."

"See. That's what I mean," Tony said. "I'd give my eyeteeth for an experience like that."

"One among many. I'll have to tell you about the Eagle River Inn someday. In the meantime, though, what comes next?"

"I'd say a call to Reynolds is in order. I've the number in my Rolodex whenever you're ready."

"I'll take it now, Tony. Can I call from here or do you want me to take it out of your building?"

"The way I see it, Roy, you're working on a story with me. Why don't you make the call from Murphy's office next door though so you have some privacy? Maybe later we can do a conference call or I can speak to him independently, but you should be making this one."

Roy took the slip of paper on which Cathers had jotted down the telephone number. "Thanks, Tony. I appreciate everything you're doing here. I'll be right back. The office door's not locked, is it?"

"Should be open."

Roy walked out the door.

"What do you think about all this, Pete?" asked Tony after Roy had left the room. "Is this all really going down or is Shea simply paranoid? From a reporter's point of view, this is a dream story, but only if all the pieces are really there and it's not just someone's overdone imagination."

"I'm taking him at his word, Tony. Remember, I was in the canoe with him as well as being out at the farm. I can't swear to everything Roy says he saw—it is Roy, after all—but something is definitely going down and he's got all three of us involved now."

"I was hoping you'd say that, Pete. I don't know Shea well, but I like him, and I'm glad he stirred up the hornet's nest before it was too late to do anything about it. I'm looking forward to seeing what comes next."

Forty-One

S O WHAT'S NEXT, MR. PAALO?" asked Pershing as they climbed back into the car.

Paalo had checked into his room in the Ramada, and after dropping off his bags they were getting ready to head back to Phoenix.

"I've a couple of calls I have to make, but I didn't want to make them from the hotel. I also want to run one more sweep of the farmhouse to make sure Newark's briefcase really is gone. I might as well make the calls from there as long as I'm at it. It's either that or from your office. With Newark dropping out I want to get you approved," Paalo noticed the quick smile as Pershing heard the promising words. "But I'm sure that's just a formality. You might want to consider it a battlefield promotion."

"Battlefield? We going to be doing some fighting? Not that I mind."

"Good soldiers don't ask questions, they just follow orders. Let's head out."

As they pulled out of the Ramada parking lot next to the lift bridge, Pershing was running through the angles in his head. He'd hitched his cart to this horse in a hurry. Paalo sounded professional and competent. To be perfectly honest, he was an intimidating figure, but then again, so had Newark been and now he was gone, out of the picture. *I wonder why he left,* Pershing thought. *He seemed like a no-nonsense sort. Well, this might be my opportunity.*

"How'd you get into this line of work anyway?" he asked Paalo.

He received a stare for his answer.

"Sorry, I didn't think you were going to be such a touchy partner," he said.

Paalo shook his head. "Look, Pershing, my partner left. You're the hired gun—no, I don't necessarily mean that literally—you're the hired help. Do a good job, follow orders and there'll definitely be something in it for you, but questions are unwelcome.

"Look, I've checked your background, Pershing. Army MP, some conduct questions, but nothing to stop you from going into local law enforcement when you got out. Thought about going state police, didn't get there. Padded out your application a little too much at the same time. What I'm giving you is a chance to get ahead with a favor or two, not a career change necessarily, but who knows? When you do a good job, sometimes opportunities continue to come your way. To be perfectly honest, that's how I got into this line of work. Now, can we just drive? I've got to work out the next steps here."

"If you talk to me about it, I might have some suggestions."

Again Pershing received a look. "I thought we covered all that," Paalo said.

The car was quiet on the last three miles into Phoenix, but as they drove through town Paalo noticed that no one acknowledged Pershing when he passed them on the street. No waves, no friendly calls.

Looks like I'm working with Mr. Popular here, he thought. *Then again, maybe it's good he doesn't attract the kind of attention Newark did in the park . . . or at the farm, for that matter.*

Well, once I get things settled, and it better be in a hurry, I'm out of here. Can't say I'll be too sorry to scrape this town off my feet.

"You wanted me to drive you straight to the farm, right, Paalo?"

"Yeah, let me get these calls out of the way, and then I'll sit down and explain what's going on to you," he said in a conciliatory tone. "I do appreciate the help of a competent fellow officer."

"That's fine, Paalo, just glad to be of service," Pershing said. *And I damn well better get paid well for it,* he thought as he turned up the drive to the farm.

He pulled the car up through the snow, parked by the porch, and the two men got out of the car. The tracks from the night before were drifted over.

"Hey, what's with this?" Pershing asked, pointing to the open window on the woodshed. "What are you doing leaving windows open in the winter? That can cause a lot of damage. This is my rental property you're screwing with here."

"We left in somewhat of a hurry, Pershing. Besides, we didn't open it. It must have been how Shea got into the place. Blame him, but keep the security deposit we gave to Ben if it makes you feel better."

"Well," Pershing said, somewhat mollified, "I guess you couldn't plan for every contingency. Maybe I should get a better lock on that window."

Paalo, who had walked over to the window, said, "Maybe you ought to get *a* lock on this window. There's none at all now."

"Shea probably knew that. It used to be in his family. I bought it for back taxes long after his granddad died. None of the kids had seemed to want it. I picked it up for a song. 'Course, like I said before, it has been a pain to keep rented."

"Shea's family owned this place?"

"Yeah, why? What difference does that make? You think he knows secret tunnels and shit?"

Paalo shook his head. "Probably doesn't make any difference, I guess. Just came as a surprise." *And,* he thought, *it could explain why it seems everything here is on his side.*

"Yeah, well, if he was here, I'll bet it's the first time since I bought it. Like I said, no one in his family wanted much to do with the place."

And maybe I know why, Paalo thought. "Well, let's get this over," he said out loud. "You've got the key or do you want me to use mine?"

"I'm here already," Pershing said from the steps. "Thanks for closing the window, by the way."

Then he pulled up short. "Wait a minute, what's going on? The key won't go in."

Paalo joined him on the porch and pulled a small pen light from his jacket pocket. "Let me take a look."

He shined the light on the door lock. It seemed to reflect the light back unusually.

"It's frozen. There's ice in the keyhole."

"That's not a good sign, Paalo. I hope that open window didn't cause problems."

"Wasn't that just leading to an unheated woodshed anyway, Pershing? The Heatrola was in the front room."

"Still makes me nervous. Damn, this thing is frozen solid. Here, I've got a torch in car. Let me go get it."

Pershing fetched the torch and igniter from the trunk of his car and returned to the porch. "When there's freezing rain we have people whose vehicles ice up. I carry this around to thaw out car locks," he explained. "Ought to work fine on this, too." He struck the igniter, lit the torch, and applied it to the metal plate holding the keyhole. "With my luck I'll probably burn it down," he said.

"You probably would be lucky to burn it down the way this place is, Pershing. Scared the shit out of my partner, I tell you."

"I've heard all the stories, but I ain't never seen anything out here, Paalo, and even if I've never stayed here myself like I said, I've been out here for maintenance. I got a guy, a dandy of a realtor who rents it out for me. Occasionally I've placed a person or two out here, and there's even been a tenant or two I come out to collect rent from directly."

"And what were those poor girls' names, might I ask?"

Pershing looked up from the task at hand and actually leered. "Girls, you got that right. I wasn't looking for a signed check from a couple of them either."

"No money needed, but they still got the short end of the stick, huh?"

"I never heard no complaints, Paalo. One of 'em was a real little sweetie, too. I put her up here after picking her up for vagrancy in Phoenix. Her family had been from around here, moved, and ran into hard times. She stuck around for a couple of weeks and then ran off one night. Stole a cooler and a radio from the house, but I figure I got my share in trade. That was back when I was married, too, but things were getting, well, strained I guess. Missus couldn't understand why I wasn't bothering her for any while I was getting it out here."

Probably just counting her blessings, thought Paalo. "You say the girl ran off, though?"

"Yeah, wasn't like we had a lease or anything. It just worked out fine for me. You find out about side jobs in a field like this, Paalo. I hear you big city guys get your perks, but out here a man can work them out, too, if he's got the right sort of attitude."

Keeping an eye of the lock, he said, "Looks like that ice is gone. Let's try the door."

He inserted the key without difficulty, turned the doorknob with his gloved hand, and opened the door to wave Paalo through.

"Always pays to come prepared, Paalo," he said, but neither man was prepared for what greeted them inside.

Down from the ceiling to the floor, the kitchen was festooned with one immense icicle after another. It looked like it would be difficult moving across the kitchen through them all. The room itself felt like a deep freeze and the walls were rime-covered.

"Water pipes must have burst, Pershing."

"You were staying here, Paalo. There's no water upstairs. There's no pipe above the kitchen to burst, damn it!"

"I hate to tell you this, but look at the top of them. It looks like they're pushing into the ceiling rather than hanging down from it."

"Christ, you're right, and it looks like they're coming up from the floor. My God, what's it like upstairs?"

Pershing pushed past the closest of the icicles and made his way into the front room of the house.

"Look! There's nothing in here at all! It's warmer, too. I'm heading upstairs. Are you coming?"

"I'm right behind you, Pershing."

Pershing climbed the stairs with Paalo behind him. As they topped the last landing and turned into the main room, they were met with a wall of ice dividing the upstairs in a straight line through the rooms and running from floor to ceiling. Looking through the wall, both men had the discomforting sense of seeing movement through the haze of the ice. One of the figures leaned into the ice wall from the other side, making binoculars of his hands to peer through to Paalo and Pershing, and then he disappeared.

"What the hell . . ." muttered Pershing.

And then the ice melted. It flowed in a downpour around their ankles and poured in a wave down the staircase. It was almost, but not quite, enough to wash the men from the landing.

"Sweet Jesus," Pershing started as he grabbed the rail and hung on as the flood waters swelled past his ankles.

Despite the sound of the water around them, there was a louder sound of shattering ice and a torrent of water from downstairs as well. As the last of the water flowed past, both men turned to follow it down the stairs.

"What am I going to do? The place will be ruined!"

"Something tells me that's the least of your worries, Pershing," Paalo shot back.

As they reached the bottom of the stairs and turned into the front room, there was no trace of water at all. In the kitchen the temperature had returned to normal, and there was no sign of the icicles, either. Here, too, the floor was bone dry.

"Where'd it all go, Paalo?" asked Pershing after standing and staring for a minute. "We did see the icicles and the ice wall, right?"

"Look at our pant legs, Pershing."

Both men were soaked through almost to the knees.

There was a sudden sound of rushing water from the basement.

"It's in the basement!"

"*What's* in the basement, you mean, Pershing. I think we're hearing special effects for a purpose."

"I've got to check it out, Paalo. There could be a lot of water damage. The foundation of this place is old."

"You really have to have water to cause water damage. I suspect you're not going to find any, but let's check it out. I've got to see now, too."

In the kitchen they approached the basement door. Just before Pershing's hand touched the door, the knob rattled. He pulled his hand back as if he'd been stung.

Paalo pulled his gun. "Who's there?" he called. They stood staring at the door for a moment, but when the rattling didn't resume, Paalo reached for the knob and opened the door. He flicked the light switch and peered down into the basement. "I don't see any water."

"Let's go down, Paalo."

"You go first, Pershing," said Paalo stepping out of the way. "It's your house, and your spooks for that matter, too."

"What's spooks got to do with burst water pipes?"

"'Burst water pipes,' yeah, that's it. Like I said, you first."

With Pershing leading they made their way down into the basement. They took each step slowly and deliberately, keeping their eyes open and looking all around. The basement floor looked dry. The temperature was cool, but only as would be expected in a basement. There was no sign of icicles or any unusual marks on the cellar ceiling.

They reached the basement floor and looked around. There was nothing out of the ordinary at all.

"Looks all right down here. What the hell is going on, Paalo? What did you two stir up out here? I've never had anything like this happen before."

"I don't know what got stirred up or who did the stirring, but Newark left because of it. I didn't do anything, at least not intentionally, and I sure don't know what's going on. I do have a question for you, though. Who rattled that doorknob?"

Pershing turned to look at him. In that instant, three things happened: The lights went out, the door at the top of the stairs slammed shut, and the basement filled with water.

As the rushing water swirled up and washed Paalo and Pershing off their feet, the two men flailed about. Paalo grabbed the railing of the stairs and pulled himself up toward the door. Pershing latched unto Paalo's feet, and in his panic braced against the stairs and almost pulled Paalo from the rail, but by sheer force and determination Paalo pulled himself and the struggling Pershing up. They managed to keep their heads mostly above water, but the level kept rising as if a river had been channeled into the dark basement.

When he reached the door Paalo discovered, as he suspected, that the door was locked. Additionally, the force of the rising water made it unlikely he could pull it open into the basement against the pressure anyway.

"Pershing," he called out, "grab the railing and hold yourself out. The door's locked. We'll never get out this way."

"What else can we do, Paalo? We're running out of room here."

"The lights are off, but weren't there windows down here?"

"Yeah, there're two," he shouted over the sound of rushing water, "and they're latched at the top and open out. We might be able to get out that way, but they're both already underwater."

"What options do we have, Pershing?" he shouted back. "Which way are they?"

"You can see a glimpse of the light coming through. There's one on the far wall and one to the side here."

"I'll try the far wall. Do you think you can reach the closest?"

"If my coat and boots don't drag me down."

"Give it a shot then. Take a breath and go!"

He followed his own advice, gulped air, and dived for the faint light showing beneath the surface.

As he kicked toward the far wall a voice cut through the torrent. *Caught in the water with no way out. It's almost like being pulled along in a river or being trapped beneath ice, isn't it? Does the situation with someone else awash seem familiar? It's somewhat fitting, isn't it?*

It's just in my head, Paalo thought, and then the water pulled him away from the wall and under.

Across the basement Pershing had reached his window, thrown the latch, and tried to push it open, but it wouldn't budge. He frantically tried to pound against the force of the water, but he was getting nowhere.

Suddenly there were faces pressed against the glass from the outside and the shape of little hands holding the window shut against his pushing. The voices of children came into his head. *They held the doors against us. We tried and tried, but we just couldn't get out. We tried until we couldn't breathe anymore. We tried to get out, but you wouldn't let us. So we died.*

Pershing pushed away from the window, his mouth involuntarily opened as he remembered holding doors shut against the screams of the dying. He remembered being there and laughing. He remembered holding the doors while the children fought for breath. He remembered while his last breath was disappearing.

And then the water disappeared, and both men fell hard to the basement floor. Soaking wet and gasping for breath, they lay against the cold cement. It was a moment before they realized the lights were back on. Paalo raised himself on an elbow to look back. Sure enough, the basement door was wide open at the top of the steps.

Paalo put his head back on the floor a moment, and then he pushed himself up and to his feet. "Come on, get up, Pershing."

"Christ, Paalo, let me catch my breath."

"I don't know about you, but I don't want to be down here if the water comes back."

"Jesus," Pershing muttered, getting to his own feet in a hurry. "Let's get out of here."

They just about ran up the stairs, although Paalo did think to turn off the basement light before he closed the door.

"I'm soaking wet! What's going on?"

"I sure don't know, but I'm not sticking around to find out either, Pershing. Maybe—forget maybe—Newark was right. We're on the wrong side of whatever's going on here." He thought about the voice he had heard in his head and added, "There's a real feel of payback here."

"I don't think I'll ever forget those kids, damn it."

"Kids? What kids?"

"Isn't that what you saw? The kids holding the window closed?"

"No, I never actually made it far as the window. The water stopped me from getting that far when I got caught in the current."

"Current? Were we in the same place? The water was rising, but it was calm beneath the surface. It was the kids that kept me from getting out. They were accusing me of holding the door, and I can remember it now. I can see it in my head. I can remember it, but it was so long ago, and I wasn't even alive then . . ."

"What was a long time ago?"

"The Italian Hall tragedy. They told me I was there and that I held the door shut so they couldn't get out. They told me that I killed them—and now I can remember it! That's not possible!"

"Take it easy, Pershing. There's something here playing with our heads. It was reminding me of something I had done, but I shouldn't have."

Taking another deep breath, Paalo continued, "The Italian Hall . . . I remember reading about it when I was studying the area before we came up, but that was—what?—nineteen-hundred?"

"Nineteen-thirteen."

"But then, you couldn't have been . . ."

"Right, I couldn't have been there, but I tell you, I remember it! It's as real to me as yesterday. I was there. I did hold the doors. I did kill those kids! It was me even though I don't know how, even though I know it's impossible."

"Look, Pershing, let's get out of here. This isn't going to help."

"'Get out of here,' right, but how am I going to get it out of my head?"

As they stepped out of the house—neither man worried about locking the door—the first thing Paalo thought was, *It's back. The barn, it's back.* And it was. Paalo felt a chill that had nothing to do with standing in the snow in wet clothes.

"You see them?" shouted Pershing. "You see the kids going in the barn? It's them! They're real."

He was obviously beyond worrying about the reality of the children when he didn't even acknowledge the appearance of a building that hadn't been there half an hour before.

"I've got to talk to them! To understand!"

And without a backward glance he jumped from the porch and ran to the barn, where the last of a group of children was just disappearing around the doorjamb.

"Pershing, wait! Don't go in there," Paalo shouted, but he saw Pershing disappear into the barn, pursuing the children. He could swear he heard them laughing and giggling.

The door slammed shut, and the barn disappeared.

With Pershing.

Paalo stood staring at the absence before him. He took a hesitant couple of steps and then began running, following the tracks Pershing had made across the lawn. The footsteps in the snow turned abruptly where Pershing had gone through the door of the barn, and then they simply disappeared. Paalo looked around in a daze and noticed there were no tracks from the children at all. He also noticed that he himself had stopped short from "entering" the space where the barn had been, and with the realization he took several steps further back.

He heard a voice behind him and spun around.

"Your friend, I don't think he'll be coming back. Payment, although delayed, is required."

It was the two men, the brothers again.

"For your part, you should go," the right-hand brother spoke. "You haven't tried your gun this time . . ."

"That's good," the other concurred.

". . . but there's still nothing for you here."

Again, the other spoke, "You are dedicated, and that can be good."

"But what you have been dedicated to, that has been wrong."

"Your partner realized this."

"Now you should, too."

"You should have gone before."

"But it's not too late."

"As it is for your friend. He turned against his own before, and even on this trip he was willing to do the same."

"He hadn't learned."

"No, he hadn't," his partner shook his head sadly.

"Perhaps next time."

"But you should go."

"Go now."

"Gentlemen," Paalo said, "consider me gone." He walked past the two men directly to the car, but then he turned back to them. "But Pershing had the keys with—" he began.

One of the men waved and said, "Look."

Paalo did. The keys were in the ignition. He started to climb into the car, but then he saw a pad on the car seat.

He stood back up and turned to the two. "Look," he said, "I know you're giving me a chance here, but there's one more thing I have to do before I leave. I need to leave Shea a message. I need to leave him a note. Do you under—" was as far as he got before the two began to nod.

"We understand."

"We approve. We will see it delivered."

"After we add our own note, perhaps," smiled Kookas.

Paalo climbed into the driver's seat, picked up the pad and with a pen from his pocket,scribbled a quick note. He hesitated before signing it, but then did so with a flourish, folded it once and wrote Shea's name on the outside. He passed the note to Pikku, closed the car door and nodded to the two men.

Starting the car, he pulled down the driveway. He took a look in the rearview just as he crested the drive and saw a small knot of people waving from in front of the house. He rolled down the window impetuously and waved back.

He drove through Phoenix into Hancock, stopped at the Ramada long enough to settle his bill and pick up his suitcases—he never made the calls he had planned to make—and then he went back to Pershing's car, got in, and drove off. As to the car, he didn't think Pershing would be needing it anytime soon.

Newark, you were right, he thought. *You have to know where to draw the line. And I need to know where I'm going. Certainly not back to the company—it's been a long time since I've seen home. It might be time to go back to Oregon.*

Decision made, Paalo took the turn off the lift bridge heading uphill and west toward Wisconsin. The Copper Country never saw him again.

Forty-Two

PERSHING RAN ACROSS THE YARD after the children. His feet almost slipped out from under him when he reached the barn, but he recovered his balance and burst through the doorway on the tail of the last of the children.

"You stop right there! Where are you kids from?"

But before he could get an answer, the door slammed behind him and the children, as a group, spun to face him. Instead of laughter and giggling, however, there was a feral silence.

"Now you kids—what are you doing here?"

The children, without a word, took a step forward.

"Now wait a minute . . ." Pershing stole a quick glimpse back at the door. He knew without looking that it wouldn't budge even if he could reach it. Instead, he took a step toward the staircase built along the wall. "I don't know where you came from or what—"

"You know," whispered one of the littlest of the girls. "You've always known. We just reminded you in the basement."

"You were there," another child whispered. "You held the door. You kept us in."

"You held the door. You killed us," a little boy chimed in.

Pershing was backing up as the children advanced. He had seen a handful of children run into the barn, but the numbers seemed to be swelling. Shadows would join the edges of the group, and then they would solidify into more solid forms. All of them stared at Pershing. A few with arms raised pointed at him, and a consistent muttering—"You were there. You held the doors. You killed us"—arose.

Pershing took a quick glance back at the door, and then turned back to the kids.

"I don't know what you're talking about. What door?"

A chorus of children answered.

"You know. You were there. The other you was there at the hall that night."

"The night we died."

"The night you killed us."

"Now just stop where you are! You're threatening an officer of the law!" Pershing yelled, and then he opened his coat to show his sidearm.

A giggle arose, "We're threatening!"

Pershing drew his gun. "You can't do this! I'm the police."

"You weren't then," the original speaker said.

"Then you were just a bully."

"Then you were a murderer."

"The other you just wanted the important people to like you."

"And to pay you."

"The other you didn't care about us at all."

"The other you . . ."

". . . is just like this you."

"But this is the you . . ."

". . . we get to settle with."

". . . to pay back for Christmas Eve."

There was a rush forward as Pershing drew his gun and simultaneously began to fall back towards the door. The children were upon him in a crush. He felt their hands and feet, their faces pressed to him, their bodies hugged against him.

His gun went off and then was torn from his grip. He couldn't see beyond the mob on him. He tried to scream, but it was impossible with no breath in his lungs. *I can't breathe,* he thought. *I can't breathe! They're killing me!*

And then they did.

Forty-Three

SO I TALKED TO DAVE, ROY. Surprisingly enough, I wasn't the first to call to inquire about your visitors. He said he had gotten a call from the representative of the company they worked for who said they hadn't been in touch in a couple of days. Dave was asked if he could use his influence to check on them as the company couldn't seem to reach the sheriff, you know, Pershing, either. They seemed concerned. You don't know of anyone who's actually dead in all this, do you?"

"Not us, Tony," Pete answered for Roy. "Roy here seems to be turning into the confrontational, gunfighter type, not the 'I buried them in the basement' sort. And you know me: 'What's So Funny 'Bout Peace, Love, and Understanding,' right?"

"Great Costello song."

"Nick Lowe wrote and recorded it five years or so earlier, but at any rate, it wasn't us. They're probably too busy trying to find me to kill me that they haven't checked in," said Roy.

"Well, I gave Dave the short form. He's already found out that Paalo checked in and out of the Ramada although Newark—that's their names, by the way, Paalo and Newark—wasn't with him. When he left he was driving an auto registered to Pershing. Both he and Newark have dropped off the map, and, as the man said, Pershing seems to have gone missing, too."

"What do you think they're up to, Roy?" Pete asked.

"I don't know, Pete. I half expected to see them show up at your place yesterday or trailing us today. That's why I still have Jeri and the kids at her folks."

"I almost hesitate to suggest this, gentlemen, but the FBI has been alerted, your story is now unpublicized, but known and about to come out. It's broad daylight. I say it's time to reconnoiter. What say you, Pete, and I go back to the farm, Roy?"

"I knew you'd be dying to see it, Tony! You're a voyeur who just has to put his nose in other people's business!" Pete laughed.

"Hey, you two brought the story to me, Pete," Tony protested, but he was laughing, too.

But Roy wasn't.

"I hate to say it, and I hate even more to do it, but I think you're right, Tony. We have to go back."

"Tony's also right about the FBI and other people knowing, too, Roy. I don't think they could just take you—let alone me, too—out of the picture anymore. They may try to quiet you up some other way, but I think the hit idea is definitely off. Maybe that's why they've gone to ground."

"You think they're sending in the lawyers, Pete? I guess that wouldn't surprise me, but what have I actually done?"

"Besides rabble rousing and surviving assassination, wasn't there trespassing, breaking and entering, and robbery in the past week's activities?" asked Tony.

"I was there, too, Roy. I can turn state's evidence and testify against you. Think they'd make me take Joyce into witness protection with me?"

"Whatever, Pete," Roy said, at least smiling now, too. "But we have to go back, and I do want to make sure it's full-blown daylight this time, too."

"Think the spooks and the thugs only come out at night, Roy?"

"You know the fighting in the apple orchard I told you about that we used to hear? That was in broad daylight, Pete."

"Well, I for one am hoping we don't hear any shots."

"Me neither."

"You both agree with me that we should check it out, though?" Tony asked.

"Yeah, Tony, I was reaching the same conclusion, too. I need to go back there," Roy said.

"I agree, Roy, but," added Pete, "something tells me we're not going to find anyone there."

"Anyone living, you mean."

"Whatever you say, Roy. No time like the present? Let's go."

Just then the phone on Tony's desk rang.

He picked it up, and Shea and Pete soon realized he was talking to the FBI agent in Marquette.

"So they both have apparently left the area, Dave? I guess that'll be a comfort to Roy. What's the next step?"

He listened while Dave must have explained the options.

"Do you want to talk to him yourself, Dave?"

He cupped the phone and turned to Roy. "You feel a need to talk to him, Roy?"

"Not just yet, Tony, but tell him thanks."

Tony turned his attention back to the phone. "Not right now, Tony. That works for you, too, I take it. He says, 'Thanks,' by the way."

He listened a little longer and then said his goodbyes. He turned to Roy and Pete. "He says they up and left, Roy. Newark was already spotted heading south toward Green Bay in Wisconsin, and Paalo seems to be heading west on U.S. 2.

"He also said the company that contacted him—it wasn't Universal, by the way—is perfectly legit and lists the two as employees with great records. Both men, incidentally, are vets with good service records. Commendations and the like are listed for both of them. Real hero types.

"And, more to the point, after hearing your story he says it's all a matter of 'he said and he said.' Even Pete says he never actually heard any shots and couldn't see clearly through the snow, and if they were brought back there's two of them and one of you to say what happened on the quarry ice. From your own admission there may have been other witnesses, but do you really think they'll put in an appearance?

"Sherriff's missing, too. I'm supposed to ask you again: There isn't something you two are leaving out about two or three bodies lying in a grave somewhere, is there?"

"Hey, Tony, like I told you," said Pete, hands outstretched, "we're all peace and love, warm and fuzzy. They were after Roy, not the other way around."

Roy had been looking at the floor. "He's right, though, isn't he? There's no real evidence to back up anything I'm saying, is there? Half the town already thinks I'm nuts, and this ought to be enough to get me locked up instead of them."

"Hate to say it, but I think you're right there, Roy. From the sound of it, though, they're gone. Maybe it's all over."

"We still need to go back out there, though, guys," said Roy.

The other two nodded in agreement.

Tony said, "Definitely, Roy. We can take my car. If there is anyone waiting out there, I don't think they've seen my vehicle yet."

"Good thinking, Tony. We'd be cramped in Pete's pick-up anyway, and I left the Blazer with Jeri."

Forty-Four

WHEN THE THREE MEN walked out to Tony's car, they discovered the day had turned simply beautiful. The sky
was completely blue and cloudless. The light was so
intense they had to squint at the snow banks.

On the way out to the farm they discussed Roy's options,
reaching a decision that too much was still up in the air to make
any real decision.

"It seems a good sign they left, though," Pete was saying
as Tony turned up the driveway, following Shea's directions.

There was no sign except for tire tracks and footprints of
anyone about as they parked behind the house.

All three got out and walked towards the house. Pete
stopped a minute and turned. "There's the site of the famous disappearing barn, Tony."

Roy had reached the front door. "It's open, guys. Ready?"

They walked through the porch into the house proper.
Outside of being a little cool, nothing seemed untoward about
the place.

"What's this?" asked Pete, reaching for a paper on the
kitchen table. "It's addressed to you, Roy," he said, passing it over.

Roy unfolded the note and read through it silently. It was
brief, and when he was done he asked, "Want me to read it to
you? I mean, you both are in this, too."

"Of course, Roy," said Pete.

"Here it is then: *To Roy Shea. You win; we lose. It's over.*

Just so you know you were on the right side. We both know it. We're gone. Once I report in there won't be anyone coming to follow up. We have enough to make sure it ends here with you and us—and them.

If ever there was proof we were backing the wrong horse, your gang there showed us.

I quit, and I'm sure my former partner does, too. Don't know about Pershing for sure—yeah, he was working with me— but I doubt he'll ever be a problem for you again. He had bigger things to worry about. I still think you're probably an asshole, but you seem to be a righteous asshole.

I'm gone; have a nice life.

Paalo

"There are two postscripts added in this old timey script, too," Roy said.

"The first one just says: *Roy, you have defeated him. Let two of them go. The third has been dealt with for past sins. Forget him. Pikku.*

"The second says: *Roy, your grandfather was an upright man, but when your grandmother was young! Oh, my. Kookas.*

Oh, say hi to Spiritooth.

"Now what in hell is that supposed to mean?" Roy asked as he finished reading.

"Sounds like it's over, and it also sounds like you have family friends working for you, Roy."

"Sounds like Granny was fun, too," Tony added with a laugh.

Roy shot him a look. "Just what I need. As if enemies aren't enough, now I have family scandal, too."

"Don't worry, Roy," Tony said, "we won't tell anyone."

"The hell we won't, Tony!" laughed Pete. "I'm telling everyone!"

Roy pulled out a chair and sat at the table, and after a second both Pete and Tony joined him.

"Can it really be over, though?" Roy asked. "I'd sure like it to be."

Pete said, "To quote every cheesy sci fi movie ever, 'We're dealing with forces we don't fully understand here,' Roy, and I think they just told you it's over and to let it go."

"Sounds like Paalo was telling you that, too," added Tony. "I'd also say you've got some pretty powerful friends."

"'With friends like these—'" started Roy.

"No!" Pete cut him off. "Without friends like these I think you'd be at the bottom of the quarry and I'd be looking for a new best friend to annoy me. Whatever you think, Roy, these folk are on your side, well, at least some of them. I don't know what rules of engagement they operate under, but look at what Paalo said. 'Your gang there showed us.' What gang? Sure wasn't me, and I don't even think he knew about Tony. You've had help. I appreciate it, and I think you should, too."

Roy was a little taken by the sincerity in Pete's voice. This wasn't buried under cynicism or even humor. This was as 'straight arrow Howie' as it got.

"I do appreciate it, Pete. It's just I'm not quite sure whom I'm supposed to be appreciative of and grateful to."

"I'm just coming in on this at what seems to be the end, Roy. You—even Pete—have been living with it longer, but I can't help feeling it's got to do with all the spirits of this place you've been talking about."

"You mean all those family ghost stories and what not, Tony?"

"Yeah, Roy, that's exactly who I think has gotten involved. And while we're here? Do you think we could look around for some of them?"

Roy just shook his head, folded the note, slipped it into his coat pocket, and laughed. "Being here with you two, I don't think there's anything else we could do. Come on, I'll give you the tour."

Roy led Pete and Tony through the house starting from the upstairs through to the basement. They found very little sign of the recent occupants except for an unmade bed upstairs, a hole in a bedroom wall, washed dishes and pans on the sink drain board, and a few items in the refrigerator.

Down in the basement were some footprints in the dirt, and that was just about it. But as they were getting ready to head back up the stairs, Tony said, "What do you think of this Roy?"

"What have you got, Tony?" asked Pete, as he and Roy headed over to stand next to Tony, who seemed to be staring up at one of the basement windows.

"Aren't those finger and palm prints all over the glass, Pete? The ones on the inside look like an adult's, but don't the ones outside look like kids' prints?"

All three stared for a time trying to outline the prints on the glass with the outside light.

"Sure looks like that to me, Tony. I wonder when the last time little kids were out here," said Roy. "I sure don't know of any, but then again the place has been out of the family for a long while."

"Somehow they look pretty fresh to me, Roy. The glass where they're smudged in is a lot cleaner than the untouched stuff," added Pete.

"Well, guys, I sure don't know what to make of it. Whoever made the ones inside must have been on a ladder, too. I can't reach that high, and I'm taller than either of you."

Roy shook his head. "Well, I don't know what it's all about, but I hardly think it's the riddle of the century. It is curious, though."

He turned to his two friends. "What do you think, gentlemen, time to go?"

"Can we take a look around outside, Roy?"

"Well, we're probably trespassing out there as well as in here. Let's go."

They climbed the basement stairs, turning off lights as they came to them.

Just as they were walking out through the mudroom off the kitchen, Roy said, "You know, the place seems quieter than when I was a kid. It almost feels like it's resting after a work out."

"Just my luck to be here when everyone's asleep," groused Tony as they went outside, closing the door behind them.

They looked around the yard from the porch and then Pete said, "What's that?" and pointed over towards where the barn used to be.

"Don't know, Pete," said Roy. "Let's check it out," and all three walked over toward the small gray object lying exposed in the snow. When they got there he bent down and fished up a gray ear-muffed cap with a standard badge attached. "SHERIFF PERSHING," was engraved on the badge.

Looking at the trampled snow, Pete said, "Looks like Pershing was here."

Roy hunkered down to examine the tracks. "He sure wasn't here alone, either. Looks like a mob was involved. Some of these look like kids' prints, too."

"Almost all of them do," said Tony. "Is there a large scout troop or something here in Phoenix?"

"Not that I'm aware of, Tony," said Roy, "and in my wildest imaginings I can't see Pershing doing more for a scout troop other than trying to arrest them for disturbing the peace and tying illegal knots."

"You've got Pershing's number all right, Roy," said Pete. "That bastard hates kids."

"Make that hates everyone, Pete."

"You guys make him sound like a fine, upstanding example of the police department. Is he really that bad?"

"You wouldn't believe it, Tony. You know how a little power goes to some peoples' heads? Pershing was born that way. I heard him bragging about 'tapping' teenagers one night up at the High Steps when he'd had too much to drink.

"Someone was talking about local history—the strike days and all—and he started in with how they knew how to handle people back then. Troublemakers were troublemakers and there were no bleeding hearts to stop the authorities from doing what needed doing.

"Someone in the crowd said, 'You mean like at Italian Hall? All those kids murdered, probably by someone working for the mining companies and supported by local law enforcement?' and Pershing just spun at him. Stood staring for a minute and then said, 'Those kids probably got what they deserved. They would have grown up to be trouble just like their parents anyways.'

"You should have heard the regulars. I think if Smitty hadn't walked him over to the door and all, Pershing would have had his comeuppance right there. I swear he sounded like he wished he had been in on it." Pete finished his story. "Anyway, that's the sort of gent we're dealing with.

"Looks like he was here, but he sure isn't here now."

"Yeah, I agree, Pete. You ready to go, Tony? Nothing seems to be shaking here right now."

"Might as well, Roy. You ready, Pete?"

Pete nodded and all three climbed into the car.

They were just heading towards the hillside when Tony looked at his rearview mirror. He thought he saw two men watching them drive off. He hit the brakes and had to turn his attention to almost slipping off the road towards the ditch, and when he regained control of the car and brought it to a halt, he looked back in the rearview. The two were gone—if they ever had been there.

"What the hell was that all about, Tony?" called Pete from the backseat. "I nearly pitched over the seat."

"Sorry, Pete, I thought I saw something and overreacted. Must be more wound up than I thought. I'll be more careful."

But he had hardly gotten underway when he hit the brakes again.

"Now what?" shouted Roy.

"I just thought—it just hit me—you know how you said the barn comes and goes? What if Pershing's in the barn?"

The three sat silent and shocked for a few seconds, and then Roy said, "It would probably serve him right."

Tony continued on toward town.

Epilogue

A COUPLE OF MONTHS LATER, Shea, Jeri, the kids and their extended family and friends were together for a post-Christmas brunch at their home. Their own kids and everybody else's were giving a pretty good review of what Christmas had been like for the volume level, minus the gift ripping and toy battles. Of course even with fewer kids, the volume level would be louder given the addition of toys.

Wassail of one sort or the other and spiritual "Auld Lang Synes" were shared along with glasses raised to absent friends on both sides of the reality border. At one point Roy, Pete, and this year's new invitee, Tony, found each other more or less sober in a more or less quiet corner on the outskirts of the hoopla.

"Merry Christmas Past, guys," said Roy, raising his Guinness. The other two joined the toast.

"And here's to the past year's events, as odd as they were," added Pete, initiating a second toast.

After they had drunk, Tony raised his glass once more. "And to the consequences of those events, too, gentlemen."

"*Slante* to that, Tony . . ." Roy started to second, and then stopped. ". . . what consequences?"

"You haven't heard, Roy? Our good sheriff is officially declared missing, not that anyone regrets his absence, and I assume in a matter of years—what do they have to wait, five? He'll be ceremoniously declared dead which will probably draw a sigh of relief from various and sundry. He was not a well-loved man.

Turns out his ex is still legally a co-owner of much of his property, and she's selling it off.

"I've heard very unofficially from our friend in Marquette that our two fall friends are living quite quietly in two very separate places on what seems to have been their prior earnings. Neither seems to be in touch with each other or their former employers. I suspect both had enough sense to set aside a suitable insurance policy concerning their company and clients, and I assume both made enough to live comfortably. Newark seems to be running a neighborhood improvement association in Chicago, and Paalo seems to spend a lot of time fishing and hunting and hanging out in his neighborhood watering hole in New Banks, Washington pretty close to the Idaho border."

"Jeeze, Tony, how do you learn these things?"

"A reporter's connections are his lifeline, Roy, you know that. Besides, like I told you, Dave told me. What he didn't tell me, though, that I have to pass along is about the Italian Hall. Did anyone talk to either of you?"

"No," said Pete, "what's up there?"

"Rumor's going round in Calumet that Reverend Englund was on his usual nightly power walk in the neighborhood Christmas Eve when he turned the corner leading to the Italian Hall. He said as he approached, he could actually see the building and not just the arch—this is all third- and fourth-hand you understand, he won't talk to me ever since the church addition story I ran—he saw the front of the building lit up. There's been nothing in there since the sixties, you know. Anyway, then he realized it was from the doorway leading to the stairway to the ballroom.

"In the light he saw a man standing there in a long black coat near the doors, and then he saw him shrug and step away.

"Then the children came out."

"The children? You mean . . . ?"

"Yep, Roy, those children with a few adults sprinkled in. They walked out, looked around, and then Reverend says they up and disappeared.

"After they all passed through he looked and saw the tall man still standing there. When he noticed the reverend he gave a little wave and disappeared, too."

"Did everybody go crazy up here?" asked Shea. "Rev seemed to have his head screwed on pretty tight."

"Well, tighter than yours at any rate, Roy, but that's not the best of it. Reverend Englund says that although he didn't recognize the man, and although he didn't look anything like our absent, unmissed Sheriff, he thought it was Pershing."

All three sat silent for a moment.

"It's minor news, too, but there seems to be a lot of land up for sale that was quietly bought up by a number of large firms over the past ten years. They're dumping it all. Property values are such that locals can pick up parcels they couldn't touch ten years ago. The land's actually going back to the people who live here."

"Yeah, that one I heard," said Pete. "Whatever they had planned for us must have shit the bed, and somehow, Roy, I think this whole business was the enema."

Tony laughed, "Well, you know, I think you may be right. Amazing what a letter to the local press will do, no?"

"So, Tony, you say the men of the press are wearing the white hats?" asked Pete. "I kind of think Shea's ghosts may have had something to do with it."

"That's what I hear, too, Pete," said Shea. "I've been having company. Piiku and Kookas, Granddad, Ami, and a flock of others have been dropping by for nights now."

"I can't even get my mom to call," said Tony.

"Yeah, well, that may be, but they were looking for something."

"Looking for something?" asked Pete.

"Yep, and after talking to Jeri and the kids I'm going to give it to them. Ties in with what you were saying about Pershing's ex, Tony."

"What? About her selling stuff?" asked Tony.

"That's it exactly," said Shea. "After discussion with significant others—namely Jeri, the children, and other family live and deceased along with a slew of other hangers on—they've talked me into it."

"Yeah?" asked Pete.

"I guess no good deed goes unpunished," said Roy. "I'm buying back the family farm."

THE END

Acknowledgments

Thank you to university libraries across Michigan, especially the Michigan Tech archives, where my digging into Italian Hall began.

Thank you to Anne and everyone else at North Star Press for the help with this book.

Although they're passed, I thank my dad, James P. Brogan, Sr., for bringing home the stereoscope pictures of Italian Hall, and Woody Guthrie for his song "1913 Massacre." These sparked my interest.

And thanks to Jim and Cheryl for providing the table and space where this was begun long ago!